EARLY PRAISE FOR BRANDT DODSON
AND *ORIGINAL SIN...*

‽

"Compelling and thought provoking, *Original Sin* reads like it was plucked from the police files, and Colton Parker is the kind of hardnosed, bloodhound P.I. you'll want to follow from case to case. Brandt Dodson has delivered a strong, intriguing first novel."

MARK MYNHEIR,
former homicide detective and author of
Rolling Thunder and *From the Belly of the Dragon.*

"Crisp. Wry. Honest. P.I. Colton Parker is as unexpected as a bullet hole in a brand new Brooks Brothers suit. You're gonna like this gumshoe!"

CLINT KELLY,
author of *Scent*

"*Original Sin* is a terrific read, packed with characters—both savory and otherwise—you couldn't forget if you tried. I'm looking forward to the next book!"

JOHN LAURENCE ROBINSON,
author of the Joe Box Mysteries: *Sock Monkey Blues* and *Until the Last Dog Dies*

ORIGINAL SIN

BRANDT DODSON

HARVEST HOUSE PUBLISHERS

EUGENE, OREGON

Cover by Garborg Design Works, Minneapolis, Minnesota

Cover photo © Benjamin Lazare/istockphoto.com

ORIGINAL SIN
Copyright © 2006 by Brandt Dodson
Published by Harvest House Publishers
Eugene, Oregon 97402
www.harvesthousepublishers.com

Library of Congress Cataloging-in-Publication Data

Dodson, Brandt, 1958-
  Original sin / Brandt Dodson.
      p. cm.—(A Colton Parker mystery ; bk. 1)
   ISBN-13: 978-0-7369-1809-1 (pbk.)
   ISBN-10: 0-7369-1809-4 (pbk.)
   1. Student counselors—Crimes against—Fiction. 2. Private investigators—Fiction. 3. Single fathers—Fiction. 4. Teenage girls—Fiction. 5. Widowers—Fiction. I. Title. II. Series.
  PS3604.O33O75 2006
  813'.6—dc22
                                                2005022897

Printed in the United States of America

06 07 08 09 10 11 12 13 14 / BC-CF / 10 9 8 7 6 5 4 3 2 1

To Jesus Christ.
May He use this book—and me—as He sees fit.

Acknowledgments

Writing a novel is impossible without the support and assistance of many kind and generous people. That has certainly been true in my case. I offer my deepest thanks...

To my wife, Karla, for being my first "first reader" and for her support and suggestions. I love you.

To my sons, Christopher and Sean, for giving up some of their time with Dad so he could spend it with his imaginary friends. I love you, guys.

To my other first readers, Jeff and Ruby Goldberg and Bob and Linda Lenn. Where are we going to eat next?

To Vicki Lane, Ph.D., child psychologist, for her advice on Callie's issues. Vicki, any errors are mine.

To the gang at the Write to Publish conference. Thanks for your support. Hang in there.

And...

To my editor, Nick Harrison. Nick, you were willing to put it on the line and take a chance. I will be forever grateful.

To all the professionals at Harvest House. You have made this a genuinely enjoyable experience. Thank you.

CHAPTER
ONE

Two days after I was fired from the FBI and five days before I opened for business as a private investigator, I was told that the best way to build a clientele was by word of mouth. That's probably true if you have enough mouths to spread the word. I didn't. So when Angie Howe came into my office early one morning and asked if she could hire me, I wanted to dance on my desk. Instead, I offered her a cup of coffee.

She sat in one of the chairs opposite mine and held the mug with both hands. She sipped from it slowly. When she lowered the mug, I noticed tears in her deeply set eyes.

Maybe the dance on the desk would have been the better way to go after all.

"Too strong?" I asked.

She shook her head.

"Would you like cream or sugar?"

She sniffled and pushed a thatch of stringy blonde hair away from her face. "No thank you," she said. "This is fine."

I eased back in my chair and sipped from my own cup as I studied the woman in front of me. She was young, probably in her late twenties, and thin—almost emaciated. She was wearing jeans, tennis shoes, and a hooded sweatshirt under a nylon jacket. There was no jewelry.

"This is good," she said. "It's cold outside."

Cold wasn't the word for it. Mid-October in Indianapolis, "the crossroads of America," rarely produces temperatures that fall into the low thirties, making the past several days exceptional.

"What can I do for you, Miss Howe?"

"Angie, please."

"Angie," I said.

She sipped the coffee again and looked around my office. It was a one-room affair with a simple wood desk, a desk chair that squeaked, and two ladder-back chairs opposite mine. I had two file cabinets, one for the files that I hope to have someday, the other for coffee supplies and paperback novels. A small half bath opened off to one side of the door, and a radiator behind my desk provided heat in the winter. Air conditioning came from an open window that looked down onto the street, three stories below.

"I've never hired a private investigator before," she said.

"Most people haven't," I said.

"How much do you charge?"

I told her my daily rate.

"I've only got, like, enough for one day," she said.

"Sure," I said. "Why don't you tell me about your problem and then maybe we can work something out."

She thought about that for a moment and then nodded as she sipped from the cup. "Yeah. That sounds good."

I pulled a notepad from the drawer. "Why don't you tell me why you're here and then we'll figure out how I can help you."

The hair fell back in front of her face. She pushed it away with one hand. "My fiancé…well, he's not *really* my fiancé, but he's more than a boyfriend, you know?"

I told her that I did.

"He's been arrested."

"For what?" I asked.

She rolled the mug between her hands. "For murder," she said.

I leaned forward in my chair.

She focused her eyes on the cup. "They think he killed his aunt, but he didn't do it. He loves her. She was the only family he had."

"What's his name?" I asked.

"Billy. Billy Caine."

I wrote the name down. "And what is...what was his aunt's name?"

"Emma. Her name was Emma Caine."

I made another note. "Why do the police think Billy killed his aunt?"

She pushed the thatch of hair from her face again. "They say he has her credit card and that it was missing from her house. They say they have proof that the card was used after she was murdered."

"How was Emma killed?"

"Her head was caved in," she said matter-of-factly.

"Was a weapon recovered?"

"I don't know. They say that he was there about the time she was killed."

"And you're telling me that the police are basing their entire case on a credit card?"

She didn't say anything but continued to keep her eyes downcast on the cup between her hands.

I shook my head. "There has to be more than that. A credit card isn't enough. They must have something else. How do they know that Billy was there? Are there witnesses?"

She nodded. "Yeah. Some people say they saw him." She rolled the cup between her hands and sniffled again. "He didn't do it though," she said, more to herself than to me.

"How do you know that?" I asked.

She kept her eyes diverted to the cup.

"Does he live with you?"

"Yeah." She looked up. "And I know what you're going to ask. And the answer is no. He wasn't home."

I put my pen down and stood. "My coffee seems to have gotten cold. How's yours?"

She shrugged.

"Would you like a warm-up?"

She nodded and held out her cup. I took it and refilled both cups. I handed hers back and sat down. My chair creaked under the sudden load.

"Angie, if Billy has the card and witnesses can put him at Emma's house and you can't say that he was with you, why do you think he didn't kill her?"

Her deep-set, red-rimmed eyes seemed to recede even further into her head. "He's no angel, Mr. Parker."

"Few of us are," I said. I eased back in the chair and blew on the coffee before drinking.

"He's been in trouble before."

"What kind of trouble?" I asked, setting the cup down and picking up my pen.

She shrugged. "DUI, possession, stuff like that. But when he gets work, he works hard."

I made a note of his record. "Does he have work now?"

She shook her head. "He can't read, so he does odd jobs like hauling trash, deliveries, things like that. But those jobs don't pay much, and when the job is over he gets laid off."

I wrote *motive* across the page. "So he doesn't have any money coming in?"

She shook her head.

"From anywhere?"

She shook her head again.

"And he had a credit card in his possession."

She nodded.

"A card," I continued, "that belonged to his murdered aunt and that was used after she was murdered."

Her eyes fell back to the mug as she began rolling it again between her hands.

"And the police have eyewitnesses who can place him at the scene?"

She raised her head from the cup and looked at me. "He isn't a killer, Mr. Parker. I know him. I know him good. He loved his Aunt Emma. He looked out for her. She was all the family he had." She lowered her eyes again. "And he's all that I have."

"Is that why you're here? Do you have any reason for your belief in his innocence other than your feelings for him?"

Her head snapped up. A flash of anger flickered in her eyes. "Isn't that enough? Wouldn't you do the same if he was yours?"

"Probably," I said. "I would at least want to know."

"I already know, Mr. Parker, and I want the world to know. Billy did not kill Emma."

"Okay. But there are some things that you need to know. First, I am not an attorney. That means that I am not your advocate. I won't spin the truth. I go where the evidence leads. Understand?"

She nodded.

"Second, if I find anything that may help your case, I will give it to you. But I can't and won't ignore evidence, regardless of who it implicates."

She remained motionless.

"If the evidence points to him, I will tell you."

"Okay," she said.

I paused to pick up my cup and down some of the coffee. I wanted time to gauge her reaction. "If you can accept that, I can take your case."

"You don't believe me," she said. "So why are you taking my case?"

"I didn't say that I don't believe you. In fact, I'm impressed that you admitted to facts that could incriminate your position."

She pushed the hair out of her face again.

"Let's just say that I'm intrigued enough to want to look into it. But I do have another question."

"Okay," she said.

"If Billy is out of work and you have no money coming in...how are you living?"

Her eyes diverted to the cup again.

I rephrased my question. "How do you pay the rent?"

"I can pay you, Mr. Parker, if that's what you're worried about. But like I said, I've only got enough for—"

I held my hand up. "We can work that out later. My question has more to do with Billy."

She gave me a look of confusion.

"I'm curious about how you two live if he's only working on occasion."

She looked at me with unfocused eyes as she continued to roll the cup between her hands. "I sell my body, Mr. Parker."

CHAPTER
TWO

M y office was located on the third floor of a three-story building, on the near south side of Indianapolis, in an area known as Fountain Square. The building in which I was located faced the fountain for which the area was named. Because it was only ten minutes from Indianapolis Police Department headquarters and the city lockup, the location was good. The fact that I could afford it made it great.

I notified the answering service that I would be out for a few hours, poured myself a third cup of coffee, and slipped on the brown leather bombardier jacket that I was using to cover my shoulder holster as much as I was for warmth.

Despite her inability to maintain eye contact, I believed that Angie was being straight with me. I had known many people in her position, both men and women, who had been down and out for so long that they had long since lost any semblance of self-respect. Often feeling trampled on by others in society, they would shrink within themselves even when the truth was on their side. If Angie was truthful, looking into her case was the least that I could do. Besides, I thought, if not me, then who?

I rewrote my notes from the conversation into some type of coherent report and filed it in the cabinet before draining the cup and jogging down the frail staircase to the first floor. I could feel the sag of every step along the way. The building was one of the many reminders of how far I had fallen. And how far I had to go.

Another reminder was sitting curbside. A tan 1986 Ford Escort with a rust hole in the left rear quarter panel that was large enough to allow a basketball to pass. I had to sell my other car, my *new* car, when I lost my job. I had needed an immediate influx of cash, so parting with a finely engineered piece of machinery had seemed like the logical thing to do. But I still needed a car, and the Escort was available. Despite its appearance, it still ran, at least most of the time, which was the only criteria that my strained budget would allow.

I pulled from the curb and moved easily through the morning traffic. It was light, so the ten-minute drive to police headquarters took less than five. When I reached the city-county building where IPD was located, I parked on Alabama Street and entered the building from the east side.

The woman sitting behind the counter was new, at least to me, and smiled when I approached her. I took it as a good sign.

"Can I help you?" she asked.

I returned the smile. It's the little things that count. "My name is Colton Parker," I said, "and I would like to speak with the detective who's investigating the Emma Caine murder."

She picked up the phone receiver and pushed a button on the switchboard in front of her. "This is Brackett," she said. "Who's investigating the Emma Caine case?" There was a pause. "Bitterman?"

I cursed under my breath. Bitterman and I had clashed several times during my years with the FBI, and I had no desire to work with him again. Others felt the same way. Nearly all cops care about the work that they do, but Bitterman loved it. He was "on" 24-7, causing many to suspect that he slept with his badge under the pillow. An aggressive cop who often walked the line between officer of the law and avenging angel, he made other type A's seem downright uncaring. Still, he was right more often than he was wrong, and he had one of the highest conviction rates in the city. In a department known for its professionalism, Bitterman was both highly respected and deeply loathed.

"Okay, I have…" she paused and looked at me.

"Colton Parker," I repeated.

"I have Colton Parker down here and he has some information on the Caine case."

"Okay…got it." She hung up the phone. "Take the elevator over there to—"

"I know where it is," I said.

"Then you know that you can't go up there without this," she said, tossing me a clip-on visitor's badge. "And you need to sign in." She pointed to a register.

I signed, deposited my gun with the woman, and took the elevator upstairs. When the door opened, Detective Daniel Bitterman was standing in the hallway outside the squad room. At six feet four and two hundred fifty pounds, he had four inches and fifty pounds on me. He was standing with both hands on his hips, his black skin reflecting the overhead lighting.

"Well, well, looks like the FBI has come to give us dumb local guys a hand. And just when we needed it the most too."

"Although most of us think of you as a little slow, I don't believe that anyone has ever actually referred to you as dumb, Bitterman. I just thought I would help you get this thing off the ground. Justice can't wait forever."

"Justice ain't waiting on this one. This dude is good for it and he's going down."

"Then maybe you won't mind telling me what you've got?"

He laughed. "Tell you what I've got? Now why would I want to go and do a thing like that?"

"Professional courtesy," I said.

He laughed again. "Sure—if you were a professional."

I was in the process of thinking up a killer comeback for that when a familiar voice came from the squad room.

"What's going on out here?" The voice belonged to Harley Wilkins, captain of detectives. He was standing in the doorway with a case file in one hand and an empty coffee cup in the other. His tie was undone and his collar was open. Like Bitterman, Wilkins was a black man—and also a man who loved his work. Unlike Bitterman, he knew where to draw the line between job and mission, and he seldom saw the need to cross over. He did what he did because it was necessary. And because he was good at it.

"Nothing, Captain," Bitterman said. "Me and ol' Colton here are just catching up on old times."

The captain and I had several opportunities to work together during my ten years with the bureau. Our relationship had always been professional.

"How are you doing, Colton?" he asked.

"I'm okay, Captain."

"We're all sorry about your loss. Anna was a fine woman."

The recent death of my wife, coming as it did on the heels of my dismissal from the FBI, had all but destroyed my interest in life. Had it not been for my daughter, I would have voluntarily joined Anna.

"Well," Wilkins said, glancing at Bitterman, then back to me, "I'll let you two get on with whatever it was you were getting on with."

He moved back into the squad room. I turned back to Bitterman.

"So what do you have for me?" he asked.

"Nothing."

He frowned. "Nothing? Brackett called up here and said—"

"I'm afraid she's a little confused," I said. "I'm here because I have a client who has an interest in seeing that justice is done."

"Client?"

I watched the detective's face go through a series of subtle changes as the reality of the situation began to form in his mind.

"You're not with the bureau?"

I could almost see the belts and pulleys working in his head as he began to realize that I was no longer an FBI agent.

"Don't tell me. Let me guess. You're a private investigator?" He almost spit the words.

"You know," I said, "despite what people say about you, you really are quite the detective."

"Then there is no way that I'm going to give you access to a pending case."

"Not even in the interest of justice?"

He jabbed his finger at me. "*Because* of the interest of justice," he said. Then, to drive home the point, he raised his voice a couple of octaves. "And if you interfere with an active police investigation of a homicide, I will get your license."

"Wow," I said, "you really do have clout."

The elevator opened, and a couple of detectives stepped out. I recognized both of them. They nodded and went into the squad room.

"Probably just as well," I said, stepping into the elevator.

"How's that?"

"This first lesson in police work was just a teaser. I was going to have to charge you for the rest." I pushed the button to go down. Just as the door was closing I saw the big detective raise his right hand and offer a distinctly unfriendly gesture.

CHAPTER THREE

I met Billy Caine in a small room off the main cell block of the Indianapolis city lockup. The room was empty except for the gray metal table at which Billy and I sat, and had concrete block walls with a steel door that provided the only means in or out. A guard stood outside the door.

From Angie's description of Billy, and from having met Angie herself, I was prepared to meet an emaciated and lethargic figure—one easily tossed by the currents of life. Instead, I found a big man, solid as stone, with a shaved head, clear blue eyes, and a quiet demeanor. He also had an arrest record that went considerably beyond DUI, possession, and "stuff like that." The three counts of assault, two counts of burglary, and four counts of battery, one of them on a police officer, along with the two counts of DUI and two counts of possession, signaled one bad dude.

"You've been in trouble before," I said.

"Ain't that the truth." He was drinking a Coke and seemed very relaxed.

I recounted some of his past arrests.

He nodded. "Yeah, that sounds about right. How'd you know all that stuff? Angie tell you?"

I shook my head. "Not hardly. I have some friends here." Actually, I had one friend there. His name was Bucky Kravitz. Bucky had spent nearly thirty years in Records and was a curmudgeon of the highest order. We hit it off during my years with the bureau and had spent many an evening playing poker as I listened to the man's endless repertoire of anecdotes. He had given me a copy of Billy's arrest record and a property room list of the items taken from Emma's house. In exchange, I owed him a box of cigars. A nice arrangement that could cost him his job and me my license.

"Oh," Billy said. He sipped from the can, and I could tell from the hollow sound it made as he set it on the table that it was nearly empty.

"Want another one?" I asked, gesturing to the can.

He shook his head.

"Unfortunately, the officer investigating your case is not a friend of mine," I said.

"Ain't that the luck," he said, flatly.

I said nothing but watched as he slowly turned the can around on the table, mulling over his situation.

"I didn't kill her, Mr. Parker," he said as he continued to spin the can around.

"The police say that you did."

He stopped turning the can and leaned back in his chair. "Yeah, well, I can't help what the police say."

"Billy, I'm going to tell you the same thing I told Angie. I'm not trying to prove your innocence. I am simply going to look into the facts and see where they line up."

"That's okay with me. I ain't got nothin' to hide."

"Okay," I said. "Why don't we start with where you were on the night of the murder."

"No problem. I was home all day until around eight thirty. I got tired of sittin' around, so I left to go see Aunt Emma."

"Is there anyone who can verify that?"

He shook his head. "No. Angie was gone all day. She didn't get home until after I did."

"So let me get this straight," I said, allowing my incredulity to seep through. "You were bored and decided to go visit your aunt?"

"Yeah," he said. "That's right."

I paused for effect. I wanted to see if he would become defensive. He didn't. "That's a little lame, Billy."

He nodded. "Yeah, I know. But what can I say? It's the truth."

I watched his body language for a sign of betrayal—a diversion of the eyes, a nervous flick of the hands, anything. Not a twitch. Nothing. "Okay," I said. "Go on."

"Well, there ain't much to tell. I called Aunt Emma and told her that I would be comin' over. She said that she was out of coffee and wanted to know if I could stop and pick some up."

"Did you?" I asked.

He nodded. "Yeah. I stopped at the Convenient Mart at around eight thirty. I picked up a pound of coffee."

"You say that you called her around eight thirty and bought the coffee around eight thirty?"

"Yeah, something like that. I don't know the exact time."

"The exact time may be critical, Billy."

"Sorry, I just don't know the exact time. I know that it was around eight thirty that I called and it was around eight thirty that I bought the coffee."

"Okay," I said. "We can get your phone records. It shouldn't be too hard to verify when you called your aunt. How far is the drive from your place to the store?"

He shrugged. "I don't know. Maybe twenty minutes?"

"How far is it from the store to your aunt's house?"

"Five minutes, tops."

I made a note of the time line on the back of the property room list. "What then?" I asked.

"Nothing much. I got to the house and she let me in. I went straight to the kitchen and made some coffee."

"How long were you there?"

"Maybe an hour."

"What did you talk about?"

He shrugged. "The usual stuff. How are you gettin' along; is there anythin' you need? You know, stuff."

"What about the credit card?"

"I told her I was a little low on cash and the car needed some work. She loaned me the card."

"Why didn't she give you the cash?"

"I didn't know how much it was goin' to cost, so she just said to take the card."

"Did you get the car fixed?"

He shook his head. "Didn't have time. I needed gas so I used it for that. But the next mornin', cops are breakin' down my door."

"Sure. Did your aunt seem okay to you?"

He folded his arms across his chest. "Yeah," he said, "except she kept actin' like there was somethin' on her mind. You know? Like there was somethin' she wanted to tell me. I asked her, 'Is everythin' okay? You act like somethin' is botherin' you,' but she said that she was okay and I just kind of let it go after that."

I leaned back in my seat. "Did she say anything that might indicate that she was in trouble?"

"Trouble?"

"Yeah. Did she mention having any problems?"

He cocked his head to one side as he paused to think, then slowly shook his head. "No."

"Did she give you any indication that she was having problems with someone else?"

"No," he said. "She didn't have no enemies."

"She had one," I said. "And right now, the police are saying that it was you."

He leaned forward and fixed a hard stare on me. "Like I told you before, I didn't kill her."

"Sure. And you will not take it personal if I don't take your word for it."

"Believe anythin' you want, man." He crushed the can.

"Do you have an attorney?"

"Yeah. Court appointed. Some guy named Benjamin Upcraft." He snorted. "Is that a name or what?"

"Has he been by?"

"Yeah. But I got to tell you, he did not sound encouragin'."

CHAPTER
FOUR

B y the time I finished meeting with Billy and retrieved my gun, the temperature had dropped to twenty-eight degrees. The previously crystalline blue sky had turned to a gunmetal gray, and the small amount of sunlight that managed to peek through promised a warmth it could not deliver.

My interview with Billy hadn't helped. I didn't get a lot of useful information from him other than the time line, and I suspected he was lying about that. I had known many cons in my career, and some of them could lie with minimal revelation of their deception. Billy was one of them. Yet, despite his relaxed demeanor, he had said that Angie wasn't at home on the night Emma was murdered, and that was what prompted him to visit Emma.

Angie had said that Billy wasn't at home that night even though she knew that that bit of information could incriminate him. For the moment, at least, I believed Angie.

I got in my car and started the engine. If Billy murdered Emma, what was the motive? A credit card? Maybe. Then again, maybe not. It didn't make sense. Why would someone who doted on Emma the way that Angie said Billy did, want to kill her in as brutal a fashion as Angie had suggested?

I phoned operator assistance for the number of Benjamin Upcraft. I was surprised when the attorney answered the phone himself.

"Short on help, Counselor?" I asked.

"Short on good help," a baritone voice said. "To whom am I speaking?"

"My name is Colton Parker. I'm a private investigator and I've been hired by—"

"Yes," he said. "I know who you are. Miss Howe telephoned this morning and told me about the arrangement she made with you. May I ask what you've been able to uncover so far?"

I glanced at my watch. "I've been on the case for just shy of two hours, so I'm afraid I don't have much. I was hoping you might be able to fill in some of the gaps."

"Of course," he said.

"Let's start by telling me what you know."

He cleared his throat. "Well, I know that Emma Caine was a much-beloved schoolteacher who has worked these past several years as a guidance counselor. She hadn't an enemy in the world except, of course, for the murderer."

"What do you know about the murder?"

"She was killed sometime around ten or ten thirty PM. The cause of death was repeated blows to her head, crushing her skull."

"Robbery?"

"The police seem to think so. Her purse was open and the contents scattered about. A credit card is missing. It was apparently used shortly after the murder. To buy gasoline, I believe."

"Used by Billy?"

"Yes. Emma had used the card not two hours before."

"For what?"

"For the purchase of computer paper."

"That's it?"

"For that particular purchase."

"Our client says he called the victim at around eight thirty. After that, he picked up a pound of coffee and spent nearly an hour at her house. Given the necessary time to drive to the store and then to her house, that would have put him leaving her place a few minutes after ten o'clock."

"Which puts him right in the time zone of the murder," Upcraft said. "And I've already verified the time he called her."

"Eight thirty?"

"Eight thirty-five."

"I was able to read some of the investigative report," I said. "I understand there are witnesses who saw him at the house."

"Correct."

"Who are they?"

"The Tooleys. Mrs. Tooley was a longtime friend of the deceased. She discovered the body early in the morning."

"I'm going to want to talk with them. Do you have an address?"

"Certainly." He asked me to hold and soon came back on the line. Judging from the address he gave me, the Tooleys lived next door to Emma.

"Doesn't all of this seem just a bit too slick?" I asked.

"I'm not sure I follow."

"Billy goes in to kill his aunt, for whom he had just stopped to buy coffee, bashes in her head, and then steals her credit card. A credit card he uses on the way home to fill up the tank. Doesn't that strike you as...too easy?"

"Not really. I once had a client who robbed a convenience store and then walked across the street to the police station and used the money to pay his overdue parking tickets."

"Did you win the case?" I asked, turning on the car's heater.

He snorted. "Even I have my limitations."

"But doesn't the style of the murder bother you? This lady wasn't shot or strangled or stabbed. She was bludgeoned to death. Whoever killed her did it with extreme prejudice."

"I believe when you talk with the Tooleys you'll see that Billy and his aunt didn't always get along as famously as he would have you believe."

"I had doubts about that when interviewing Billy," I said. "During our talk, I didn't seen any signs of remorse over Emma's death."

"Neither did I," Upcraft said.

"Have you talked with the Tooleys?"

"Yes. Any attorney worth his salt always checks the facts."

"One more question," I said. "What's your take on Billy?"

"With respect to his innocence or guilt?"

"Yes."

"I think he's guilty as sin."

FIVE

The Tooleys lived in a single-story brick house with a sloping roofline and a well-maintained lawn. A sidewalk of aggregate concrete wound its way from the curb to the house and shimmered with a coat of sealant.

When I rang the bell, I was greeted by Mr. Tooley. He was a tall man with thick white hair and a pair of black-framed glasses that rode low on his nose under the weight of very thick lenses. He looked to be about eighty years old.

I displayed my ID and told him I was a private investigator and that I would like to ask him a few questions. He studied my ID and then my face before motioning me into his home.

I stepped into a living room that was clean, orderly, and quiet except for the ticking of a few clocks. The house was small and had a cozy feel to it. The house and its occupants seemed to complement each other.

"This is Colton Parker," Mr. Tooley shouted to his wife. "He wants to ask us a few questions."

Mrs. Tooley was a short, round woman of about the same age as her husband. She fidgeted with her hearing aide with one hand while rolling a small hanky with the other.

"I'm sorry," she said, "but this thing just hasn't been right since I got it."

"That's what my mother used to say about me," I said.

"What was that you said?" she asked.

"He was making a joke," Mr. Tooley said, almost shouting.

She looked at him and then back at me. "Well, it wasn't very funny."

"No ma'am. It wasn't," I said.

Mr. Tooley gestured for me to have a seat. I sat on the sofa and faced the couple, who sat in matching wing back chairs. A cluster of prescription bottles and several issues of *Seniors Monthly* sat on the coffee table between us.

"So you're a private detective," Mr. Tooley said.

"Yes, sir."

"That must be pretty exciting."

I shrugged.

"I was a minister myself. Forty-one years."

"That's a long time," I said.

He chuckled. "Probably longer than you've been alive."

"Yes, sir," I said.

A cat jumped onto the sofa and began to study me.

"Don't mind him," Mrs. Tooley said. "He isn't mean—if he likes you."

"So what can we do for you?" Mr. Tooley asked.

"I'm investigating the death of Emma Caine and I'd like to ask you a few questions."

Tooley shook his head. "A shame is what it is. We never had any trouble in this neighborhood before."

"What's he asking about?" Mrs. Tooley said, nearly shouting.

He leaned over toward her chair and cupped a hand to his mouth. "He's asking about Emma," he said. Then pointed a finger in the direction of Emma's house.

"Oh, such a thing. It was such a sight. Blood all over the place," Mrs. Tooley said.

I glanced at the cat. It seemed to be analyzing me. "I understand that you are the one who found her. Is that right?" I asked.

Her husband repeated the question and then said to me, "You're going to have to talk a little louder." He moved his hand up and down to signal an increase in volume.

Mrs. Tooley nodded. "I found her."

"When was that?" I asked, near shouting.

"When was it, Marvin? Seven o'clock?"

He thought for a minute. "Yeah, that sounds about right."

"Why were you at her house?"

"I wanted to see if she would meet me for breakfast. We went out sometimes, and I wanted to see if she felt up to going," she said.

"I was going to drive the ladies to breakfast," Marvin said. "They go to eat and socialize but I usually just drink coffee."

"How did you find her?" I asked.

"How?" She looked at Marvin with an expression that made it clear she thought she was talking to one of the great dummies of all time. "Dead. I found her *dead*. How else did you think I found her?" she asked

"I mean, was the door unlocked? How did you—"

She was shaking her head. "No, the door wasn't unlocked. I could see through the front door window. She was lying face down in a pool of blood. Her head was…" she paused. Her eyes began to redden. The memory of her discovery of Emma was filling her with anguish. I suspected that it would for a long time to come. "Her head was…" she paused again.

"Take your time," I said as she dabbed at her tearing eyes with the small hanky.

"Her head was…squashed like a pumpkin," she said. "Why would anyone do that? Emma didn't hurt nobody."

"Did she have any enemies or problems with anyone that you know of?" I asked.

Mr. Tooley answered for his wife. "Not a one. She was kind to everyone. Always helping the kids. Always had a pack of them coming in and out all the time. She helped them in school, out of school, with problems at home…you name it."

"Did she have any hobbies? Any interests outside of her work?"

Mrs. Tooley adjusted her hearing aid and looked at her husband.

"She liked the ponies," he said. "It wasn't anything harmful. Just a few dollars here and there. Of course, I couldn't approve of it. I tried to lead her to the Lord. But," he shrugged, "it's a difficult thing to acknowledge one's sin and yield to the Creator. Even when He calls, we just don't want to listen."

I could see where this was going, and I needed to get the Tooleys back on track. "Did you see anyone lurking around the house?"

"Sure did," Mr. Tooley said.

"When was that?"

"The night of the murder."

"Have you ever seen anyone lurking around there before?"

"Well sure. That nephew of hers."

"Nephew?"

"Well sure. What's his name?" He leaned toward Mrs. Tooley and yelled again. "Opal, what was the name of that nephew?"

"Billy," she said, wiping her nose with the embroidered hanky. "Mr. Billy No-Good."

"That's it," he said, leaning back in his chair with a satisfied look. "His name is Billy."

The cat narrowed its eyes as it continued to study me. I was beginning to feel like prey on the Serengeti.

"And you saw him at the house?"

The old man nodded. "Yep."

"Do you remember when?"

The cat jumped onto my lap and began pushing its paws up and down, trying to determine if I was an adequate cushion.

"Just tell kitty to get down," Mrs. Tooley said.

"Get down, kitty," I said.

Kitty curled up in a ball.

"Oh, look, Marvin, he likes the detective."

Marvin shook his head. "Dumb cat."

"Do you remember what time you saw Billy at Emma's?" I asked again.

"Sure do. It was ten o'clock."

"Are you sure about that?"

"It's what I told the police. I wouldn't have told them that if I wasn't sure."

"Are you sure that it was Billy you saw?"

"Sure I'm sure."

"Do you remember what he was wearing?"

"What he was wearing?" he asked.

I nodded. I was testing him, trying to determine the power of his recall.

"Well, let's see," he said, gazing upward as he tried to recall. "No, I can't say that I do. Why? Is that important?"

"Maybe not. How do you know that it was Billy?" I was fishing. There was no doubt that Billy had been at Emma's house around the time of the murder, but I wanted to know if Marvin could have seen someone else.

"'Cause I seen him before."

"What does he look like?"

Mr. Tooley looked at the cat on my lap. "We've had that old thing for years. Kind of grows on you after a while. If you want him down, just push him off."

The cat was purring.

"He's okay," I said.

"I'm sorry," Marvin said, "what was your question?"

I asked him again.

"He's tall," he said. "Tall, big, and as bald as a hockey puck."

"Can you remember anything else about him?"

He shook his head. "What else is there to remember? He was there. I saw him."

"Sure. But I was wondering, did you get a close look at his face?"

His eyes narrowed. "Why?"

"I'm wondering if who you actually saw was who you *think* you saw." I focused on his glasses.

"I know who I saw."

"Billy?"

"That's right. It was Billy. He was over there a lot. I even heard him and Emma going at it one night. There was no love lost between them."

"What were they arguing about?"

"That girlfriend of his." He leaned toward Mrs. Tooley. "What was the name of that girl? The one that was seeing Emma's nephew."

She dabbled at her nose, pausing to think. "Angie," she said.

He leaned back in his chair. "That's it. Angie."

"Emma couldn't stand her," Opal said. "She called her a 'gold digging hussy.'"

"Did Billy have any gold to dig?" I asked.

Marvin shrugged. "It's none of my business if he did or not. It still doesn't give him the right to kill Emma the way that he did."

"But I understand that he was over there all the time. If they didn't get along, what was he doing over there so often?"

"Emma loved the boy," Mr. Tooley said. "She was always fretting over him like he was something special. Best I could see, he was just a bum."

"Why do you think he killed her?" I asked.

"I don't know," he said. "It isn't really any of my business why he killed her so long as he pays for doing it."

"Now Marvin," Opal said, "the boy's got a soul."

A sheepish look crept over Marvin's face. "A man's got a right to feel secure in his own home."

After I left the Tooleys, I drove around the block to get a better look at Emma's house. Like the Tooleys' home, it was a single-story brick building on a manicured lawn. Both houses were situated on the north side of East Tenth Street with Cherry Street running between them. A streetlight hung over the corner of Tenth and Cherry. Behind Emma's house, a narrow unpaved alley ran between Cherry and Sunset Street, which was one block east.

So far, my investigation was leading me to believe that Billy was guilty. He had lied about Angie not being home, he was at the house at the time of the murder, and he had shown no remorse over Emma's death. Shortly after the murder, he used a credit card that Emma had used shortly before. It didn't look good for Angie.

I drove around the block again to get another look at Emma's house. It was surrounded by yellow CRIME SCENE tape left by the police after their initial investigation.

I didn't have any solid evidence and few leads. If I was going to make headway on this, I was going to have to get more of both— even if I had to cross over the line to do it.

I left the Tooleys' neighborhood and stopped at a McDonald's drive-through. I had a double cheeseburger, fries, and a Coke and dined in my car on the way to Tifton High School. The school was named after former Indianapolis city councilman Lloyd Tifton and was located in one of the poorer areas of town. Emma had served as a teacher and guidance counselor there for her entire career, and by all accounts, she had been well liked by everyone. But years of law enforcement experience had jaded me enough to realize that we all wear masks. I was hoping that someone had seen behind Emma's. Enough, at least, to shed some light on who she really was and to help me get a handle on why Billy would want to kill her.

The school was housed in a three-story brick building with ivy growing up one side, giving it an Ivy League look. But that was where the illusion ended. Local gang symbols were spray painted on the side of the building opposite the ivy, and several young men that I estimated to be in their early twenties were playing basketball in an area to the north of the parking lot. The area was cordoned off by a high chain-link fence that had gaping holes in some sections and paved with asphalt that had clearly seen better days. Some of the men were shirtless, despite the cold weather, and others wore gang colors. All of them watched as I pulled into the parking lot.

It was half past three, and the kids were leaving school. Some of them were leaving in school buses, some were driving their own cars, and others were walking. I stopped a girl who was coming out of the building with a book bag slung over her shoulder and who was dressed similar to the way Angie had been dressed earlier that morning. I asked for directions to the guidance office and was told to turn left as soon as I entered the building.

"You can't miss it," she said. "One of our counselors, Miss Caine, was murdered. There's a picture of her in the hallway by the offices."

I thanked her and climbed the steps to the front door. The men on the court stopped playing and watched as I entered the building. I looked at them and smiled, resisting the temptation to give them a thumbs-up. I wasn't sure what that signal meant anymore, and I didn't want to do anything that might trigger an inner-city gang war before I had a chance to talk with the principal.

The hallway was dark, and my eyes took a minute to adjust to the sudden change in lighting. The sound of slamming lockers and squeaking shoes threw me back to the days when I was a kid. A time when eight-track tapes, the Bee Gees, and *Saturday Night Fever* glued a generation together. Or maybe it just seemed that way. We were different then, that much was certain. The times were different too. We didn't kill our teachers.

I turned left and immediately saw a large black and white photo of Emma. It was resting on an easel outside a door that, I assumed, led to her office. Judging from the picture, she was quite attractive, had a pleasant smile, and was a fashionable dresser. She photographed well. Across the hall from the easel was another office with a sign, which read Mrs. Presky. The light was on and the door was open. Inside sat a well-groomed woman whom I judged to be about Emma's age. She was wearing an olive-green business suit with a white blouse. A pair of gold-rimmed glasses rested on her nose. She was deeply engaged in her work when I tapped on the door.

"Yes?" she said, looking up from her desk.

"Mrs. Presky, my name is Colton Parker. I'm a private investigator, and I'm looking into the death of Emma Caine."

"You mean the murder, don't you?"

"Yes ma'am."

"Call it what it is, young man. No need to euphemize it." She gestured to one of the two chairs in front of her desk. "Have a seat."

I left the door open and took a seat. The office was professional. The diplomas on the wall, the books on the shelves, and the computer on her desk gave it that air. But some framed photos of grandchildren, a vase of flowers, and a couple of stuffed dachshunds placed about the room created a personal touch as well.

"Weenie dogs," I said, looking at the stuffed toys.

"Yes. I have two of them. My students know how fond I am of them and gave me these two as a gift. I treasure them almost as much as the real ones. Do you like dogs, Mr. Parker?"

"Sure, but I never had one. Always felt like I missed out on something," I said.

"You never had a dog?" she asked. "Even as a boy?"

I shook my head. "No." It was mostly true. I was bounced from foster home to foster home as a child. One of the homes I lived in had had a Boston terrier named Peanuts, and I became very attached to him. When I was moved out of that home and into another one, I missed Peanuts the most.

A look of profound sadness crossed her face. "What can I do for you?" she asked.

"I'm trying to learn more about Emma."

"What do you need to know?"

"How she spent her time, whom she might have befriended, what kind of a person she was."

"I see," she said. "And I can assume that someone has hired you?"

"Yes."

"And it's reasonable to assume that your client is the guilty party. After all, one would not need to hire a private detective to prove guilt. The prosecutorial arm of our government is quite capable of doing that."

"My client may be guilty and he may not. Let's just say that for the moment, he is the *alleged* and is presumed innocent."

"Ah," she said, leaning back in her chair, "the presumption of innocence. A pillar of the American constitution. Well, Mr. Parker, I'm afraid you're going to be disappointed. Emma was well liked." She paused to correct herself. "No," she said as an after thought, "she was well *loved* by everyone with whom she had contact. Especially the girls here at Tifton."

"She was their counselor?"

"And more. Her job was to guide them through the college admission process, aid them with difficult studies, and work as a sort of…ombudsman. That was her job. But she did a whole lot more."

"Beyond the call?"

"Of course."

"Like what?" I asked.

"Like not just guiding them through the admission process but actually helping them to find the money to go to college. She helped them with scholarships and grant searches, part-time work, anything that would help some young girl to attend college who otherwise might not have had the opportunity to do so."

"No enemies?" I asked, wondering why she hadn't done the same thing for Billy.

"None of which I am aware."

"Who was her closest friend?"

She crossed her legs and looked upward as people do when thinking. "I don't think I can say that she had any really close friends. Just a lot of people that admired her. Especially her students."

"Did she confide in anyone? Befriend anyone in some special way? Someone with whom she ate lunch regularly? Or carpooled?"

She thought for a moment. "Maybe…June Seidel," she said.

"Does she teach here?"

"Family life science."

I shook my head. "I'm sorry. You lost me."

"We used to call it home economics," she said, smiling.

"Could I speak with her?"

"She left earlier today, but I don't see any reason why not. Ultimately, that would be up to her of course."

"Sure," I said. "Did Emma have any male companions?"

She shook her head. "No. Now I can't say for sure, but if she did, I certainly never saw any evidence of it."

"Know anything about her personal life?"

"A little. I know that she was a strong person."

"How so?"

"From her background mostly. She came from a home with no father but many…'uncles.' Her mother was eventually arrested for prostitution, leaving Emma to fend for herself at seventeen."

"What happened to her then?" I asked.

"I don't know, really," she said. "Emma would only say that she worked to put herself through college, choosing to help young girls who, like herself, have no real family structure."

"Anything else that you can tell me?" I asked.

She shook her head.

"Proclivities? Interests? Hobbies?"

"No, sorry."

"Was she ever married?"

She paused to think. "I don't believe so."

"Okay," I said and stood. She stood with me, and we shook hands.

"I believe that I have taken up quite enough of your time," I said. "Thank you for talking with me."

"I wish I could say that I wish you well," she said, "but I do believe that your client is guilty as charged."

"A lot of people are saying that," I said.

CHAPTER
SEVEN

I live in half of a rented double that sits along the periphery of Garfield Park. The park, renamed in honor of assassinated President James Garfield, has been an Indianapolis south-side fixture for decades. Like most public parks, it slid into disrepair and began to attract the underside of big-city life. Hookers, drug dealers, and anyone else looking for illicit activity were beginning to congregate, forcing out the law-abiding citizens who paid the taxes that kept the park alive. Outrage lead to action, and the park underwent a renovation. Now, with a public bandstand, new shelters, and refurbished walkways, the park had become the perfect place for many of the area's younger inhabitants to stroll with their children or have a simple picnic with their family or friends. But the seamier side isn't necessarily gone. Just less conspicuous.

When I arrived home I grabbed my mail from the mailbox attached to the front of the house and found the usual cluster of utility bills, fliers, and credit card offers. I dropped them on the living room table and sat on the sofa. I emptied the bag of items I had purchased and spread them out on the coffee table. I ran through them again to be sure I had all of the things I would need: a small adjustable flashlight with belt clip, a box of latex gloves, and a small set of wire snips. Given my new line of work, I probably should have already had some of this stuff, but I didn't. I hadn't planned on needing them before tonight. In fact, the only required item that I did have was a set of lock picks. I had taken them off a suspect once and had kept them. "Burglary is against the law," I had told him. But then so is possession of burglary tools.

I bagged the items again and noticed that it seemed almost as cold inside as it was outside. I hadn't yet bothered to replace the rotted weather stripping around the door frame, so the house was drafty. I kept my jacket on and moved the thermostat off the usual sixty-eight and up to seventy-two. The phone and answering machine were on a table near the thermostat, and I noticed I had a call. I pushed the button.

"Colton? It's Mary. I didn't want anything important. I'm just calling to see how you're getting along. Listen, call me and maybe we can do lunch. You know, have your people call my people...Bye."

Mary Christopher and I had worked several cases together when I was still with the FBI. I considered her to be one of the best agents I knew. She was intelligent with an innately inquisitive mind, and she rarely let anything rattle her. Since Anna's death, she had stayed in close contact.

There was another beep.

"Dad? It's me. Just wanted to let you know that I have a game on Saturday, and I wanted to see if you could come. Can you? It's going to be at ten o'clock at the school." A pause. "Oh, I almost forgot. Grandma and Grandpa wanted to know if you could have dinner with us that night too." There was another pause. "Anyway, I just wanted to check. Bye." The message was followed by another beep, and the tape began to rewind.

I picked up the phone and called Anna's parents. Corrin, Anna's mother. answered.

"Corrin, it's Colton."

"Hi, honey. How are you doing?"

"I'm doing okay. How are you and Frank getting along?"

There was a pause. I sometimes forgot that when I lost a wife, they lost a daughter—their only child. Anna's death had been sudden and senseless. A car accident. Another highway statistic. Yet behind that statistic was a wife, a mother, and a daughter.

"We're holding up okay. Did you want to talk to Callie?"

"You bet," I said.

The phone was silent for a moment before my thirteen-year-old daughter came on the line.

"Hi, Dad," she said.

"Hi, sweetie. So you have a game on Saturday?"

"Yeah. Are going to come?"

"I'll be there," I said, "and tell Grandma and Grandpa that I'll be there for dinner too."

"Okay. We're eating at six."

"I'll be there," I said again.

"Promise?"

That stung. Prior to Anna's death, I had been so consumed with my career that I had left the day-to-day raising of our daughter to my wife. I had missed more than my share of school plays and soccer games, and now, without a stable source of income, I found it necessary for Callie to live with the Shapiros. Although I knew it wasn't a permanent arrangement, I also knew that it was a necessary one. At least for now.

"I promise," I said. "I'll be there." I hung up and made a mental note to be with my daughter on Saturday.

I reached Emma's neighborhood at half past midnight. As I cruised past the house, heading west on East Tenth Street, I saw that none of the homes bordering hers still had their lights on, which I took as good indication that the neighbors were asleep.

I circled around and came back east for one last check. No lights and no squad cars meant no problems.

I turned north onto Sunset, perpendicular to East Tenth and one block east of Emma's house. I parked along the curb, killing the lights and engine. Despite the cold, I rolled the window down and sat motionless. The best burglar alarm in the world is a barking dog. I didn't hear any, which meant they hadn't heard me. Or else there were no dogs in this neighborhood.

I waited twenty minutes to be sure that I was undetected and, after not seeing or hearing anything, rolled up the window. I made one last check to be sure that I had my tools, including the nine millimeter Ruger semiautomatic I had under my left arm, and zipped up my jacket before getting out of the car.

The dome light hadn't worked since I bought the car, and as I exited, I eased the door closed. I'm a stickler for avoiding detection.

The alley I had seen earlier in the day seemed to offer the best access to Emma's house with the least chance of problems. I jogged down the narrow path to an area just behind her house and crouched, pausing momentarily in the darkness that lay just beyond the periphery of light from the overhead streetlight. The light made Tooley's statement that he had seen Billy, and not someone else, more credible.

I didn't see or hear anything, so I jumped the chain-link fence that separated Emma's backyard from the alley and moved alongside the back of the house. I stepped onto the concrete stoop, slipped on the latex gloves, and tried the back door. It was locked. I pulled the set of lock picks from inside my jacket pocket and went to work. In a little over two minutes I had the tumblers in place. Before going into the house, I tucked the picks back into my pocket and pulled the Ruger from my holster. I have a personal rule developed from years of acrid experience. Never enter a darkened building without a gun in your hand.

The rear door opened into the kitchen with a faint squeak. I eased myself into the room and closed the door.

The kitchen was sparsely furnished with a small refrigerator, microwave, stove, and dining table. Except for a calendar on the wall, there wasn't much in the way of decorations. No plants, flowers, or pictures. There was, however, a window over the kitchen sink that looked out onto Cherry Street. The window had a set of venetian blinds that were open, giving me an excellent view of the Tooleys' living room. I closed them. Given what I had seen of Marvin's glasses I was probably overreacting, but he had seen Billy, or someone, and I didn't see any reason to ask for trouble.

The house was quiet, dark, and cool. The police had probably reset the thermostat lower than usual and locked up until their investigation was done. That meant that they would undoubtedly be back tomorrow to wrap up any loose ends and would discover that someone had burgled the house.

I focused the beam of the flashlight on the floor and moved across the kitchen and through the doorway that lay straight ahead. It opened directly into the living room, which was equally dark and which already had the window coverings closed. I swung the beam around the room. Emma had been as sparse in her decorating habits in this part of the house as she had been in the kitchen.

The room contained a sofa that looked as if it folded out into a bed, two chairs in matching upholstery, a couple of end tables with nondescript lamps, a bookshelf with a smattering of books, a computer desk, and a television. I also noticed large blood stains on the carpet, walls, and front door. The room smelled like spoiled hamburger.

I knelt beside the computer desk and shined my light along the backside. Wiring of the type necessary to support a computer and modem was visible, but the computer was gone. The desk had a drawer, but except for a small stack of blank paper, it was empty. The monitor remained on top of the desk alongside the printer.

I used the flashlight to guide my steps to the bookcase, being careful to not step on blood patterns in the carpet. My job was to investigate, not to interfere with someone else's investigation.

I was interested in seeing what books Emma read. You can learn a lot about someone by what they read and by what they throw away. I would hit the trash can on my way out. But for now, I was learning a lot about Emma from her bookcase.

On the top shelf were two books on law, three books on adolescent psychology, and a dictionary. The second shelf held a small stereo CD player, and the third shelf held an Indianapolis area Yellow Pages. Emma was not one for fun. There were no novels, magazines, or even a Bible. Only reference books. Spartan decorating. Spartan reading. Spartan woman.

I turned to move toward the bedrooms when a car passed the house, its headlights casting a swathe of light into the living room. I instinctively ducked until the danger had passed before standing again and cautiously moving around the forensic evidence in the carpet.

The house had two bedrooms that were connected by a short hallway with a bathroom in between.

The first bedroom appeared to be a guest room. A nice-looking yet inexpensive bedroom suite was in place, but the closet was empty, and the chest of drawers held only a few clean towels, wash cloths, and linens.

The other bedroom, however, had an expensive-looking four-poster bed—oddly out of place with the rest of the house—a desk, a nightstand, and a dresser. A mirror was suspended on the back of the door. On the nightstand was a telephone, an alarm clock with a large digital display, and a comb. I punched the alarm button on the clock, and the display read 5:00 AM. Emma had been an early riser.

I picked up the phone, dialed *69, and was told "the last number that called your line was..." followed by an out-of-town number. I jotted the number down and tucked the note into my pocket.

I examined her desk next. The lower drawer was open, and I guessed it had contained file folders that the detectives had taken to get a better handle on Emma and to build their case against Billy. I would have done the same thing.

The main desk drawer held a tray of paper clips, note pads, and pencils. I pulled the drawer out farther, and behind the tray was a large chrome paper clip bearing the logo of two *Fs* facing each other with an ampersand between them. I took the clip and pocketed it.

I opened the drawers of her dresser and found the type of articles I expected to find. Underclothes, a few sweaters, and some costume jewelry. If there were any clues there, I wasn't seeing them.

Emma's closet was as unremarkable as her house, and the only information I could gather from it tended to support my opinion of her based on the photo that I had seen at Tifton. Despite her lackluster social life and Spartan decorating habits, she had been a snappy dresser.

I slipped into the tiny bathroom, which was situated between the bedrooms. It was decorated in yellow ceramic tile with black bordering, making it the most colorful room in the house. The shallow medicine cabinet over the sink held no prescription medicines. A tube of cortisone cream, a bottle of over-the-counter pain relievers, toothpaste, and a toothbrush were all that spoke of Emma's health and hygiene.

I worked my way back into the kitchen, checking the various trash cans in all the rooms. All of them had been emptied, and if I knew Bitterman, the contents had probably already been thoroughly inspected. The paper clip I had taken from the bedroom was all I had been able to find. A clue is a clue, but I had the sinking feeling of a man in quicksand reaching for the nearest branch. Anything would do. But almost anything else would be better. Nevertheless, if Billy was the killer, so be it. But if not, I wanted to know who. And why.

On the way out, I didn't lock the door. The Indianapolis Police Department is one of the best law enforcement agencies in the country, and they wouldn't take long to realize someone had been here. Besides, I needed to get back to my car. I have a personal time limit of fifteen minutes for a burglary, and I had already exceeded that.

NINE

By eight AM I had been up for more than an hour and downed two cups of coffee, two pieces of toast, four eggs, and four strips of bacon. I had washed the dishes and was placing them in the drainer when the phone rang. It was Mary.

She asked if I had gotten her message the other night and wanted to know if I would be able to meet her for lunch. I told her that I had and that I could. She had to testify on a case that was still at trial, but she expected to be out by noon. We agreed to meet at a downtown restaurant.

After we hung up, I went downstairs to the basement. Over the years, I had accumulated some free weights, a bench, and a chin-up bar. Since a club membership would mean no meals or paid utilities, I do my grunting and wheezing in a small corner of my subterranean gym. Almost everything else that Anna and I had accumulated during our marriage had been sold to finance the opening of the business.

When my chest, back, shoulders, arms, legs, and abs were sufficiently stressed, I grabbed a jacket, tucked my Taurus .38 snub nose into my waistband and ran around the periphery of the park. I finished three miles in time to shower, shave, run a few errands, and meet Mary for lunch.

We had agreed to meet at Houlihan's, and by the time I arrived, Mary was already sitting at a booth. I joined her and ordered a hamburger with iced tea.

"Tea?"

"Sure," I said. "Two thirds of the world drink it. You ought to try it."

"I am trying it," she said. "The question is, why are you?"

"What do you mean?"

The server returned with my tea and refilled Mary's.

"I mean, I've seen you drink. A lot. And it wasn't tea."

I squeezed juice from a lemon wedge into my drink then dropped the lemon into the glass. "Would you want to hire a private eye that reeked of alcohol?" I asked.

She grinned, stirring a packet of Sweet'n Low into her glass. "Aren't you supposed to? I mean, don't all you guys wear snap-brim fedoras and trench coats and keep a half-full bottle of Jack Daniel's in your bottom drawer?"

"You rented *The Maltese Falcon* again, didn't you?" I asked.

"Actually, I bought it," she said. "They just don't make 'em like Bogie anymore."

"Good thing. In case you hadn't noticed, he's dead."

She sipped from her glass and studied me over the rim. "So how are you doing?"

"I'm doing okay," I said. "It's been six months and I'm still here. Guess that means I'm probably good for another six."

"And Callie?"

I shrugged. "She's playing soccer."

"That's not what I mean."

"I know."

The server came and set the hamburger in front of me and a chicken Caesar salad in front of Mary. After asking if he could get us anything else and being told that we were fine, he left the table.

"I'm not trying to pry," she said, continuing where she had left off.

"I know."

"I'm concerned." She placed her hand on mine.

Under normal conditions, having a tall, athletic, raven haired, green-eyed beauty like Mary place her hand on mine and tell me that she was "concerned" would have been enough to stop my heart. But these were not normal conditions. Anna was dead, and it was her death that helped me see what I'd had and how much I lost. No woman, not even Mary, could fill the void left by my wife.

"Callie's with Anna's parents," I said in a raspy voice. "Until my job situation stabilizes I just thought it was best that she live with them. They did such a good job with Anna…"

Mary frowned. Her expression showed concern, tinged with disapproval. I decided to change the subject.

"Do you know what this is?" I asked, showing her the paper clip that I had obtained from Emma's house.

Mary smiled. "You're ducking the issue."

"Yes I am," I said.

She took the clip and examined it. "What does the 'F&F' stand for?"

"I was hoping you could tell me."

She shook her head. "Nope. Sorry. What is it?"

"It's a paper clip."

"Yes, I can see that. I meant what relevance does it have in your life?"

I couldn't help smiling. "It may be a clue in a case that I'm working."

"What kind of a case?"

I told her about Angie, Billy, Emma, and the overwhelming cooperation I was receiving from Bitterman. I did not mention the burglary.

"I heard about her," she said, referring to Emma. "Nice little old lady who was murdered in her home."

"That's the one," I said.

"And you want my help?"

I shrugged.

She smiled. "Okay. Let me see what I can do."

"I appreciate that," I said.

"Can I keep this?" she asked.

"Sure."

She pocketed the clip. "Is there something about this that I should know?"

"What do you mean?"

She leaned forward across the table and lowered her voice. "I mean that I know you, Colton. So I'm not going to ask where this came from or how you obtained it. But I can trust that this isn't something that will get us both in trouble, right?"

"I'm glad you called," I said. "It's been a long time since I had a hamburger this good."

After lunch, I stopped to pick up the cigars I owed Bucky and then drove to the office to get the mail and check in with the answering service. Going to the office wasn't something I had to do, and I wasn't expecting any mail, and I could have checked in with the service from home. But going in gave me the illusion of being busy.

When I reached the top of the stairs, I saw Bitterman. He was leaning against the door frame in a rumpled overcoat and a rumpled shirt that was open at the collar. He did not look pleased.

"You and me," he said, jabbing a finger at me, "we gotta talk. Now."

"Did you get all gussied up for me? You really shouldn't have, you know. I'm a down-to-earth kind of guy."

"Keep it up, funny man," he said, gesturing toward my office.

I unlocked the door and left it open for Bitterman to follow. He did and then slammed the door with such force that I thought the opaque glass would shatter.

"Well mannered too," I said, dropping the box of expensive cigars on my desk. I sat behind the desk, motioning for the detective to have a seat.

"What's on your mind?" I asked.

"Someone broke into Emma Caine's house last night."

"Crime," I said. "It's ever on the increase."

He leaned across the desk and pointed a finger at me. "I know you did it."

"You've always known so much more than me, Bitterman. That's why I always feel so stupid when we're together."

"We dusted for prints," he said. "If I find anything there, you're gone."

I pulled open the lower drawer of my desk and rested my feet on it as I leaned back in my chair. "Bitterman, do you really think I would be inept enough to leave fingerprints? Hypothetically speaking, of course."

He eased back in his chair, allowing his overcoat to fall open and expose the badge on his belt. "Ex-FBI or not, if you interfere with my case again, I'll run you into the ground."

"Look," I said, "I've been where you are. I've had the badge, the gun, and the power. It just doesn't intimidate me."

He stood, towering over the desk. I rose to meet him.

"And neither do you," I said.

He outweighed me by fifty pounds, but he was fat and out of shape. I knew it and so did he.

"I have a little old lady who was murdered for nothing more than a credit card." He raised his finger again and jabbed it at me. "I don't care if I intimidate you or not. If you do anything to jeopardize my investigation, I'll personally see to it that you never work again. When I'm through with you, you won't be able to work security at a rock concert." He lowered his finger and moved toward the door. "Just remember what I told you. Stay out of my investigation." He opened the door and paused. "Or I'll be back."

"Arnold Schwarzenegger," I said. "Wow, that was good. Can you do anybody else?"

He stood at the open door and glared.

"On second thought, 'I'll be back' just doesn't sound as menacing coming from you," I said.

He left, slamming the door behind him.

After Bitterman left, I put on half a pot of coffee and pulled out the property list that Bucky had given me, which listed the items taken from Emma's house. Each of the stolen articles had the potential of becoming state's evidence, so each item was carefully labeled and logged at the IPD property room to ensure the integrity of the chain of evidence.

I poured myself a cup of coffee and sat at the desk with my feet up and the property list on my lap. I went over everything that was listed on the inventory, item by item. Nothing that had been taken by the police surprised me. The contents of Emma's trash cans were cataloged, along with the folders from her desk. Those folders were listed as containing telephone records as well as her checking and savings account information. Even the clothing she had been wearing on the night of her murder was recorded.

"Maybe if you'd bothered to look at the list in the first place, Parker, you could've avoided a felony break-in," I said to myself.

I went to the file cabinet on which I kept the coffee pot and poured myself another cup before sitting down again and going over the list a second time. Only then did I notice that something wasn't right. Something that should have been on the list but wasn't. There was no computer.

When I had been in Emma's house, I had seen a computer desk, a printer, and a monitor, but the computer was gone. And Upcraft had mentioned that Emma had just used her credit card to buy paper and ink. The computer from her home was missing, yet it wasn't showing up on the property list.

People use their computers for a lot of things. Games, banking, travel arrangements, and Internet activity are all common pursuits, and all of these would be obtainable from the computer's hard drive. It should have been the first thing that the police would have taken, yet it wasn't listed.

I picked up the phone and called Bucky.

"Are you sure the list you gave me is accurate?"

"What do you mean, 'accurate'? Course it is. I've been doin' this since you were in high school." Bucky had a gravely voice that sounded more like it belonged to a merchant marine than to a property room clerk.

"But the computer isn't listed," I said, regretting the words immediately.

"What computer? What makes you think the old lady had a computer?"

"Uh...I guess I just assumed. Doesn't everybody have one?"

"I don't."

"Of course not."

"Now what is that supposed to mean? You don't think I can use one of those things?"

"Sorry. I didn't mean anything by it," I said. "Listen, thanks for your help. I owe you one."

"You owe me a lot more than that," he said. "I'm still waiting on those cigars."

"I have them," I said. "How about getting some of the guys together?"

"Poker?"

"Sure. Or we can watch the game or—"

"Poker."

"Or…poker," I said. We set a date, and I hung up.

I went over the list again. Whoever killed Emma didn't want that computer to fall into police hands. That meant that Emma surely had an enemy. Someone on whom she may have had incriminating information stored in her computer. Someone who couldn't afford to have that information get out. Maybe someone to whom she owed money. A great deal of it. Tooley had said that Emma played the ponies. So did someone else I knew. Someone who could send me in the right direction.

I eased my feet off the desk and tucked the list into my jacket. One thing was for sure, whoever the killer was, it wasn't Billy. There was very little about him that wasn't a matter of public record already, and certainly nothing could be any more incriminating than his arrest record. Besides, Angie had said that Billy couldn't read. That made his use for a computer unnecessary.

I glanced at my watch. It was a little early for dinner, but I was hungry, and if I was going to get a handle on Emma's gambling habits, I knew just the place to go.

TWELVE

I had dinner that evening at Armatzio's. The restaurant was a long-time Indianapolis favorite and a frequent hangout for the city's law enforcement community. Tony Armatzio had inherited the business from his father and had managed it well. Then his son, Nick, announced that he had no interest in continuing the business, and that was spelling the end for the south side Indianapolis establishment.

The restaurant was small and had that "hole in the wall" feel. Outside, patrons parked on a gravel parking lot that had more holes in it than Bugsy Siegel and that was partially lit by an old neon sign that actually worked part of the time and buzzed when it did.

Inside, booths lined the periphery of the room, surrounding several tables in the center. A cash register sat over a glass display case that was full of gum, mints, and candy, and a framed one-dollar bill hung on the wall. Canned Italian music came from a boom box sitting on a chair behind the display case, and an easel announcing the daily special stood to one side. Despite appearances, though, the food was excellent.

"Colton? Is that you?" Francesca Armatzio, Tony's wife, was a large, plump woman who appeared to come straight from central casting's idea of the way a large, plump Italian woman ought to look.

She had an olive complexion with gray-streaked hair that she wore pulled back. A pair of thick lenses sat on the end of her nose, and she wore a dark blue dress flecked with small white polka dots. A pair of white canvas tennis shoes and an apron laced over the dress completed the ensemble.

"It's me," I said, hugging her.

"How have you been?" she asked.

"So, so," I said.

She looked around as though she was about to tell me the darkest secret of all. "You know," she whispered, "we were all shocked to hear about Anna."

"I know," I said. "It shocked us all."

"But you. You are doing okay, no?"

"Yes. I'm going to be okay." I wasn't as sure as I made it sound.

She smiled and patted me on the back. "Good, *good*. Are you hungry?"

"Always."

"Here," she said, leading me to a booth at the rear of the dining room, "let me get you something. What would you like?"

I told her.

"I will get Tony. He will want to see you."

She left the table, and I scanned the room. Most nights that I came here I would see at least one or two people that I knew, but it was still early, and the dining room was mostly empty.

"He-ey, Colton." It was Tony. He was approaching from the kitchen, wiping his hands on a stained apron that partially covered his equally stained white shirt. A big man with thinning white hair and a thick white mustache, he matched Francesca's Italianess, point for point. He slid into the booth across the table from me, barely managing to pack his ample frame into the limited space.

"We haven't seen you in so long a time."

"I've been busy."

He nodded his head. "Yes. We know." He placed a hand on mine. "We are all so sorry to hear about your Anna. She was a fine woman."

I thanked him.

"Listen," he said, "how is your daughter. She is fine, no?"

"Yes. She is doing fine," I said.

He smiled. "That is good." He leaned forward and lowered his voice. "Is she okay? With the loss of her mother? You know, a girl needs a mother."

"She had a rough time with it, Tony," I said. "Callie and Anna were very close."

"But you two," he said, "you are close now too, no?"

I shook my head. "I'm afraid not. I was always involved with my work. Now that Anna's gone, I'm not sure I know how to raise a child. Much less a daughter. She's living with Anna's parents."

He recoiled. "No, no," he said, shaking his head. "That is no good. A girl needs her family."

"They are family, Tony. They take good care of her and can give her things that I can't. Besides, it's temporary."

"They can't give her you. They can't replace her father."

"I'm around. I'll always be around. But they did such a wonderful job raising Anna, and they have the resources to do it right. How can I give Callie that?"

"You give her love. If you do that, everything else will come."

Francesca appeared from the kitchen and set a plate of linguini in front of me. "Here you go, young man. Eat."

Tony watched her move away and leaned closer. "You remember what we talk about. A girl needs her father."

"I'll remember. Listen," I said, changing the subject, "who makes book in this town?"

He gave me his "I'm just a poor immigrant who doesn't understand" look.

"Come on, Tony. I know you play the ponies. It's okay. But I need to know who runs the bets in this town. Who would you go to if you were looking for some off-track action?"

He looked over his shoulder to where Francesca was standing by the door. She was greeting a young couple and was out of earshot. "You are FBI man. Don't you know?"

I shook my head. "Never had any reason to know until now."

"How come you need to know now?"

"It's for a case that I'm working. A lady was murdered and I heard that she played the ponies. I want to know if—"

"If she owe anybody money?"

I nodded. "Yeah. Something like that."

He looked back at Francesca before leaning across the table. He lowered his voice. "Do you know Frankie DiCenza?"

"No." I stirred the pasta with my fork.

"He's my bookie. He is the bookie for a lot of people I know."

"Where can I find him?"

He recoiled, casting a nervous eye toward Francesca.

"I won't tell him, Tony. I just need to talk with him."

He was hesitant. I couldn't tell who he feared the most—the bookie or the wife.

"Okay," he said. "I will tell you. But you did not hear this from me."

THIRTEEN

It's impossible for a strip joint to be classy. Regardless of the chrome fixtures, fancy lighting, or "statuesque dancers," those places have always left me feeling oily and unkempt. Before my years as an FBI special agent, my work as a beat cop with the Chicago Police Department often required me to involve myself in the seedy affairs of places like DeNights. More often than not, I would have preferred running someone down a dark alley.

Located on the near north side of Indianapolis, DeNights catered to the convention crowd. Men, mostly, who would never visit a strip joint in their own town but who, when here, away from home and hearth, took on a different hue. One that their wives would have never recognized.

I parked in the side parking lot and could immediately hear the thumping music that seemed to exude through the pink stucco walls. A few men, mostly of the upwardly mobile persuasion, were gathered in a couple of groups around the lot, which was full of newer cars, trucks, and motorcycles. The night was cold, and most of them huddled against the breeze as they smoked and stomped their feet in a vain attempt to get warm. None of them paid any attention to me.

As soon as I entered the building, a short, thick-necked, barrel-chested bouncer in a black T-shirt with the DeNights logo approached me.

"There's a minimum here, bud."

"Minimum what?" I asked.

He looked at me for a moment as though he was wondering if I had missed the mother ship for the trip home.

"Cover charge," he said. "A minimum." He pointed to a sign that was posted just inside the door. The sign said that a cover charge of five dollars was the norm. I slipped him a five.

"Sorry," I said. "I thought you were talking about the size of my neck."

I walked past him and went to the bar. A young woman, no more than twenty-five, came over to my end. "What can I get ya?" she asked, leaning over the bar to hear my answer.

"I'm supposed to meet Frankie," I said.

She leaned closer. "What's that?"

I told her again, only louder this time.

"What's your name?"

I told her.

She told me to wait a minute and walked to a phone at the other end of the bar. After she had a few words, she hung up and returned. "Go through that door," she said, pointing to a door that was left of center stage.

I thanked her and crossed the floor where a large group of men were lining up to tuck their kids' lunch money into the dancer's G-string. By the time I reached the door, I was getting that oily feel.

The door opened into a hallway with two more doors. One to my left was unmarked, the other, straight ahead, had a sign that read Office. I went through that one.

The room was small and contained DiCenza's desk along with two file cabinets off to my right. It was sodden with the smell of tobacco smoke, and the only light was from a green-shaded desk lamp.

"You Parker?" The voice came from a sinewy, swarthy-looking guy with thick black hair whose face was partially obscured by the desk lamp. He wore a tan sport coat over an open-collared shirt that revealed a significant amount of gold chain buried in a patch of chest hair. He sat with his feet up on the desk.

When my eyes adjusted to the darkness, I could see a bouncer, just as thick as the one who had greeted me in the bar, standing off to my left. He was wearing the same T-shirt. You've got to love a man in uniform.

"I'm Parker," I said.

"What did you want to talk to me about?" He lit a cigarette and tilted his head back as he blew the smoke upward. From this angle, I saw the fine features of a round-faced man who appeared to be thirty-five or forty years old.

I had called Frankie before I came, telling him that I had information that could save both of us a lot of trouble. It was a lie, of course. He was the one with the information, but I knew that he would have never volunteered to meet with me if I hadn't given him a reason.

"I want to know if the name Emma Caine rings a bell with you."

He looked at me, then to the bouncer. "What is this?"

"It's a question and answer session," I said. "Commonly referred to as the Q and A."

"I don't have time for this. Take off," Frankie said.

I didn't move.

"I believe Mr. DiCenza told you to take a hike," the bouncer said.

I could feel myself tightening. "Sorry. But Frankie, here, is going to tell me what he knows about Emma."

The bouncer was surprisingly agile. He covered the distance between us in a couple of steps and caught me on the left side of the head with a straight right that sent me into the file cabinets. The blow had caught me by surprise and rang my chimes like a church bell choir.

I shook my head to stop the ringing as he began to follow with another. I blocked his punch and, using the cabinets for leverage, caught him in the chest with a straight right. It knocked some of the wind out of him, causing him to exhale sharply, but otherwise it had little effect. He flashed a grin and came at me again with the right. I was able to pivot and step to my right, deflecting most of his punch. Still, he caught me on the upper left shoulder and, again, sent me into the file cabinets. From the position I was in, I had little room to maneuver and even less time. The bouncer was big and solid, outweighing me by fifty pounds, and he was moving forward, closing the small distance between us. I knew that if I didn't gain the upper hand soon, I was going to find myself in a very untenable position.

I came at him again, this time with a right of my own, and caught him firmly in the gut. Again, it had little effect.

DiCenza had surrounded himself with some able talent. This guy was no slouch.

He swung at me again, this time with a left hook that caught me on the right shoulder and spun me into the wall. I now had my back partially open, providing him with an inviting and vulnerable target. I knew he would take advantage, so I instinctively ducked just as he let loose with another left, landing his fist into the wall. He yelped in pain, giving me the opening I needed.

Spinning to my right, I was now face-to-face with him again with the file cabinets to my back. My ability to maneuver was still poor, but his injury was compensating for the lack of room.

I aimed for his gut again and landed a straight left. His injured left hand had left him with little time to react, so he was not able to prepare himself for the blow. It knocked the wind out of him and caused him to stumble backward, giving me more room.

I moved toward him, followed with a left hook to the side of his head, and then hit him with all I had in a straight right. He stumbled backward and landed on his back.

Frankie sat motionless for a second as he seemingly was trying to process all that had just happened. Then he began to reach for the upper left-hand drawer of his desk. I pulled the Ruger from its holster.

"Now we can do this the hard way or the easy way. Personally, I prefer the easy way."

"You must be crazy to come in here and threaten me like this," Frankie said.

"Maybe," I said. "But right now, I don't really care all that much whether I live or die. Which means," I cocked the hammer of the gun, "that I sure don't care if you live or die."

The bouncer groaned. He was on his knees now.

"All that I want to know," I said, "is if you have made book for Emma Caine. And how much she owed you."

"I don't know no—"

"Don't play games with me, Frankie. I'm in no mood. It's late and I want to get out of this sleaze pit." I gestured with the gun toward the computer that sat on his desk. "You know every dime that everyone has owed you since you muscled your way into your first paper route. Look it up."

Anger danced in his eyes. "What's the name?"

I told him.

He glanced at the gun and then toward the computer as he began to type. "Yeah, I know her," he said. "Or at least my computer does."

"How much was she into you for?"

He looked from the screen to me. "Was?"

"She's dead."

It took a minute for him to process why I was here. "I didn't have the broad killed."

"Sure. And you didn't just threaten me." The bouncer was up now, studying me with glassy eyes.

"This broad was into me for a thousand a week—every week."

"Did she owe you anything?"

He scrolled down. "No. All of our books are clear."

I walked over to where he sat and looked at the monitor. The spreadsheet listed all bets and outstanding debts. Emma had nothing in the outstanding debts column.

"See? All of this was for nothing," Frankie said.

"Not for nothing," I said. "I needed to clear you off the books. I've done that."

"Yeah. Except now, I need to clear you off my books."

I spun his chair around so that he faced me and leaned down to a position that put me inches from his face. "Listen, I will only say this once. I have nothing against you personally. I came in here to do a job and it's done. I owe you one for that and I always pay my debts. But if I have so much as a bad day, and I even *suspect* that you're behind it, I'll be back."

He looked at the Ruger in my hand. "Get out of here."

I stood erect and moved toward the door, holstering the gun. The bouncer kept his focus on me but said nothing.

"And don't think that I won't be calling for that debt," I heard DiCenza say as I left the room.

CHAPTER
FOURTEEN

The air is warm. The sky is clear. A gentle breeze blows. A wisp of Anna's dark hair is moving, and I reach to lay it back in place. She smiles. There is, for now, no one in the world but us. We have escaped to that place. Our place. And to a time that belongs only to us.

I tell her that I love her. She smiles again. She leans toward me to say that she loves me too and that it will always be as it is now. She begins to speak and her words begin to ring. And ring. And ring.

"Yeah?" I said, yanking the receiver off the hook.

"Geessh," Mary said, "Who spit in your cornflakes?"

I held the alarm clock up to my face and squinted at it. "It's almost five AM," I said. In truth, the alarm was set to go off at five. But the dream with Anna had seemed real, and I resented Mary's intrusion.

"I know, but I'm leaving to go on surveillance soon and I thought you might want what I've got."

"Got on what?" I asked, rubbing the sleep from my eyes.

"On your paper clip."

I eased myself into an upright position. "Okay," I said. "What have you got?"

"The logo is used by a company out of St. Louis called F&F. It stands for Fun and Frank."

66

"What do they do?"

"They're an Internet site. They specialize in pornographic material."

"You're kidding," I said.

The inflection in her voice had a seriousness that is normally reserved for heart surgeons and military commandos. "I never kid about my work."

"Why would a high school guidance counselor be involved with an Internet porn site?" I asked, more to myself than to Mary.

"Maybe she wasn't. Who knows how she came across that paper clip?"

"Maybe," I said. "Does the bureau have any interest in F&F?"

"We keep an eye on them but most of their problems have come from the postal inspector. Interstate shipments of obscene material—things like that."

"Any Indianapolis connections?"

"Nothing current. At least nothing that the bureau is aware of. But I was able to find a couple of possible leads. The first is a man named Brad Thornton. Records indicate that he was a private contractor for F&F. He was a photographer. Records also indicate that he was arrested and charged with the molestation of a child, but the charges were dropped."

"Dropped?"

"Correct. The child's mother suddenly became hostile to having the child testify. On top of that, the child was very young and unwilling, so—"

"Without the mother's assistance and with an impeachable witness, the prosecutor had no case."

"Seems that way. There was some suspicion of witness tampering, but—"

"They couldn't prove it," I said.

"Correct again. So the case fell apart."

"And he walked."

"Yes."

There was silence on the line as we mulled over the news.

"Maybe he didn't do it," I said, breaking the silence.

"Maybe he did."

"I was just playing devil's advocate."

"Don't," she said. "He has the judicial system to do it for him."

"He's not a registered sex offender," I said, "which means we don't have an address."

"Sex offender? Probably. Registered? No. But I do have a last known address." She gave it to me.

"Anything else on him?"

"Just that this guy has an 'approach with extreme caution' attached to him."

I made note of it. "You said that you had a couple of local leads?"

"Right. The other is an accountant."

"Accountant? You've got to be kidding." I caught myself as soon as the words slipped my lips. "Sorry," I said.

"Pornography is a multimillion-dollar business. They have more accountants than the federal government," she said.

I rubbed my eyes with my free hand. "Does this accountant have a name?"

"Pat Evigan. I have an address."

"Shoot," I said.

"DuVries and White, Certified Public Accountants." She gave me an address in the three thousand block of East Forty-Sixth Street.

"Anything else?"

"That's it. Now, if you don't mind, we have a group that may be planning on hitting a bank later this morning, and we want to be there before they are."

"Thanks for your help," I said.

"Where would you be without me?"

Still dreaming about Anna, I thought.

FIFTEEN

After Mary's call, I now had two leads into F&F, and I wanted to move on them as quickly as possible.

I started some coffee and turned on the small black and white television that I kept in the kitchen. I've never been one for watching the tube, and I couldn't afford cable anyway. But I'm a newshound, so I flicked the channel to one of the local morning news programs.

Overnight, a gas station on the west side had been robbed, a shooting had occurred on the near north side, and a truck had over-turned on I-465. After commercials and a word from my station, I learned that the weather pattern was going to remain essentially the same for the foreseeable future and that the Pacers were going to square off against the Knicks at Conseco Fieldhouse. I flicked off the set and poured a cup of coffee.

The dream I had been having before Mary called seemed real. I had those often, and they almost always seemed real. Real enough, at least, to make waking up a real chore.

I went into the living room and grabbed a photo album off the small wall unit I had kept from my previous life. On it, I also had a few of the various roosters that Anna had managed to collect since she had been a child. Figurines, soap dispensers, cups, towels—any-thing that depicted a rooster became fair game. I had left a few of the figures on the shelf simply because they reminded me of Anna and better times. The rest of her collection, I had boxed and placed in the attic because they had reminded me of Anna and better times.

I sat on the sofa, flipped open the album, and for the next twenty minutes, reviewed a prior life. Most of the photos in this one were of us bringing Callie home from the hospital shortly after her birth. There were the usual baby photos, including the ones that the hospital takes a few minutes after the baby is born that made her look more like an angry cantaloupe than a child.

But there were the others too. Anna smiling and holding Callie as Frank and Corrin beamed, Callie's first birthday—her face nearly hidden by the balloons, Callie and Anna having ice cream and playing with a ball in the backyard. I flipped forward in the album.

There were photos of our trip to Florida, when Callie had gotten excited at the dolphin show and giggled when she had been splashed by their antics. There was a photo of Anna, me, and Callie swinging in the park; a photo of Frank, Corrin, and Anna posing in the Shapiros' home; photos of Callie on Christmas morning; photos of a three-year-old Callie playing with a soccer ball, something which would become an obsession...I closed the album.

There were photos of a happy child with a mother who loved her, photos of a happy and secure family—one that had disappeared in an instant.

I stood to place the album on the shelf. When I did, I noticed how quiet the house had become. Much more, in fact, than it had been just a few minutes ago.

SIXTEEN

The office of Carson DuVries, managing partner of DuVries and White, was well-appointed with burgundy leather furniture and a cherry desk, behind which the distinguished-looking public accountant was sitting.

"Are these Hon?" I asked.

"I'm sorry?" he said.

I leaned over to examine the underside of the chair in which I sat. The tag did not read Hon. "I wanted some Hon chairs for my office but I couldn't swing it," I said. "Is this real leather?" I patted the chair's arms.

He rested his elbows on the desk and tented his fingers. "Yes, they are."

I let out a whistle. "Must have set you back a penny or two," I said.

He smiled. "We do…quite well here at DuVries and White."

I looked around the office. "I bet."

He cleared his throat hinting that he didn't have all day. "What can I do for you, Mr. Parker? My secretary said that you're conducting a preemployment background check on Pat and that you had some questions for me. I'm quite busy, so…"

"Sure. Why did he leave DuVries and White?"

"She. And it is our policy to not discuss the reasons for an employee leaving the firm."

"Problems?"

"Not of a public nature."

"Of a private nature?"

He shifted in his chair. "What I am trying to say is that I am not at liberty to discuss her employment history in depth."

"Sure," I said. "What did she do here?"

He sighed. "I suppose I can discuss her title." He leaned back in his chair, resting his elbows on well-padded armrests. He kept his fingers tented. "Pat was one of our staff accountants."

"Certified?"

"Working toward it. She passed her CPA exam, with flying colors I might add, and at that point, had only to underscore that achievement with practical experience."

"But then she up and left."

"Essentially, yes."

"Isn't that a little unusual?" I asked.

He shifted in his chair. "Uh…well, people come and go for different reasons, Mr. Parker. Not all of them are nefarious."

"Sure," I said. "But I'm paid to look for the nefarious reasons."

He shrugged. "Sorry. I don't believe I can help you in that area. And now, I'd like to ask you a question, Mr. Parker. Who hired you? For what position is Pat applying?"

"I've been hired by a large concern," I lied, "and Miss Evigan has applied for a position there. My client is interested in finding out why she would leave this firm so suddenly."

He nodded his understanding.

"How do you work here?" I asked.

He cocked his head. "I'm not sure I understand your question."

"When someone is hired on, what happens next? In a career sense."

He cleared his throat again. "Well, a new accountant will typically be relegated to a staff position. In that capacity they will concentrate on audits, some tax preparation, but little else. As they acquire skill and, hopefully, bring new clients to the firm, they can expect to see their position and responsibility escalate. It is largely based on their willingness to work and, of course, their innate ability."

"Did she work hard?"

"I recall her as a hard worker."

"Innate ability?"

He nodded his head. "Yes, I would say that she had talent."

"Did she succeed in bringing new clients to the firm?"

He looked at his watch. "As I said, Mr. Parker, I am not at liberty to discuss her employment history. I'm also afraid that I am going to have to end our meeting. I am expecting a client shortly and I have some final preparations to complete." He stood, and I stood with him.

"I wish that I could have been of more help to you," he said.

"You have been," I said.

We shook hands. His was sweaty.

I was ushered from the inner sanctum to the secretary's office, which wasn't much of an office at all. Her desk sat in an area of the hallway in front of DuVries' door. She was a pleasant woman in her late thirties, approachable yet professionally detached. A name plate on her desk read Clarissa.

"Is there anything else we can do for you, Mr. Parker?"

"Maybe. Did you know Pat Evigan?"

She smiled. "Of course. I've been with DuVries and White for more than fifteen years. Very few people have crossed through these doors that I don't know."

"Why did she leave?"

She shook her head. "Sorry, I can't divulge that."

I smiled. "Sure. Did she have any problems here?"

She smiled. "Sorry, I can't divulge that."

I nodded. "Of course. Did she fulfill the corporate vision statement?"

She laughed. "We don't have a vision statement, Mr. Parker. We're an accounting firm with ten CPAs. Small potatoes compared to the big players."

"Sure, sorry. Did she fit with the corporate image?"

The smile began to recede. It was replaced by an expression of annoyance. "Now, you know that I—"

"Can't divulge that…yes, I know. Were you a friend of hers?"

"Still am," she said.

"Do you stay in contact?"

She hesitated. "Yes. Occasionally we will have dinner, catch a movie, go shopping."

"Could you give her a message?"

She nodded. "I don't think that there would be any harm in that."

I reached across her desk and pulled a yellow Post-it note from a note feeder and wrote "F&F. Call me." I wrote my name and cell number across the bottom. She took the note and put it in her desk drawer.

"May I ask, do you anticipate hiring her? She has a natural talent for accounting, but I always believed she would fit better in the corporate structure with a single client than the world of public accounting."

I smiled. "Sorry, I can't divulge that."

CHAPTER
SEVENTEEN

The last known address for Brad Thornton was a house on the east side that sat on Lincoln Street, which intersected with Michigan a couple of blocks north of US 40. The houses on the street were of the same design—shotgun, and spaced less than thirty feet apart. Some were abandoned. Most of the others probably should have been.

I parked in front of the house and got out of the car. The sidewalk was broken and uneven with patches of grass sprouting through the cracks. A mailbox sat on a rotting wooden post in front of the chain-link fence that surrounded the yard. A sign on the gate said Beware of Dog, and the gate was chained and padlocked.

I hopped the fence and walked to the front of the house. I could hear cartoons blaring on the television as I approached the stoop. I reached through a tear in the door's screen and knocked. A dog started barking.

After a period that seemed forever, the door was opened by a young woman wearing a T-shirt and cargo pants. She was restraining a Rottweiler with a choke chain, and a cigarette dangled from her lips.

"Yeah?"

"Good morning," I said, pleasantly. "May I speak with Bradley Thornton?"

The dog stared. The woman stared.

"Who are you?" she asked.

"Colton Parker."

"You a cop?"

"No."

"I don't know no Colton Parker."

"Well then, you see?" I said. "You can make new friends every day."

"Kiss off." She slammed the door.

I knocked again. The dog barked again. The woman opened the door.

"Do I have to sic Buster on you?" she said.

Buster stared. A large string of drool dangled from one corner of his mouth.

"No ma'am," I said. "You don't have to do that."

"If you knock on my door again, I'll sic him on you."

"With all due respect, if you sic him on me I will shoot him."

Her tough exterior cracked. A little. "What do you want?"

"I told you. I want to talk with Bradley."

"He don't go by that name. Everybody calls him Brad."

I looked past the woman and saw a young girl, no more than four years old, sitting on the floor. She had a half-eaten piece of toast in one hand and a capped sipping cup in the other. She was so engrossed in the television that she hadn't noticed the door was open.

"Is she his?"

"None of your business," the woman said.

"True," I said. "But if she isn't—and maybe, even if she is, you don't want him around."

"That ain't none of your business."

"True again," I said. "But it is your business."

I reached into my jacket and pulled out one of my cards. She refused to take it, so I tucked it into the door jamb.

"If you see him, call me."

She slammed the door. A blast of chilled wind blew across the lawn, and I ran the zipper on my jacket up a little higher as I headed toward my car.

The woman's house sat two doors down from the intersection with Michigan and diagonally from a gas station and mini-mart.

I drove across the intersection and parked in the service station lot, where I could keep an eye on the house. If Thornton moved in or out, I wanted to be there.

During the next couple of hours, I sat in the car, trying to keep my feet warm as I watched a bevy of people drift in and out of the gas station. Some of them bought gas, but most of them were there for lottery tickets, beer, chips, and antifreeze. A fine mist of rain began to fall.

I slipped out of the car and into the station to get a large coffee. I could still see the house from my position inside the building. As I stepped up to pay for the coffee, I saw the woman come out of the house. She was carrying the child to a 1970s Chevy Impala that was parked several doors down from her house. I dropped the change into the clerk's hand and ran to my car.

The woman drove down her street, away from my position, turned the car around, and headed back for Michigan Street, which she crossed, heading south on Lincoln. I could see that the child was standing in the back seat, unsecured. I followed.

I stayed three car lengths behind them, sipping the coffee and watching as she drove to Washington Street and began heading east. She drove as far as the intersection with LaSalle and then turned into the White Castle hamburger stand on the northwest corner of the intersection. I followed her and parked in the rear of the lot.

She drove through the drive-up window and bought a bag of hamburgers. I watched as she then circled around the lot and turned onto LaSalle, heading north.

We crossed Michigan again and continued north until we came to Virginia. She turned left onto the residential street and began to slow down. I found an open parking area in front of a house near the corner and pulled against the curb. I killed the engine and slid down to avoid detection. Ever the professional.

Like the woman's house, this one was shotgun with peeling paint, a missing piece of siding, and a large section of plywood over one of the side windows. I slid up partway in the seat to get a better look.

I watched as the woman and her child got out of the car with the bag of hamburgers, walked to the front door, and knocked. The woman stamped her feet as she waited for the door to open. When it did, I sat straight up.

The person who opened the door was Angie Howe.

EIGHTEEN

For the next two hours I waited in a cold car for something to happen, but nothing did. So I took some investigational initiative and wrote down the license number of the woman's car. I called Mary to ask her to run the woman's tag, but the operator said she was in a meeting and asked if I would like to leave a message. I declined and said I would call back later.

The next hour wasn't quite as exciting, and by half past three, I was counting the number of cracks in my dashboard, when finally the woman emerged. The little girl was asleep with her head resting on her mother's shoulder as the woman stood on the step, talking to Angie.

After a couple of minutes, Angie went back into the house and the woman and child drove away. I followed, dialing my cell phone. After a couple of rings someone answered on the other end.

"FBI," a woman said.

This voice was different, and I thought I recognized it, but I wasn't in the mood for small talk. "Special Agent Mary Christopher, please."

There was a pause. Probably checking the register, I thought. The register was a spinning carousel of fawn-colored three-by-five cards used by the supervisors to keep track of their agents. "I'm sorry, but Special Agent Christopher is out. May I take a message?"

"No thanks. I'll try again later." I hung up.

We had turned and turned again until we were back on Washington Street, heading west. I concentrated on staying several car lengths behind her, but as soon as it was clear that she was headed back to her house, I allowed my thoughts to shift to the connection between her and my client.

Which was what? Why did they meet, and what was so important that they would meet for almost three hours? If Angie knew the woman, did she also know Thornton? Was Angie connected to F&F? For that matter, was Emma connected to F&F? And if so, how? And why?

I followed the woman and child home and resumed my position at the service station. I watched as she parked in front of the house, removed the little girl from the front seat, and pulled a few envelopes from the mailbox before going back into the house.

I had something. I wasn't sure what it was exactly, but I knew that I was on to something that would shed light on this case. A chrome paper clip and a meeting between my client and someone who was connected to F&F, even if indirectly, was beginning to look like a pattern. And that pattern was revolving around two simple letters.

"Colton, you intrepid investigator," I said. "You just might be onto something."

When I saw the lights in the house come on, I started my car and drove away.

NINETEEN

When I arrived home, my head was still swirling from the sudden revelation that my client may not be everything I had assumed. Given her occupation, I shouldn't have been surprised. Over a decade in law enforcement, ten years of dealing with the underside of life, had hardened me. Yet I still found myself caught unaware by people and the events in which they engaged themselves. From time to time, they just flat took me by surprise.

"Get a grip, Colton," I said to myself as I dropped my jacket onto the sofa on the way into the kitchen. "It isn't the first time, and it won't be the last."

I opened the refrigerator in search of dinner. I found a quart of milk, half a dozen eggs, a few strips of bacon, and a pound of bologna. I smelled the bologna and threw it in the trash. "I've got to get to the store," I said, realizing that I was talking to myself again.

I grabbed three of the eggs and closed the door, glancing at the wall clock as I did. It was nearly four thirty, and I wanted to get ahold of Mary and see if she could run the woman's tags for me.

I set the eggs on the counter and slid two pieces of bread into the toaster without pushing the lever down as I grabbed the phone and tried to reach Mary again. And again, I was told that she was out and asked if I wanted to leave a message. I didn't.

After cracking the eggs and dumping them into the bowl, I began to scramble them. Eggs are one of the few things I can cook.

My attempts at contacting Brad Thornton had led to my surveillance of his girlfriend—or wife, I wasn't sure which—and that had led to my finding a connection between the woman and Angie. That, of course, was inevitably going to lead to my going out again tonight to try a second time to connect with Thornton.

As I thought about the events of the case, suddenly realizing that I was scrambling the eggs with more fury than was required, the phone rang.

"Dad?"

I balanced the phone between my ear and shoulder as I continued beating the eggs without mercy.

"Hi, honey."

"Dad, where were you?" There were strong undertones of irritation in her voice.

"What do you mean, 'where were you'?"

There was a pause. "Dad, it's Saturday."

I began flipping through my mental rolodex, but I was coming up empty.

"Dad? The game? Remember?"

The game. "Oh, honey, I'm sorry." I sat the bowl on the counter.

"You promised."

"I know…I know. I just…got busy."

Silence.

"I'm sorry," I repeated.

"Are you at least going to come to dinner?"

I looked at the bowl of beaten eggs. "What time?"

"Six. At Grandma's. Remember?"

I glanced at the wall clock. I could still make it in time. "I'll be there," I said.

"Are you sure this time?" she asked before hanging up.

CHAPTER
TWENTY

I arrived at the Shapiros' at precisely six o'clock. Anna's parents had
always been meticulous about everything they did, and it showed
in the level of care they lavished on their home. Simple by anyone's
standards, the house was a three-bedroom ranch with two baths and
a wood deck attached to the back. A flock of mums were in place
around the perimeter, and a large garden of wildflowers was waiting
to bloom when spring rolled around once again. The lawn was lush
and green with only a smattering of fallen leaves lacing the yard. The
asphalt driveway shimmered with a recent coat of sealant.

I recognized the Shapiros' late-model Pontiac. Parked behind it
was a red Ford minivan. I pulled my car tightly behind the Ford and
shifted into park. I had a sinking feeling as I approached the door.

"Colton." Frank answered the door. "Come on in."

The living room was illuminated in the amber glow of a crackling
fire. It was one of the few spots on earth where I felt comfortable,
one of the few places where love and security were nearly tangible.
In a world that is fueled by change, the Shapiros' home seemed to
be the one constant in life.

"Colton," Corrin said, coming from the kitchen and drying her
hands on a dishtowel. She was dressed in a full apron wrapped over
a cotton housedress. Despite a recent degenerative hip problem for

which she was taking pain medication, she moved with a level of grace and elegance that I had not seen since Anna. We hugged.

"Hi, Corrin, how are you?" I said.

"Colton," her eyes filled with tears, "we have seen so little of you since..."

"I know," I said. "But with the new business and—"

"Sure, we understand," Frank said, placing a big hand on my shoulder, "it's just that with Anna gone...you and Callie are all we have left."

They had taken me into their lives the minute Anna and I met. I was the only son they would ever have. They were the only parents I had ever known.

"Colton, how are you?"

My sinking feeling had been justified.

"Colton, you remember Pastor Millikin, don't you?" Corrin asked.

I took his outstretched hand and shook it. "Sure do," I said. "I'm fine, Pastor. How are you?"

He was a tall man with thinning gray hair and sharp, angular features. He looked as though his face had been purposefully designed. He was wearing a brown sport coat over a beige crew-necked sweater. "Call me Dale," he said. "And I'm fine."

Six months prior to her death, Anna had declared herself "born again." She began attending her parents' church, and Dale Millikin was their pastor. He had officiated at her funeral, and seeing him again reminded me of that difficult time.

I turned to see Callie coming from the bedroom area of the house. She was dressed like any typical teenager—jeans, polo shirt, and tennis shoes. She did not make eye contact with me.

"Hi, sweetie," I said, hugging her. "I am so sorry about missing your game today."

She put her arms around me but said nothing.

"They won." Frank said. "Ten to nine, and Callie scored the first point."

I leaned back to look into Callie's face. "Wow. That was a squeaker wasn't it?"

"It only takes one point to win." Callie said, flatly. The air had gotten decidedly chillier.

"Well now," Corrin said, "dinner's ready, and I don't want to let it get cold."

We all gathered in the dining room. I sat and began to spoon the potatoes onto my plate when I realized that no one else was following suit. I looked up into the faces of the others.

"We're going to ask Pastor Millikin to say grace," Frank said.

"Of course."

"Let's bow our heads," Millikin said. We all bowed.

"Heavenly Father, we thank You this evening for the food that You have provided and for the hands that have prepared it. For those who are gathered here together, we ask Your blessing and that they may find Your peace. It is in Jesus' name that we pray. Amen."

We all said amen.

"Okay," Frank said, glancing in my direction, "now we can eat."

After dinner, I asked to see Callie's room. She led me down the hall to a rear bedroom and showed me the new decorating job that Corrin and Frank had done for her. The room had once been Anna's but now reflected the tastes of a different teenager of a different time. Papered in pastels and fitted with new furniture, it was apparent that Anna's parents were doing all they could to make Callie feel as secure as she had once felt in her own home.

A line of dolls that had once been Anna's, and that she had given to Callie several years ago, sat on the bed. A student desk with a computer stood in one corner, along with some books and several soccer trophies.

"This is really nice, honey," I said. "Grandma and Grandpa have put a lot of time into this."

She looked around the room. "I helped."

I acted astonished. "You did? Well, they took a chance didn't they?"

She nodded without expression.

I put my arm around her. "You did a fine job. This looks great."

From the look in her eyes, I could sense that she was looking for the right time to spring a question. Like two brown searchlights, they darted back and forth, yet never lost contact with my own. I could see Anna in them.

"Dad?"

"Yes?"

"When can I come home?"

"Let's have a seat." I guided her to the bed where we sat. I kept my arm around her. "Honey, it's really not that simple."

"Why isn't it?"

I took a deep breath. "Look around this room. Look at how nice it is, how much money that Grandma and Grandpa have spent on you."

"So?"

"So, I can't give you this. If you come to live with me right now, you will be living in half of a rented house. Half of a drafty house," I said, mostly to myself. "You won't be able to go to the school that you go to now, you won't be able to play on the same soccer team, you won't—"

"There's nothing wrong with the schools where you live," she said.

"I know," I said. "But wouldn't you miss your friends? This is the only place that you know. If you pack up and move to the south side with me, it'll mean making new contacts and leaving old ones behind and…just a lot of changes."

"So?"

I stood from the bed and walked around the room. She repositioned herself with her back against the headboard. She pulled one of the dolls to her and hugged it.

"So…I can't afford to care for you right now, honey."

She clenched the doll tighter and looked at the floor. "Oh."

The truth often hurts. It hurt me. And I knew that it had hurt her.

"How's school going?" I said. It was a clumsy way of changing the subject.

She continued to clench the doll and shrugged.

"Do you have any homework?"

"It's done," she said.

The conversation had become stilted, and I was desperately searching for the next thought when Corrin came into the room.

"Dessert," she said. "Frank is making ice cream."

"Thanks, Corrin. We'll be right there."

She left the room, and I sat on the bed, putting my arm around Callie again. "It won't always be like this," I said. "The business will pick up and then we can be together."

She shrugged.

"There's a Pacers-Knicks game coming up. If I can get tickets, would you want to go?"

She nodded, still clenching the doll.

I was hoping for more. For some enthusiasm, maybe even a little excitement. But there wasn't going to be any that night.

"Come on," I said. "Let's go get some of Grandpa's ice cream before it's all gone."

TWENTY-ONE

After dessert and clearing the dishes, we all played a round of Monopoly. Callie got rich, I went broke, and no one seemed surprised. When the game was over and Callie said her goodnights, Frank, Millikin, and I gathered in the living room. Corrin soon joined us, bringing several cups and a carafe of coffee when she did.

Each of us had a cup as we sat and watched the fire. No one spoke, which was okay with me. I knew once the conversation began, it would turn to Anna and then...the inevitable.

"Colton," Millikin said, stirring his coffee, "how are you getting along?"

Here we go, I thought. "It isn't easy, but I'm getting it done."

"Day at a time?" he said.

"Yeah, something like that."

"You know," he said, "all of us loved Anna."

I shifted uncomfortably. This was exactly the scenario I had wanted to avoid.

"The entire congregation has taken her loss particularly hard. She left a huge void."

Tell me about it, I thought.

"We appreciate the words you had to say at the funeral," Frank said. "They meant a lot to us."

"Yes," Corrin said. "You and the church were very kind to us throughout this whole ordeal. We can't thank you—or them—enough." Tears formed in her eyes, and I could feel a heaviness beginning to settle on me.

"We're glad we could help and be with you in a time of need, Corrin," Millikin said. "All of us have times when we must lean on someone."

The heavy feeling was beginning to coagulate. I could feel the bile rising in my throat as I choked back the bitterness.

He turned to me. "I know that no one knows more about the void she left behind than you."

"And exactly how would you know that?" I asked.

Frank shifted uncomfortably.

"Because I lost my wife too," Millikin said. "And my son was only seven at the time. And it took me a while to realize that while I had lost a wife, he had lost a mother. And for a long time I focused on work as a way of avoiding the pain. But in the process, I left my son to deal with his mother's death on his own." He continued to stir his coffee as he stared vacantly. "It was too much for a little boy."

"Callie and I will be fine," I said, struggling to suppress the growing anger.

"Of course," the minister said. "It's just that sometimes we can lean so heavily on ourselves that we can forget where the real source of strength lies."

"And exactly where would that be, Pastor?" I asked.

Frank glanced at Corrin.

"In Christ."

I snorted.

"I know that life hasn't always been kind to you, Colton. Anna and I had several talks about it."

"About me?" My voice was beginning to raise an octave. "Anna talked to you about me?"

He nodded. "Yes. She was concerned."

I could feel the muscles of my chest and arms tighten. "Concerned?"

"She told me how you were raised. Moved from one foster home to another. Never having the opportunity to develop any close ties with anyone. No father figure in your life. She was concerned that you had become so self-reliant that you would never see a need to place your life in the hands of Christ. She wanted you to find salvation."

"What I really need," I said, standing, "is to get going." I was afraid of what I might say next.

The three of them looked up at me.

"So soon?" Frank said.

"I really have a lot of work to do. Early day tomorrow," I said.

Millikin set his cup and saucer down on the coffee table and stood. "I'm afraid I have to get going too," he said.

Frank and Corrin stood, voicing a few protests about us not having to rush off so soon. Neither I nor Millikin gave in, and eventually they walked both of us to the door and saw us off.

The outside air had gotten considerably colder, seeming to eerily reflect the mood between the pastor and me as we walked to our cars. He followed me to mine and paused as I opened the door.

"Colton, you know that death is a part of life."

"Sure," I said. "And you'll pardon me if I say that observation doesn't add a whole lot to my situation right now."

"No, I don't suppose it does. But this should. Anna was a Christian. A follower of Christ. That means that although she may die here, she will live forever."

"Sure. And what are her daughter and husband supposed to do in the meantime?"

"Talk to God. Tell Him about your concerns. He understands."

"He understands?"

Millikin nodded.

"Does He understand that there's a thirteen-year-old girl in that house who will grow up without her mother? Does He understand that someday that thirteen-year-old girl will be a young woman and will walk down the aisle without a mother to share that day?"

"Colton, God lost a Son too. He knows the pain of death."

"Jesus wept. Is that right?" I said.

He nodded.

"Did Jesus weep when I lost my job because I beat the snot out of a young woman's kidnapper? Or did He leap for joy when that beating helped us find her in time?"

"Colton," Millikin said.

The gate was beginning to open. I had been struggling to keep it closed, and I was losing. "No, Pastor. I have questions for God. Fair questions."

"Colton, give God a chance."

"It doesn't seem like I have much choice now, does it, Pastor?"

"Maybe not on some things. Like, for instance, the tragedies that sometimes come into our lives. But we do on others. Like how we will respond to those tragedies. And if we'll allow God to do what He does best." He paused, waiting for a response. I didn't give him one. "God gave us a free will. We can choose our path in life, just like Adam did. But our ability to make choices doesn't free us of the consequences. God is in control." He paused again. "Callie misses you, Colton. She needs to be home with her father."

I could feel the heat rising to dangerous levels. "Aren't you delving into an area that isn't your concern?"

He held up both hands. "You're right," he said. "You're absolutely right. I didn't mean to pry. But think about this. What we do affects our children. Take it from me. I know. My son and I never talk. I haven't seen him in years."

"And you're giving me advice?"

"I'm trying to help. Callie will grow up whether you're in her life or not. Anna's death has cast you into a new role. One that you were not prepared for. But it's yours now regardless. And you can't do it alone."

"I've gotten through life just fine, Pastor."

"Sure, for now. But the time comes for every man when there's nowhere else to go. When the challenges become so great that we can't find the answer in ourselves or in anyone else. There comes a time in life when we realize that God is in control." He paused again, waiting for a reaction. And again I didn't give him one.

"Adam was the father of us all," he continued. "Through him, sin entered into the world. Because of his failings, because of his desire to do things his own way and ignore God's parameters, we all live in a world that does not function as God designed it. That is why He sent His Son to die. To redeem the world."

"I've got to go," I said, trying to avoid what was surely going to be a confrontation that I would later regret.

He paused to raise the collar of his jacket. "Talk to Mary, Colton."

"Mary? Christopher?"

He nodded.

"How do you know Mary?" I asked.

"She was at Anna's funeral. Remember?"

Mary had indeed been at Anna's funeral. It had been her constant support that had carried me through that difficult day.

"After it was over, she asked if we could talk."

"About what?" I asked.

"Talk to her, Colton," he said, sidestepping my question. "You might find some very interesting facts about a very interesting woman."

TWENTY-TWO

I slept fitfully that night and was awake by five. The conversation with Millikin was still on my mind as I ran several laps around the park. The sun hadn't yet risen, and the area surrounding the park was quiet except for the echo of my shoes striking the pavement and my own labored breathing.

I wasn't sure how well Millikin knew Mary or what he meant by his suggestion that I talk to her, but my interest had been piqued. I knew that I would eventually have to ask her, and I suspected that Millikin knew it too.

I rounded the park for the last lap. Usually I will see at least one other runner when doing my laps, regardless of how early or late I'm out. But this time I didn't see a soul, which only added to my feelings of isolation.

I finished my run in what I thought was a personal best but with little sense of accomplishment. Given the magnitude of what lay ahead, a solid run just didn't seem to add up to a whole lot in the scheme of things.

After finishing my last lap and making my way back to the house, I showered, allowing the warm water to counter the effects of the chilled morning air. It didn't help. The chill I felt was as much internal as external. My anger toward Millikin hadn't come from his perceived intrusion. It had come from fearing he was right.

I didn't have a lot in the fridge, so I skipped breakfast and downed two cups of coffee before leaving around seven. I drove back to the woman's house to see if I could pick up Brad Thornton. I was working on the assumption that he was not an early riser or a regular church attendee, which should mean that he would leave the house after I was in position. That was assuming, of course, that he was in the house. If not, I had more time to count the cracks in my dashboard. Maybe even start to catalog them.

My mood began to lift when, two hours later, I saw that I had been correct.

Twenty minutes after ten, a tall, muscular man of about thirty with dark shoulder-length hair left the house. He was dressed in a black T-shirt, black jeans, black boots, and a black leather jacket. Underneath one side of the jacket, I could see a wallet that was tucked in his hip pocket and chained to one side of his belt. The sheath for a knife protruded from the other side.

He climbed into an '84 Ford and lit a cigarette as he pulled away from the curb. He drove in my direction and turned west on Michigan. I waited until he passed before following.

Since most people tend to sleep in on Sunday morning, the traffic was light. That makes for fewer traffic jams and the road rage that accompanies them but significantly increases the chance of being spotted when tailing someone. I kept as far back as possible while still maintaining a useful vigil. It wasn't easy, and several times I thought he might be trying to shake a tail. Something that someone in his line of work would feel compelled to do even when no one was there.

He wove in and out of traffic, made sudden lane changes, and even pulled to the curb once, allowing the cars behind him to pass, which I did. I picked him up again several blocks down the road.

I continued to follow as he headed for the downtown metropolitan area of Indianapolis. When we arrived downtown, he parked on Ohio Street. I paralleled several slots behind him and killed the engine.

After a few moments, he got out of the car and flicked a cigarette butt to the ground. He looked both ways and jogged toward the staircase that led to the brick patio of the Indiana Historical Society, which lined one side of the canal.

When I was confident that he hadn't made me, I chambered a round in the Ruger and left my car. My original goal had been to talk with Thornton so I could get a better handle on F&F. Maybe even get a lock on Emma and see what dealings she had with F&F, if any. But after seeing his woman meet with my client, my professional interest in him had changed.

I stayed a few dozen yards behind and watched as he moved down the steps. He paused and cupped his hands against the breeze to light another cigarette. The day remained as cold as it had been all week. His breath and the exhaled smoke condensed into clouds of vapor.

I paused to lean over the railing and watch the ducks as they moved along the canal.

He glanced in my general direction but was soon diverted by another man who joined him as the two of them continued down the steps. Thornton looked back in my direction one more time before turning away. I remained in place, keeping an eye on the canal and on him.

The other man was neither as tall as my subject nor as solidly built, but he too was dressed all in black, including a bandana with a Harley-Davidson logo imprinted on it. After the two of them turned along the canal, I began to move.

I went down the same steps and took a seat at one of the tables on the patio. From where I sat, I could see Thornton and the man sitting on the bank of the canal some thirty yards away. They appeared to be in animated conversation, with Thornton jabbing his finger into the man's chest several times. After what seemed to be an eternity, Thornton handed the man a package in exchange for another package that the man handed him. After the swap, the two stood, and the man continued walking along the canal heading north. Thornton moved back toward the same steps he had come down, passing me as he did. If he made me, he gave no indication. I waited until he had moved up the steps before I followed him. By the time I reached the top, I realized that I had lost him.

I kept moving. Years of surveillance had taught me that the best way to remain inconspicuous is to *be* inconspicuous. If I was being observed, I didn't want my body language to show signs that I had lost the person that I was following. Unfortunately, I only speak one language, and *body* isn't it. Ten feet ahead, Thornton emerged from behind the doorway of the Indiana State Library, grabbing the front of my jacket with one hand while brandishing a very large knife with the other.

CHAPTER
TWENTY THREE

L ook," I said, "I don't want—"
"Shut up and keep your hands out to your side where I can see 'em."

I spread my hands out to my side and kept an eye on the knife. It was large. A lot like the one Sylvester Stallone preferred in *Rambo*. He pressed the point firmly against my chest.

"Is this the guy?" The voice came from behind me. It was the man I had seen meeting with Thornton on the bank of the canal. He was out of breath. He had apparently doubled back when I followed Thornton after their meeting. My surveillance technique was going to need some work.

Thornton ignored the man's question. "See if he's got a gun."

The man, no more than twenty-one or two, frisked me and quickly found the Ruger. He pulled it from its holster and held it in his left hand.

"You that dude that came around? Messing with Melissa?" Thornton asked.

"I came looking for you."

"Why'd you mess with Melissa?"

"I didn't mess with her. I was looking for you."

"Is that so?" He moved close, keeping the knife pressed into my chest. It was beginning to hurt.

"It's so," I said.

"Well, now" he said, "looks like you found me."

I looked at the knife. "It appears that way."

"So what'd you want?"

"I want to know what you can tell me about F&F."

"Nothing you need to know."

"I'll be the judge of what I need to know," I said.

He pushed firmly on the knife. "Don't look like you're in a position to be judging nothing," he said.

I nodded toward the knife. "Why don't you put that away? All I want is information."

He grinned as he released my jacket and used his free hand to pull my business card, the one that I had left with Melissa, from his left jacket pocket. He kept the point of the knife in my chest. "Says, 'Colton Parker, Private Investigator.'" He lowered the card. "That you?" The grin faded. "Or are you a cop?"

"I'm not a cop."

"You was followin' us like you was one," the other man said.

"I'm not a cop," I repeated.

"Who hired you?" Thornton asked.

Since I didn't know to what extent my client was involved with Thornton or Melissa, I didn't want to tip him off that I knew anything and then have him take it back to Angie before I could piece all of this together. "Sorry," I said, "but I can't tell you that."

Thornton looked around, furtively, as he kept the point of the knife pressed firmly in my chest. Any thoughts that I had to take the knife from him were overshadowed by the kid who had my gun.

"We oughta off him," Thornton said, glancing at the kid.

There were a few people beginning to move about the city, but none closer than a hundred yards.

"I don't know, man," the kid said. "I don't think we—"

"Shut up," Thornton said. "Let me think."

"I ain't goin' back. Not for no murder," the kid said.

"I said, shut up."

I decided to seize the moment. Divide and conquer. "If he pushes that knife in, you're going down with him, kid. Accessory to murder."

"You shut up," the kid said. He licked his lips as he rocked from one foot to the other, keeping his eyes on Thornton and the knife. He still had my gun in his left hand.

"You talk too much," Thornton said, grabbing me by the jacket again.

"Easy," the kid said. "I ain't doin' no killin'."

"You're in up to your eyeballs now, kid," I said.

Thornton shoved me toward the secluded doorway from which he had emerged. "That's it," he said. "I've had enough."

I dropped my hands as I began a reach for the knife, when suddenly the kid lunged for Thornton, tearing me from his grip and pushing me backward with the force of his body.

Thornton was caught off guard by the kid's sudden movement and swung at him with his free hand. He missed, and the kid grabbed Thornton around the waist with my gun still gripped firmly in his left hand.

As I started to move forward, Thornton struck the kid in the side of the head with the hilt of the knife. The kid reacted, slamming into me again and again, driving me backward.

Then, in one fluid movement, Thornton thrust the knife forward, plunging it into the kid's abdomen.

He stiffened with a sudden gasp, grabbing the knife with both hands. His back was pressed firmly against my chest, and I could feel the slackness begin to take over as he dropped my gun and began to slide. As he began to sink, I caught him and eased him to the sidewalk.

"Easy kid," I said. "Hang on."

I looked up at Thornton, who was looking at the bloody knife in his hand. Then his gaze shifted, simultaneously with mine, to the Ruger lying on the concrete.

I reached across the kid for the gun, only to see Thornton take off as he moved west down Ohio Street, for the anonymity of Military Park.

Cell phones can be incredibly intrusive. Still, I was glad to have one. It improved the kid's chances for survival.

The police were the first to arrive, followed seconds later by the paramedics.

I was keeping pressure on the kid's abdomen with both hands, using the Harley-Davidson bandanna he had been wearing. It was a nearly futile attempt to stem the flow of blood.

As the two police officers emerged, it was apparent that they were new to the force. Both were young, probably no more than twenty-five, and not quite sure what was happening. Like most calls for help, this one had most likely been misinterpreted as it was passed from me to a dispatcher and then to the officers. They reacted to the situation as they saw it. A severely injured man with blood all over the place and a gun lying on the sidewalk not two feet away. And, of course, me kneeling over the victim. One of the cops pulled his weapon.

"On the ground, now!"

I kept the pressure on the kid's abdomen, waiting for the paramedics to get their equipment out of the truck.

"Did you hear my partner?" the other cop asked, as he grabbed me and shoved me, face down, into the sidewalk. The bleeding immediately began to increase.

"What've we got here?" one of the paramedics asked as he snapped on a pair of latex gloves.

"Looks like a shooting," the cop with the gun said.

The second paramedic set his box on the ground and knelt along-side his partner, who was already wrapping the kid's arm with an inflatable cuff.

"No," I said. "It's not a—"

"Quiet!" the cop on top of me said, as he reached for my hands.

"This guy's lost a lot of blood," the second paramedic said, as he began to cut through the kid's shirt.

"He wasn't shot. He—"

The cop forced my face into the concrete.

"He wasn't shot," one of the paramedics said. "This guy was stabbed."

"See?" I said, from the sidewalk.

The cop on top of me kept his knee in my back as he jerked my hands behind me and slapped on the cuffs. "Tell it downtown," he said. "Got any ID?"

"In my right rear pocket," I said.

He fished around and pulled out my ID. "It says he's a P.I."

"No way," gun-cop said as he holstered his weapon. "That is so cool, man, we busted Kojak."

"Kojak was a cop," I said.

"What was that?"

"I said Kojak was a cop."

They both looked at me and blinked.

"He was a New York City Police Detective," I said. "He wasn't a private investigator."

They looked at each other. Gun-cop grinned. "Book 'im, Danno," he said.

TWENTY-FOUR

A re you here in an official capacity?"
"No. Purely humanitarian," I heard Mary say from somewhere outside my cell.

I stood and peered through the bars in time to see Harley Wilkins and Mary round the corner. They stopped in front of the holding cell and studied me without speaking.

After a few seconds, Wilkins turned to Mary and said, "One of our society's darkest moments is when a human being is incarcerated."

Mary crossed her arms and nodded thoughtfully. "I agree, Captain. Such things only serve to further underscore our judicial system's inadequacies."

"Tragic." Wilkins said. "So much potential, lost."

"The only thing around here that is lost on me," I said, "is your act."

Mary looked at Wilkins. "It's a pity to see what even a little time behind bars can do to a man's spirit."

"Tragic," Wilkins repeated.

I was getting tired. I knew that they were trying to pump me up on what had been a bad day, but their humor was lost on me. "Look," I said, "it's two o'clock in the afternoon. I haven't had breakfast or lunch. I've been threatened, nearly gutted by a nut with a knife, and watched a young man stabbed. If you two are going to subject me to any more of this, I'm going to want to speak with my lawyer."

"I'm noting an increase in hostilities," Mary said, clinically.

"I agree. I'm picking up on some of that as well. Are you sure that he can be successfully reintegrated into society?"

I sighed.

"Well," Mary said, "one can only try. If you release him to me, Captain, I will see to it that this social malcontent will not cause you or your officers any further embarrassment."

Wilkins motioned at someone sitting down the hall. The doors slid open with a hum. "I would appreciate that very much, Special Agent Christopher," he said with a grin.

As I stepped out of my cell, Wilkins said, "Bitterman is a tad upset that you are still poking your face into his case. You might want to go a little easy. You know?" He walked away, leaving me with Mary.

"Well now," she said, looking me over, "let's see what we can do about getting you rehabilitated."

Mary took me by the house so I could clean up and change out of the bloody clothes. Thirty minutes later, we were sitting in a booth at Armatzio's. I was having a plate of pasta, and Mary had a salad.

"So tell me again," she said, "about this Brad Thornton."

I shrugged. "Proceed with extreme caution," I said. "He stuck that kid like he was nothing. Just a piece of meat that got in the way." I twirled my fork in the pasta. "On the other hand, when he thought I had been messing around with Melissa, it seemed like he cared for her."

"Maybe he does."

"Maybe," I said. "Even cobras can take care of their own." I ate a bite of the pasta.

"Are you okay?" she asked.

"Yeah, I'm fine," I said. "I hope the kid makes it, though."

She flipped open her phone and called Wishard Memorial Hospital. "Let's find out."

The ER told Mary that the kid was in surgery but expected to survive. I was glad to hear the news.

"So," she said, flipping the phone closed, "changing the subject, what have you got so far?"

I set my fork down. "Well, let's see," I said, counting off the fingers of one hand. "First, I've got a client who has hired me to investigate her boyfriend's involvement in the murder of his aunt, a much-loved, well-respected schoolteacher who, by all accounts, was active in the lives of troubled kids well beyond her required duties. Second, I find that the aforementioned, much-loved schoolteacher, who lived a quiet life, was active in horse betting. Very active."

"Any possibility that she owed money to someone?" Mary asked.

I shook my head. "No, I already looked into that. Third," I continued, "I find a connection between this much-beloved schoolteacher and a porno production company."

"Possible connection," Mary said, taking a bite of the salad.

"Possible," I said, correcting myself.

"And the totality of that connection consists of a paper clip."

"True," I said, acknowledging the weakness of my lead. "And, as we have indicated, my connection may not be a connection at all. And fourth," I continued, "I find that one of my leads into this porno production company may be connected to my client by way of his girlfriend."

"And this would be the same lead that tried to kill you today."

"That would be correct," I said.

Mary nodded. "And you're getting concerned that your client may have a role in all of this."

"The thought has occurred to me. According to the Tooleys, there was no love lost between Angie and Emma."

"Who are the Tooleys?" Mary asked.

"Emma's next-door neighbors. Marvin, Opal, and Kitty."

"Kitty?"

"The cat."

Mary shook her head. "Your life is like a soap opera."

I concentrated on my pasta as neither of us said anything for a couple of minutes.

"Has the possibility that Billy is actually guilty of the crime crossed your mind?" Mary asked, breaking the silence.

"Sure. It did at first. I can put him at the scene at the time of the murder. I also know that his record makes him out to be someone who is capable of violence, and he had at least one argument with the victim," I said, taking another bite. "Add to those his lack of emotion over the loss of someone who was allegedly very dear to him, and he becomes a very solid suspect." I twirled more pasta onto my fork. "I also know Bitterman. He's very thorough. If he thinks Billy did it, I need to listen."

"So why did you take this case?"

"A hunch." I set my fork down again. "You know how it is. You can't work in this business as long as we have and ignore those hairs on the back of your neck. I spent five years with the Chicago PD before I applied with the bureau. I've worked the streets and I've worked the boardrooms, and I've found one thing they have in common."

"Nothing is as it appears to be," Mary said.

"Bingo."

"Why don't you think that Billy is the murderer?"

I reluctantly told her about the burglary and everything related to the missing computer, including the fact that Billy couldn't read. I didn't want to involve her in my illegal affairs, but I felt as if I had no other choice. She didn't flinch at the news.

"It's starting to look more and more like Emma knew her killer. Possibly too well," she said. "And if you can find that computer, you'll have your murderer."

"I agree," I said. "Of course, that computer is probably long gone by now."

She nodded her agreement. "So is that all you have?"

I shook my head. "Not quite." I pulled a crumpled piece of paper from my pocket and slid it across the table to Mary.

"What's this?"

"It's the tag number of the woman I tailed."

"Thornton's girlfriend?"

"I think so. Or she's his ex...or maybe the mother of his child. Either way, she's somebody he cares about."

"You want me to check this out?"

"If it wouldn't be too much trouble," I said, taking another bite of the pasta.

"No, not at all. I mean, after all, if the FBI can't be at your disposal and bail you out of the slammer once in a while and run down your leads for you, what good would we be?"

I smiled. "It's nice to see my tax dollars at work."

She called the office on her mobile phone and asked for the NCIC operator. When they answered, she asked them to run the tag. "It'll be a couple of seconds," she said.

I ate another bite of the pasta.

She shook her head. "You eat like you're starved."

"I am."

Mary diverted her attention to the phone. "Who? Any history? Got it. And thanks."

"Well?" I asked.

"It comes back registered to a Melissa King. Twenty-six years old with no previous arrests or warrants."

I set my fork down. "Melissa—that's the name he used. But what is someone with no record doing with a guy like Thornton?"

"The same thing could be said about me," she said. "Didn't I just get you out of jail?"

TWENTY-FIVE

After lunch, Mary took me back to my car, and I drove to the office. I told her I had some work to do and that I wanted to think on the case and try to make some sense out of what I had developed. That was all true, of course, but I also had another reason.

When Anna had been alive, she had been the spirit of our home. But when she died, that spirit was gone, and I could no longer live in the house we had once shared.

So I sold the house and downsized to one I thought I could better afford on the uncertain income I now had. The result, of course, was that there weren't as many familiar sights. Fewer memories. But the pain of her loss was still acute, and each day was still a struggle—more difficult than the one before. And the change of scenery, even if it was to the office, helped alleviate some of the tensions of being alone in an empty house.

I thought again of my conversation with Millikin. His words continued to resonate with me. Still, how could I trust a God who would turn His back on a thirteen-year-old girl? How, for that matter, could I trust a God who had turned His back on me when, as a child, I had been shuttled from home to home, never really knowing exactly how long I would be in any one of them? A God who never allowed me to have anyone that I could call parents, forcing me to live a life of total self-reliance? How could I trust a God who would allow that and then punish me for being the type of a person that lifestyle had forced me to become?

I sat at my desk and rubbed the fatigue from my eyes. "Enough," I said. "You've got work to do."

I settled in behind my desk and made a handwritten record of the case as I understood it so far. I made a list of the events of the investigation in chronological order and tried to make a connection. By a consensus of all involved, Billy was good for the murder. Tooley's description, as impeachable as it was, was as accurate as my own would have been given the dark of night. Upcraft was convinced of Billy's guilt, and one of IPD's best homicide detectives was convinced as well. But my own doubts remained. Billy couldn't read, and there was little anyone could use to blackmail him. Which meant that if Billy did kill Emma, why? And how did the missing computer tie in to her death?

Also, Tooley's description, good as it was given the circumstances, was not rock solid. Was Billy the man Tooley actually saw or the man he remembered from past sightings? And if Billy wasn't the man Tooley saw, who did he see? And what about Emma? What was she into, if anything, that would have driven someone to hate her enough to kill her with such violence? And why take the computer? What was on it, and who did it incriminate?

I replayed the details in my mind again and again. The conversation with Billy. The phone call to Upcraft. The investigation of Emma's house, where my only tangible clue was a paper clip...

I remembered the phone number that I had lifted off of Emma's phone. I found the scrap of paper still in my jacket. I dialed the area code and number.

"F&F, may I help you?" I hung up.

I rubbed the fatigue from my eyes again. It was certainly starting to look like Emma had some type of connection with F&F. Something that went beyond a paper clip.

Whatever the peculiarities of this case, one thing was certain. It would all hinge on finding out the extent of Emma's involvement in F&F and what information she possessed that someone else didn't want her to know—or at least didn't want her to tell—badly enough to kill her.

TWENTY-SIX

I finished my three laps around the park by eight and was in the office by nine. Monday mornings had always held a particularly low wattage in my energy grid, and this particular Monday wasn't shaping up to be much of an exception. I had two messages from my answering service, and neither was likely to brighten my day.

The first was from my landlord, telling me that the rent on my office was overdue. The second was from Angie, wanting to know if I had made any progress.

The rent money I had, even if I had forgotten to give it to the landlord. But progress, on the other hand, was a little harder to come by.

I chambered a round in the Ruger and tucked the gun into position under my left arm. After my run-in with Thornton, I didn't want to be caught with my defenses down. The day was going to involve a meeting with Angie and, if her connections with Melissa were as solid as their meeting had seemed to indicate, there was a chance that I would run into him again. I could only hope.

I dropped the rent check in the mail before stopping to pick up a dozen red and white carnations. They had been Anna's favorite.

I drove to the cemetery and followed the path that the hearse had taken only six months ago. The same path that I had taken every week since.

The Garden of Peace provided nothing of the kind for me. This section of the cemetery was new with freshly mined graves. Many of them, like Anna's, were beginning to settle. They served as a reminder that only a few days or weeks before, the people in them had been alive. They had watched the sun rise with all of the hopes, dreams, and ambitions that we all share. These people had known that their "someday" would come, that they would ultimately have to relinquish life. Yet each had held out for the long haul. Live for today, build for tomorrow. But the clock was ticking. For some, death would come slowly. Like a coiling snake, it would tighten its grip until the release of life was welcome. For others, death would come suddenly—violently—dragging the damned into an eternity they weren't willing to embrace.

The graves were mute reminders of a future that awaits everyone. For me, life without Anna had become a living death…but without the release. The Garden would hold no peace for me until I assumed my position next to her.

Fallen leaves had accumulated on her headstone. I knelt and swept them aside with one hand as I inserted the flowers into the in-ground holder with the other.

"I'm sorry," I whispered. Sorry for not being a better husband. Sorry for not being a better father. Sorry for not being there when she died. Sorry it hadn't been me.

A gust of wind blew, stirring the cluster of leaves that lay around her grave. I zipped my jacket against the wind, aware of the nine-millimeter under my arm. For a moment, my hand hesitated over the bulge in my jacket. The gun was enticing, inviting me to complete the circle of life and join Anna—right there, right then. But as it had many times since her death, my hand dropped away. I knew that Anna would have to wait just a little while longer.

TWENTY-SEVEN

I was on my way out of the cemetery when my cell phone rang. I flipped it open. "Yeah?"

"Who is this?" a woman's voice said.

"Who's this?" I said, so engrossed in my phone that I barely managed to avoid hitting a kid on a bicycle.

"You left a message with Clarissa."

My mind raced through the events of the last several days trying to recall Clarissa.

"I'm Pat Evigan. I believe that you are with F&F and were trying to reach me at DuVries and White." Her voice was clear, her words well enunciated.

"I need to meet with you," I said, allowing her misconception to remain in place.

"I have already spoken to Boyle. The proper adjustments can be made when I have the paperwork to substantiate it."

This was good. I didn't understand any of it, but it was good. "I need to discuss another matter."

She sighed. "What?"

"Not on a wireless. Where can we meet?"

"Who are you?" she asked.

"That's not important. What's important is that we close this thing before we get closed. Do you get my meaning?" I was deliberately being vague.

There was a moment's pause. "When and where?" she asked.

I made arrangements to meet her in an hour at a Taco Bell on the corner of Washington and LaSalle Street, not far from where I had followed Melissa to her meeting with Angie. I told her that I would be wearing a brown leather jacket over a blue T-shirt and jeans. She didn't tell me what she would be wearing.

I arrived at the Taco Bell ten minutes before our appointed time and ordered a taco salad and medium Coke. I was busy drenching the salad in extra-hot sauce when a tall, well-built young woman with blonde hair focused her attention on me. She was wearing a smoke-gray business suit and could easily have been mistaken for a FOX anchorwoman. I motioned for her to have a seat.

"Want something to eat?" I asked.

She shook her head. "Who are you and what do you want?"

I wiped my mouth with a napkin and pulled a business card from my wallet. I handed it to her.

"Private investigator?" Her expression changed from one of uncertainty to one of utter disdain. I picked up on it. Sixteen weeks at the FBI academy hadn't gone to waste.

"Emma Caine was murdered," I said.

There was another change in her expression. This one was less perceptible.

"I've been hired to find out who did it," I said.

She slid the card toward me. "We have an excellent police department for that sort of thing."

"Yes, we do. Except that I have an interested party who doesn't believe that the man currently incarcerated is guilty of Emma's murder."

She shifted slightly in her seat and crossed her legs.

"And why would you want to talk with me?" she asked.

"Because you're an accountant whom I've been able to connect to F&F. I have reason to believe that Emma was also connected to F&F or, at the very least, knew someone else who is...or was."

"F&F is a client. I'm not at liberty to divulge confidential information about my clients' business practices."

I took a bite of the salad. "This is great," I said. "I love Mexican food. In fact, I love any ethnic food. Are you sure you don't want something?"

She frowned as she looked at my salad. "I'm absolutely sure."

"So," I said around a mouthful of salad, "you don't want to talk about Emma and her connection to F&F?"

"I believe you misunderstood me. I said that I'm not at liberty to discuss the affairs of my clients."

"Sure. Except that Emma is not your client. In fact, technically speaking, she is no one's client, seeing as how she is dead and all. So that kind of leaves you open to talk about her and not put yourself in a compromising position."

"Emma Caine was an employee of my client and, dead or alive, I cannot and will not discuss her relationship with them."

"Yes you will." I said, finally getting my first official confirmation that Emma was connected to F&F.

Anger filled her face. "Excuse me?" she said, loudly enough to attract the attention of the restaurant's patrons.

"You might want to hold it down a bit," I said. "I don't think you need for everyone in here to know the type of clients that you service or the fact that they are the reason you lost your position with DuVries and White."

"That's it. I'm leaving." She stood to go.

"Brad Thornton."

She paused.

"What's your connection to him?"

"I don't know any Brad Thornton and I'm..."

"Yes you do," I said. "And if you don't sit down and tell me how Emma Caine was connected to F&F, I will go to the police with what I have and let them sort it out. Somehow I don't think your bosses would like that. Especially when I tell them that it was avoidable."

She hesitated but then sat down with a glare that was meant to singe my soul. It didn't.

"Let's start at the beginning," I said. "How was Emma connected to F&F?"

She hesitated. I figured she was probably trying to give her "this is my angry look" more time to work its magic. Her face must have gotten tired because she sighed and said, "Emma was a regional director of talent."

I broke off a part of the taco salad's edible bowl and ate it. "No kidding," I said. "What does that mean?"

"It means that she was responsible for recruiting the...talent."

"The girls."

"Yes."

"And how did she do this?"

She shook her head. "I don't know. That's not part of my responsibility. I'm an accountant. I handle the financial matters. Not the legal ones."

"Sure," I said. "Given the high caliber of your other clients, you probably wouldn't want to mix with those low-life legal types."

Her face reddened with anger again.

"So how much did Emma pull down? Annually."

Her expression said that she was deciding whether she wanted to answer, but apparently she thought better of it. "About fifty K a year."

"Is that a lot? For what she did, I mean."

She shrugged. "It's par for someone who works as hard as she did."

"How was she paid?"

"Flat rate. Five thousand per girl."

"So she was churning ten girls per year?"

"Something like that. Sometimes less. Sometimes more."

"Did she have any legal bouts?"

"Like I said, I'm an accountant. I don't handle the legal matters."

I ate another piece of the bowl. "Oh yeah. That's right. You did say that."

She made an obvious gesture of looking at her watch. "Anything else?"

"Brad Thornton. What does he do and where can I find him?"

"I don't—"

"Yes, you do. Don't kid a kidder, lady. I'm better at it than you are."

"Okay, look, I don't know him. I've heard the name, and I've heard enough to know that he's nobody to fool with."

"Where can I find him?"

"I don't know, and that's the truth."

"Did Emma have any trouble with him?"

She held up both hands. "I don't know. That's the honest to God truth. All I know is that she worked hard and had a competitor for her job."

"Who?"

"I don't know. Some chick."

"Name?"

"I don't know."

I paused to study her. Most people cannot lie effectively. They will tip their hand in some way or another. Maybe a glance at their feet, or a look away...I didn't see any of that. "Okay," I said, "but I want to know where I can reach you if I have any more questions."

She sighed again and paused to think about it before reaching into her purse and pulling out a gold Cross pen. "This is my mobile phone number," she said, writing a number down on the business card I had given her.

"Thank you," I said.

"Don't thank me. I'm doing this under duress." She stood. "But let me make this clear, I will only go so far in being intimidated. Threaten me once more, and I will call you on it."

I broke off another piece of the bowl. "Let's hope that it doesn't come to that," I said. "Because I will surely do exactly what I say."

TWENTY-EIGHT

After my impromptu meeting with Evigan, I decided to drop in on Angie and give her the update she had requested. Ever since I had seen her meet with Melissa, my curiosity had been aroused. Updating her in person would give me a chance to gauge her reactions in a way that a phone conversation could not.

The place that Angie and Billy occupied was located on the near east side of Indianapolis. The Villa Italiana was a series of little apartments sequestered in an area off of Emerson, near US 40. Most of the apartments were unoccupied with pieces of plywood nailed over the windows. The few that did still have tenants were scattered about the complex. Some were located at the front, but most were in the rear. Angie's was one of those at the back.

I got out of the car and a young girl, no more than five, pedaled past me on a squeaking tricycle. Despite the unusually cold temperatures, the little girl was dressed only in a corduroy jumper over a cotton T-shirt. She had a sucker in her mouth.

I reached through the screen door where a screen had once been and knocked on a solid wooden door that had been severely warped by years of inclement weather. The door was stuck and required several pulls before it opened with a deep, sucking sound.

"Mr. Parker," Angie said, surprised.

"I got your message. Just thought I would drop by," I said. "Maybe give you an update on what I've found." I glanced over her shoulder, hoping to see either Melissa or Thornton.

"Come in," she said, stepping aside.

The tiny apartment was minimally furnished. A small television sat on a cart on one side of the room, and a love seat was carefully balanced on a stack of books on another side. A distressed coffee table rested between the two pieces of furniture with a floor lamp in one corner. The carpet was worn and dirty. What had once been a plush, maroon-colored floor covering was now a thin-crust pizza of mud and beer. It crunched as I moved across the room.

"Can I get you anything?"

"No thanks," I said.

She brushed the stringy hair from her face and then slid both hands into the rear pockets of her jeans.

"Have you been able to find anything that can help Billy?" she asked.

I shook my head. "Not much. I have my doubts about the credibility of the eyewitness but other than that," I shrugged, "not a whole lot." I tried to gauge her reaction.

"Oh," she said, revealing her disappointment. "I was hoping to get this thing cleared up soon." Her gaze fell to the floor.

"Billy looked like he was doing all right to me. It isn't the first time he's been in jail."

She wrapped her arms around herself, seeming to shrink within full view. "Detective Bitterman was by earlier."

"What did he want?" I asked, suspecting that Angie was another way to get at me.

"He wanted to know if I had talked with you. Said if I really cared for Billy, I would spend the money on a decent lawyer and not on..." she glanced at me, "some ex-FBI guy who couldn't find his own feet in his shoes."

I laughed. "He is the clever one, isn't he?"

She didn't seem amused. Bitterman had her scared.

"Relax, Angie. Bitterman is a good cop. A thorough cop. But he's not infallible. If Billy didn't do it, I will find the evidence sooner or later."

She nodded but kept her arms wrapped about her.

"Actually, I have more questions than answers. What do you know about F&F?"

Her eyes flickered. "F&F?" She shook her head. "I've never heard of it. What is it?"

"Probably nothing," I said. "Sometimes during an investigation, things will tend to pop up. I like to be thorough. You understand, I'm sure."

She nodded her understanding.

"Do you know anyone named Melissa?"

"No," she said, shaking her head, and sweeping back a lock of hair that had fallen over her face, as a result.

"Brad Thornton?"

"No, why?"

"Like I said, just some names that have come up. Probably means nothing."

The shock of unruly hair fell into her face again. She swiped it from her face.

"Well," I said, moving toward the door, "sorry that I don't know more."

"Billy didn't do it, Mr. Parker. Please keep looking."

"I'm sure that Billy didn't do it," I said, turning to face her. "And you can bet that I'll keep looking."

TWENTY-NINE

H ow's the pesto sauce?"
Mary made an *O* with her thumb and forefinger.

"Mine too," I said. "I love this place."

"You know, as good as it is, there are other places to go."

"Like where for instance?" I said, twirling my fork in the pasta.

"For instance," Mary said, pausing to butter her roll, "my place."

"You cook?"

She looked at me with genuine indignation. "Is Rush Limbaugh conservative?"

"I don't know," I said. "I don't listen to radio much."

She shook her head. "You really are a putz."

"Sure," I said. "Whatever that is."

The banter stopped while we concentrated on the dinner that sat before us. We had ordered the same thing, a fact that had not escaped Tony's eye. "Like two peas in the same pod," he had said earlier. "You should try something different. Mix and match just a little."

I put my fork down and looked at Mary. "My client is lying to me."

"What do you mean?"

"When she hired me, she said that Billy was not home on the

evening of the murder. But when I talked to Billy, he said that Angie wasn't home and that's why he went to see Emma."

"Maybe she was confused, or maybe Billy is confused."

I shook my head. "When I asked her if she had ever heard of F&F or Melissa, she lied. Now call me a master of the obvious, but I think that she has something to hide."

Mary swallowed a fork of pasta and drained her wineglass. "We all have something to hide, Colton."

"True. But most of us don't have something to hide that can send us to jail."

"You think she's doing something criminal?"

I poured Mary some more wine. "If she isn't doing it herself, she's certainly privy to someone who is."

"Like who?"

"Melissa. Or maybe Brad Thornton."

"I told you he was a bad dude."

"Now how did I know that you were going to say that?" I said.

"I'm not kidding, Colton. Thornton is the kind of guy who would kill his grandmother for fun and then sell off her dentures to pay for the bullets."

I gave her a look of indignation. "I'm not exactly Mary Poppins," I said.

"I know. But if you keep playing this game, you are going to have to take it more seriously. Thornton will kill you."

I erased my look of indignation and gave her my "I'm offended" look. My repertoire was endless.

"I'm not kidding, Colton," she said again, raising her voice and causing others to look in our direction.

"You want to keep it down a little?" I asked.

She glanced around the room, then leaned across the table, lowering her voice. "This guy has an 'approach with extreme caution tag.' Doesn't that mean anything to you?"

"Sure," I said.

She leaned back in her seat. "You don't act like it."

"Well, there's a reason for that. It's not that I don't recognize what Thornton is or what he's capable of doing; it's that I don't care. Not since Anna died."

She groaned. "You'd better care. He had you the other day."

"He *almost* had me," I said.

"No, Colton. He had you. He could have shoved that knife into you at any time."

"Okay," I said. "Point taken. No pun intended."

"This isn't funny."

"No, you're right. It's not. Trust me, I know. I was there."

She sighed and fixed her eyes on me like two emerald lasers. "You just be careful," she said.

"Always," I said. "But I think it's Thornton who needs to be careful now."

"And that's another problem," she said.

"What?" I ate a bite of roll.

"You can't go gunning for people, Colton. You don't have a badge anymore. You don't have any official status. If you don't wind up dead, you could wind up in jail."

"I don't plan on winding up in either."

She pushed her plate aside. It was a clear signal that our conversation had ruined her appetite. "Sometimes, things don't go according to plan."

"Tell me about it," I said.

"Besides, you have Callie to think about."

"I am thinking about Callie," I said. "She's why I do all of this."

Mary stood to leave, tossing her napkin on the table. "Are you sure?"

THIRTY

I had promised Callie I would take her to a Pacers game, and it was a promise I wanted and needed to keep. I drove to Conseco Fieldhouse to see if I could pick up two tickets to the game against the Knicks. The game was later that night, and I knew I had waited until the last minute. I was surprised when I found that tickets still were available.

I paid the cashier and took the tickets. For the most part, my mind was on Thornton and Angie. I wasn't sure of the connection, or why Angie had felt the need to lie to me about her relationship with Melissa. But I was satisfied enough that there was a relationship to make me want to look into it further. As I walked to my car, I saw a mother and daughter heading toward the Circle Center Mall. I watched as they passed by, talking lightheartedly, seeming to truly enjoy each other's company. It reminded me of the relationship between Callie and Anna. Shopping excursions, lunch out, a movie or just simply going over homework—they treasured those times the most. Callie went to Anna when life became challenging. And she went to Anna when she won some recognition for an achievement. Anna doted on our daughter, and the loss of their relationship was having a profound impact.

As I slipped the tickets into my pocket, Millikin's admonition of the other night began to reverberate within me. "Callie will grow up whether you're in her life or not." And I began to feel ashamed. Almost dirty. I knew that I had to work, yet my job was ruling my life. Callie was indeed going to grow up whether I participated in her life or not. And the lack of my participation in her life prior to Anna's death was leaving me without the knowledge or skills to be the parent I needed to be.

Millikin had struck a chord in me when he had told me about the estrangement with his son. I didn't want the same thing happening to Callie and me. And yet that was exactly what was going to happen if I didn't get my priorities in line.

I paused at my car. In the window, I could see the reflection of the mother-daughter team heading toward the mall. I watched as they moved on, seemingly oblivious at what they had and how quickly it could be taken away.

"If you want to keep lookin' at them tickets, you can have another one."

I looked up and saw an officer approaching my car. The meter had expired.

"I'm moving," I said, unlocking the door.

As I pulled away, I began going over my mental list of errands to do before the game. Mundane things like laundry and grocery shopping had always seemed to be intrusions in the day. Now, as I shot one more glance at the mother and daughter, those mundane things seemed to give order to an otherwise out-of-order life.

"It's Colton," I said to Frank on the phone. "I told Callie I would pick up tickets to a game." I was stocking the house with enough food to get me through the week.

"Great. She's been looking forward to it."

"They're for tonight. So I thought—"

"Not so great," Frank said.

"Why not?" I slid a carton of milk into the refrigerator and closed the door.

There was a protracted pause. "Tonight is a school night."

"I'll have her back before midnight."

"I don't know, Colton. That's awfully late."

"I made her a promise, Frank. I'm going to keep it." I put a loaf of bread into the breadbox and fished a can of coffee from the grocery sack.

Another disapproving pause. "Colton, Callie isn't doing as well in school as you might believe."

"What's wrong?" I paused with the can of coffee in my hand.

"Her report card came in today. Her grades are down."

"Much?"

"Considerably down from last year."

"I don't understand. She told me she was doing well."

"Actually, I believe she told you she was doing well in soccer."

"Why didn't you or Corrin say something?"

"We didn't want to worry you. We think that with her mother's death and your…job situation, the stress may be playing itself out. We just think it's important to create some sense of stability for her."

"A night out with her dad is going to destabilize her?"

He sighed. "No, of course not. We just think that on a school night, she should be working on improving her grades and getting a good night's rest."

"I can't argue with that, Frank, and I wouldn't want to. But Callie has had life break its promise to her. It promised a normal life with her father and mother. A normal life in a secure home. But the promise was broken. And I have broken promises to her too. I don't want to let her down again." I moved across the kitchen, sliding the can of coffee into the cupboard over the sink.

"Life doesn't promise anyone anything, Colton. Life is rocky. Tenuous at best. We didn't contemplate losing a daughter. But that's what happened. We have the right to hope, of course, and we should plan. But we must be willing to deal with the unexpected turns that life throws our way."

"Maybe," I said, "but I have let her down too often. I am not going to break any more promises."

"You will, Colton. Out of necessity, you will break more promises. None of us can guarantee anything. We don't even know if we will be alive tomorrow, much less guarantee that we can keep all of the promises we will make. Things will come up. Unexpected turns will happen and you won't always be able to navigate them. Broken promises and broken dreams don't mean that life is unkind. They are a part of life."

"Maybe," I said. "But tonight, if I'm alive, I'm going to pick Callie up at six. We're going to dinner and then to the game and then I'm going to bring her home."

He sighed again. "Okay," he said, "she'll be ready, but try to have her home by twelve, Colton."

I promised I would, with every intention of keeping my word.

THIRTY-ONE

I picked Callie up at precisely six.

"When will you be home?" Frank asked.

"No later than twelve. Probably earlier," I said.

He stood on the front porch with both hands in his pockets. "Okay. But just remember, tonight's a school night."

We left the Shapiros' and drove south from Carmel to Indianapolis, stopping to get a pizza before the game. Callie had been quiet the entire ride despite my attempts to stir some conversation, and as we pulled into the parking lot of the pizza place that she and Anna preferred most, she seemed to recede even further into herself.

The restaurant hadn't changed since the last time we visited and was filled with high school and college kids. Some of the kids were on dates; the others were in groups of friends, clustered together. A juke box stood silent among the chatter of youth.

It's odd, in moments like these, how the little things can come to mind. I remembered how Anna, unlike Callie, had never cared for mushrooms and anchovies, preferring instead a basic pepperoni on thin crust. And I recalled how our last visit here had been upbeat and pleasant. Like tonight, it had been on a Sunday evening. I had picked Callie and Anna up from a church service they had attended while I finished paperwork at the office. The evening had been pleasant, but I remembered steering the conversation off of church-related topics and back to something more relevant. How I wished now, as I sat there with Callie, that I could go back to that night even if the conversation was centered around church.

"What do you want on your pizza?" I asked.

"Pepperoni." She kept her eyes focused on the menu.

"Are you sure? That's what Mom always ordered. You can have anything that—"

She looked at me over the top of the menu. "Just pepperoni."

"Sure. Pepperoni it is," I said.

The server came to the table. She was a pleasant young woman of about twenty with a name tag that read Tammy.

"What can I get for you?"

"We'll have a large pepperoni..." I glanced at Callie..."and a pitcher of Coke?"

She shook her head. "I'd rather have Sprite." It had been Anna's choice.

"Sprite for her," I said, "and a Coke for me."

Tammy smiled. "A large pepperoni, one Coke and one Sprite. Do you want to go for the Biggie?"

"The Biggie?" I said.

"Yeah. It's a twenty-ounce drink with free refills."

"Do you have people who do that?" I asked. "Drink twenty ounces and then ask for a refill?"

"Oh sure," she said enthusiastically. "It happens all the time."

I looked at Callie. She shook her head.

"No, we're fine," I said.

"Okay," she said, "I'll get this in and have your drinks to you in just a minute." She spun away, writing our order on her order pad.

"I've been looking forward to this," I said.

"Me too."

I pulled the tickets out of my pocket and slid them across the table. "They're not center court, but not bad on short notice." Actually, they were terrible. But nosebleeds were never a problem for me. I couldn't afford for them to be.

Callie looked at the tickets. "They're fine, Dad," she said.

"Listen," I said, "I—"

"Here we go," Tammy said, bringing our drinks to the table. "A Sprite for you," she set Callie's drink in front of her, "and a Coke for you." She set two straws on the table. "Your pizza should be up soon. Will there be anything else?"

"We're fine, thanks," I said as she left the table.

I turned back to Callie. "I'm sorry I missed your game the other day," I said.

She tapped her straw on the table until the wrapper slid off and then stuck the straw into her drink. "I know," she said.

"Are we going to be okay?"

She nodded. "Yeah. We're okay."

I smiled. "Good. And I promise as soon as the business is up and running, I'll come get you."

She looked at the table. "I know," she murmured.

I changed the subject. "Listen," I said, seizing the goodwill of the moment. "We have to talk about your grades."

She paused sucking on the straw. "Why?"

"Grandpa said that they're slipping."

She shrugged and reached for the previously discarded straw paper.

"How much is 'slipping'?"

She shrugged again. "I can get them back up." She was fiddling with the wrapper.

"How much is 'slipping'?" I repeated.

A young man in baggy jeans and an oversized shirt sauntered to the jukebox and selected a song that sounded like two cats fighting. I raised my voice over the din.

Callie continued to fidget with the paper.

"How many Cs did you get?" I said, picking a starting point.

"One."

"That's all?"

She nodded.

"The rest were Bs? Any As?"

She shook her head.

"All Bs?"

She shook her head.

I thought for a moment. With only one C...

She continued playing with the wrapper. I took it from her. "Ds? You got all Ds?"

She shook her head.

"One C and the rest were not all Ds?" I put my head in my hands. "Did you get any Fs?"

She shrugged.

"How many?" I asked.

She slid lower in the booth and hesitated before holding up one finger.

"One C, one F, and the rest Ds? What did you get the C in?"

Her face turned red. "Art."

"Art? You used to get As in art. I can't believe you got all Ds and Fs." My voice had reached the upper limits of its range, partly out of anger and partly so that I could clear the racket from the jukebox, when I noticed that the song had ended. My last line was hanging out there for all who cared to listen. The room grew quiet as the other kids turned in our direction and Callie's face grew a deep red.

"Here we go," Tammy said, more chipper than I needed. She set the pizza on the table. "Anything else?"

Callie slid from her seat and ran to the restroom. "Just a box," I said. "And the check."

We didn't make it to the game, and Callie was quiet the entire ride home. When I arrived at the Shapiros', she ran into the house, leaving me standing on the front step. Frank came out.

"What's wrong?"

"I don't know. I tried to have a talk with her about her grades, and she just blew up."

He looked back at the house then to me. "You talked to her about her grades? Tonight?"

"Sure. Why not?"

"On a night that was supposed to be a bonding night? A fun night?"

"Frank, I'm her dad. I have to talk to her about her grades."

"Yes, I know, but..." he let his thought trail off, but the look on his face said enough.

"I'm no good at this," I said. "And I know it."

"But you see, Colton," he said, placing a hand on my shoulder, "you're going to have to *get* good at this. You're her father, and as hard as Corrin and I try, we can't fill that void. Anna's death has hit her especially hard. They were very close."

"I know," I said, painfully aware of my shortcomings. "I know."

THIRTY-TWO

I didn't sleep well that night. It was getting to be a habit.

When I woke the next morning, I skipped breakfast, preferring to have only a cup of coffee. My mind was still on the events of the night before, and I began to despair of ever developing the skills to be the kind of a father that Callie needed.

Looking for a diversion, I flicked on the kitchen television and saw a news report about the city's war on drugs. That piece of news reminded me of the scourge that drug abuse had become and the lives it ruined, which reminded me of all the drug dealers I had run across in my career, which reminded me of Thornton, which reminded me of work. Despite my concern with the larger issue of raising my daughter, a single piece of news had managed to assemble all the cars of my train of thought and push them down familiar track. I was soon focusing on work again.

If I was going to make any headway on this case, I was going to have to find Thornton. He was the link between Emma and F&F, himself and Angie, and Angie and Melissa. The best place to find a bear is in the honey jar, so I decided to pay Melissa another visit.

After showering, I slipped into a flannel shirt, jeans, and the leather jacket that I had grown attached to since Anna had gotten it for me on our second anniversary. I also had the gun under my arm. I had gotten attached to it too.

I parked in front of Melissa's house at around eight. I didn't see Thornton's car, which didn't entirely surprise me. I had known a lot of men like Thornton, and few of them see the women in their life as anything more than a government paycheck or a convenient source of pleasure. Despite his seemingly caring attitude for her during our confrontation, he was a rolling stone. Here today, gone tomorrow.

As I got out of the car, the morning wind was strong, nearly ripping the door from my hand. A few dried leaves, raptured by a current of air, danced over a cluster of dew-laden ones. I hopped over the fence and went to the front door. I heard no television blaring this time and couldn't see lights on inside. I pounded on the door.

Nothing.

I pounded again. And again. I paused as I began to hear stirrings in the house and, finally, the sound of a chain being slid away from inside the door. It opened and there was Melissa, fresh out of bed, in all her morning shine.

"What do you want?" she said.

She was dressed in a light blue, see-through teddy that would have served her better if it had not been see-through. Her black hair was pulled back, and her face was still swollen from sleep. A tattoo, consisting of a pair of crossed arrows, decorated one arm. I hadn't noticed it before.

"Morning ma'am," I said. "I was wandering if you could direct me to Bradley Thornton?"

She crossed her arms and leaned against the door frame. "Haven't we been through this once already?"

"Déjà vu."

"And what did I say about this the last time?"

"I believe it was kiss off, buzz off, or words to that affect."

"And what makes you think that my answer is going to be any different this time?"

"Because I'm not willing to accept the same answer you gave me the last time."

"Is that right?"

"Yes, it is. Look," I said, "I just have a few questions for the man. All I need to know is where I can find him."

She studied me for a moment, but her face had begun to soften. A bit. "I already told him about you."

"I know," I said.

"He told me to tell him if you came 'round again."

"So, tell him," I said.

"You ain't afraid?"

"No. I'm not."

She snorted. "You should be."

"I should be a lot of things that I'm not," I said.

She didn't say anything.

"Are you going to help me or not?"

"I'm helping you by not telling you where he is. If he sees you again, he's going to kill you."

"He can try," I said.

"He won't just try. He'll do it."

I said nothing. She said nothing. Each of us was looking the other over, waiting to see who would blink first.

She sighed. "Stay here," she said.

She left the doorway, leaving the door partially open. A gust of wind whipped across the barren front yard. I raised the collar of my jacket and blew into my cupped hands.

"Here," she said, opening the door a little wider and handing me a handwritten note.

"The Busy Bee?"

"It's on West Tenth," she said. "I'm not going to tell you where he lives. If you want to talk to him, you can find him there."

"Okay. One place is as good as another."

She shook her head. "No, this is better." She pointed at the slip of paper in my hand. "He's not as likely to draw down on you there."

"Melissa," I said, in mock surprise, "I didn't know you cared."

She snorted again. "I don't. But if he kills you, he goes back to prison. And that's not good for either of us."

"Your assuming he'll beat me to the draw."

"It don't make no difference. If he kills you, he goes to prison and I lose. You kill him, I kill you, and I go to prison. See? I lose either way."

"Well," I said, tucking the note into my pocket, "here's hoping that we all come out winners."

THIRTY-THREE

The temperature remained just above freezing as the sleet fell like shards of glass poured from a cosmic bucket, landing with a tinkle on my windshield. My wipers thumped back and forth, keeping an oddly rhythmical beat with the falling sleet.

The Busy Bee was a concrete block building surrounded by a small gravel parking lot. In the lot were several motorcycles and pickup trucks. A painting of a bee in repose decorated the front of the solid black door.

The interior of the bar was done in classic bar-dark. The bar itself was on my left with a couple of bowls of nuts and some napkins at each end. There was a smattering of tables and booths on my right and a pool table at the rear. A few of the patrons glanced at me, but most kept their focus on their drinks.

It was nearly one in the afternoon, and the place was full. That didn't surprise me. Most bars are filled to capacity on days like this, when the weather doesn't permit doing anything else. And they are filled with men and women. All of them lonely. All of them looking for something and hoping to find it in each other.

"What can I getcha?"

The bartender was older than me, late forties to early fifties, with the face of a man who has seen and done it all. His head was shaven, and a string of tattoos decorated his muscular forearms. His attention was only partially directed toward me. Most of it was focused on a game show that was blaring from a television that was suspended over the bar.

"I'm looking for a friend of mine," I said.

"Yeah? Who's that?" He was looking at the TV.

"Brad Thornton," I said.

He turned from the TV and gave me his full attention. His eyes, void of any warmth, rolled in his head like two black marbles set within deep pockets. "You don't look like no friend of Brad's to me."

"What does a friend of Brad's look like?" I asked, scooping a handful of nuts from one of the bowls.

I saw a frail kid at the end of the bar swig the last of his beer and leave.

"Who are you?" he asked.

"Someone who wants to talk to Brad."

He kept his serpentine gaze fixed on me for a minute and then said, "Leave your name and number. If I see him, I'll let him know you were in." He turned his back to me as he leaned on the bar and resumed his game show.

"I was told he comes in here often."

"He does."

"Any idea when he'll be back?"

"Nope."

A bell rang on the TV show, and the host called for the final round.

"Brad a friend of yours?" I asked.

"He's a customer. Customers aren't friends."

"Sure," I said.

I downed a few more handfuls of the nuts and watched the final round with my new friend. When the show ended, he turned to face me again.

"You a cop?"

"Would it help?"

"To find Brad?" He shook his head. "No, I don't think so."

"Then I'm not a cop."

"You got the look, though."

He was right. Years in law enforcement can take a toll, and it isn't long before the strain begins to show. I had yet to meet a con, ex or otherwise, who didn't recognize a cop when he saw one. I motioned at one of the tattoos on his arm. It was in black ink.

"Where were you?" I asked.

He glanced at the tattoo. "Riker's."

"You're a long way from home," I said.

He nodded. "Yeah. I'm a long way from a lot of places."

Neither of us said a word for a second or two as we both dipped into the bowl.

"What do you want Brad for?" he asked.

"To talk."

He snorted. "Brad ain't the talking kind. You got something to say, say it and I'll get it to him. Otherwise, your best bet is to leave well enough alone."

I glanced around the room. The others were either too bored or too engaged in their drinks to pay much attention to what was going on at the bar.

"Tell him the kid is going to be okay," I said. Then, I poured the nuts onto the bar and set the bowl down on top of them. "Tell him I'm going to turn his world upside down."

I walked outside. The cold air had gotten colder, and a crust of ice had formed on the windshield of my car.

"Hey," a voice whispered from off to my right.

I turned and saw the frail kid who had left the bar earlier. He had his hands in his pocket and was stomping his feet to stay warm.

"You want me?"

He nodded, keeping an eye on the bar door. "You looking for Thornton?" he asked. He had a strong southern accent that I couldn't localize.

"Yeah. You know where I can find him?"

"He lives at Riley Towers."

Riley Towers was one of the finer places in Indianapolis. Brad Thornton didn't fit.

"How do you know that?" I asked.

"'Cause he gave me this," he said, holding out his crooked left leg.

"I take it he's no friend of yours," I said.

"Not hardly. I want the man dead."

"I'm not out to kill the guy," I said. "I just need to talk with him."

"If he doesn't take a shine to you, he might make you kill him."

"Maybe."

The kid glanced at the door again. "And you would too, right? Kill him, I mean."

"I don't want to kill anyone," I said, ignoring the kid's need to see me kill his nemesis. It was information I wanted.

He frowned.

"Where's Thornton?" I asked.

"He lives on the fourth floor of tower one."

"Do you know where? Specifically?"

He gave me the apartment number.

"Has he been here lately?" I asked, nodding toward the bar.

He shook his head. "Haven't seen him around."

"Okay," I said. "And thanks."

I turned back toward the car.

"Hey."

I turned back toward the young man.

"That information. It's worth something, ain't it?"

I opened my wallet and found ten one-dollar bills. I gave them to him.

"Thanks," he said, thrusting the money into the pocket of his jeans.

"What's your name?" I asked.

"Lenny."

"Lenny what?"

"Just Lenny. You can ask around. Everybody knows me."

"Does everyone know you have it out for Thornton?"

"I don't make no secret 'bout it."

"Probably best if no one sees us talking. If word gets back to Thornton before I can get to him…"

"Yeah," he said, glancing again at the bar. "Yeah, that's right."

"Take care of yourself, Lenny."

"You too, man. You too."

I watched as Lenny limped away. I felt sorry for him. I wanted to make Thornton pay for what he did to the kid and for all that he had done to others.

I fingered the wound he had given me, knowing that Mary had been right. He could have killed me. And Callie would have lost both parents. Both of them in six months. The thought angered me.

I began to scrape the ice that had formed on my windshield.

Thornton and I were more alike than I cared to admit. Our side of the issues may be different, but the route we chose for victory was the same. I knew the kid was right. If Thornton challenged me again, I would kill him. And I would see it as nothing more than a means to an end. Much the way Thornton had during our confrontation at the canal.

I finished removing the ice from my car and knocked off the last bit from the mirror of my door. As I readjusted it, I caught a view of myself. I didn't like what I saw.

THIRTY-FOUR

The last time I had run into Brad Thornton, I had tried to be inconspicuous without trying to be inconspicuous. That hadn't worked. So, knowing I was going to need a different approach this time, I decided to be inconspicuous while trying to be inconspicuous—sort of. So when Brad Thornton and his bimbo of the week entered the foyer of Riley Towers the next evening, I was not leaning against a lamppost reading the newspaper. I was sitting in one of the two wingback chairs that faced the elevators—reading the newspaper.

The girl, probably twenty-two at most, was tall, leggy, and blonde. She giggled a lot and held tightly to Thornton's arm. She wore a clingy red skirt with a slit up one side, a tight blouse, a red vinyl jacket, and bright red lipstick. The purse she carried didn't look big enough to hold anything.

Thornton, ever the snappy dresser, was wearing black jeans, black boots, and a black leather jacket. A red bandana was tied over his head. Any thoughts I had entertained about his caring for Melissa were discarded. If he cared, it wasn't love. It was more like property rights.

It was a busy night with a lot of people moving in and out of the building. Thornton and the girl got into an overcrowded elevator as

I followed another group into one of the other elevators and pushed the fourth-floor button. When I stepped off onto the fourth floor, I was a few steps behind Thornton and the girl as I saw them round the corner. I jogged down the hall to the apartment number that Lenny had given me. My watch read 9:15.

I gave them time to get comfortable and was approaching the door when it opened. I slipped around the corner and out of sight.

"Jack Daniel's?" the girl was saying as she was leaving. "Anything else?"

"Yeah. Get me some cigarettes too, will you, babe?"

"Sure thing," she said, closing the door.

I waited until she reached the elevator. When she stepped in and the doors closed behind her, I made my move.

I pulled the Ruger from my holster and knocked on Thornton's door. I kept my thumb over the peephole.

The expression on his face when he opened the door told me that he had expected to see the girl coming back for something she had forgotten. Instead, he saw me.

I kicked the door in and shoved Thornton back with one hand. He made a move for me but stopped when I put the barrel of the gun against his forehead.

"Looks like we meet again," I said, kicking the door closed behind me.

He didn't have his jacket on, revealing that he wasn't armed.

"You better pull that trigger," he said. "'Cause if you don't, when this is over, I'm coming for you."

I kicked his right knee and he fell to the floor with a groan.

"Did you see how easy that was?"

"You're dead, man. I mean it. You're dead," he said, clutching his knee.

"I've been dead for six months," I said.

I pulled the bandana off and grabbed a handful of hair. I half dragged, half pulled him toward the door to the balcony, keeping the gun trained on him as we crossed the living room. I was aware that my rage was taking over, but I felt no compulsion to stop it.

"Open it," I said.

He hesitated.

I struck him across the face with the gun. "Open it."

He wiped the blood from his mouth and glared at me with serpent's eyes. He opened the patio door.

"Out," I said, motioning with the gun.

We stepped out onto the balcony, four floors above Indianapolis. The temperature had dropped to near freezing, and a brisk wind was blowing the sleet in a near ninety-degree angle. I pulled a pair of handcuffs from my jacket.

"Put these on. Lace them through the banister." He kept an eye on the Ruger as he slipped one cuff on his right wrist and laced the other through a railing in the balcony's banister. He cuffed the other wrist, securing himself.

"I mean it," he said. "You're dead. I'm talking to a dead man."

I kicked him in the same knee. He fell to the floor of the balcony.

"None of this was necessary," I said. "All I wanted to do—all that I still want to do—is to talk with you and ask a few questions."

He looked up at me and spit, landing a clump of saliva near my feet.

I kicked his knee again. He groaned and cursed.

"Save yourself—and me—the unnecessary roughness and just answer a few questions," I said.

"What do you want?" he said, near growling

"I want to know what you know about F&F."

He was breathing hard from the pain. "I don't know what that is."

I kicked him in the knee again. He cursed again.

"I don't have time to play games. I need to know what you know about F&F."

His breathing became more rapid and shallow. "It's out of St. Louis," he said.

"What do they do?"

"They dabble in a lot of things but mostly adult-type stuff."

"What 'adult-type stuff'?" I asked.

"You know, porn. Internet mostly."

"How are you connected?"

"I ain't."

I drew back to kick him again.

"Whoa, whoa, man. Hold on. I mean I ain't now. But I used to be."

"What did you do for them?" I asked.

He groaned and rocked. "I used to do some photography."

"You still doing that?"

"Not regularly. I used to do it a lot. But I do it freelance now."

"What does Emma Caine have to do with F&F?"

"Emma? Aw, man, I should've known that was what this was all about."

The wind howled and the cold bit hard.

"What do you mean?"

"Listen, can we go inside? My hands are going numb."

"Answer the questions or your body is going over the rail."

He sighed and began moving his knee back and forth as he winced from pain. "That old broad was into everything."

"Like what?"

"Like everything. You know. Gambling, prostitution—everything."

"How deep?"

"I don't know—deep, I guess."

"Tell me about her gambling."

"Don't know much." He moved the knee again. "I know she was into the horses. Had a hard time paying her debts."

This was contrary to what DiCenza had said. "How much did she owe?"

He winced as he moved the knee again. "I don't know, man, I really don't. All I know is that the last time I seen her, she was having money troubles. She owed a dude that runs the books in this town. He was on her and she was in need of cash. Quick."

"Frankie DiCenza?"

"Yeah, that's the guy."

"Did she get it? The cash, I mean?"

He nodded. "Yeah, I think so. I saw her a week before she got whacked. I just assumed those dudes did it. They're a tough bunch. You don't owe them money for long and live."

"How do you know these guys?"

"I used to do some work for them."

"Photography?"

"Naw, man. I just do that on the side. Lot of underground stuff in this city." He rotated the knee. "I did some enforcing for them."

"How long ago was that?"

He paused to think. "Year. Maybe two."

"Why did you quit?"

"Pay wasn't that good."

"Whatever it was, you were overpaid."

He shot me a look of anger.

"Do you know Billy Caine?"

He shook his head. "Who's he?"

"He's the guy the police have in custody for killing Emma."

He shook his head again. "Don't know him. Did he work for Frankie?"

It was a good question. One that hadn't occurred to me. Did Billy work for DiCenza? Angie said that Billy did odd jobs, and his size and build certainly made him capable of enforcing. Could Billy have killed Emma on orders of DiCenza? I thought back to my interview of Billy. He had shown no remorse over Emma's death, and Upcraft had said that the two of them did not get along as well as everyone thought. In fact, the only one who did seem to feel that Emma and Billy did get along well was Angie. Add to that the fact that Angie had lied to me on other matters, and I now had reason to suspect Billy again.

"Tell me about Emma and F&F," I said. "What did she do for them?"

"Anything that F&F wanted done, she offered to do. She was a regional..." he paused to move his knee again, "a regional something or other. She found the girls, set up the studio, you name it. The old lady even rolled some of her hookers into the business. It was safer."

"She have any enemies?"

He shrugged as he continued to move his knee. "You mean except for Frankie?"

I nodded.

"I don't know. Probably. Kind of hard to be in this business and not have enemies."

"Who were they?"

"I don't know, man. I really don't. The person that would know that stuff is her friend."

"What's the friend's name?"

He paused to think.

"What's the friend's name?" I asked again. I was beginning to lose the struggle for control. The desire to shoot him and toss his carcass over the banister was close to becoming an impulse.

"I'm thinking, man."

I waited as he strained his limited mental abilities. After what seemed an eternity, he shook his head. "I don't know. I can't remember her name. She works at the same school with Emma."

"Does the name 'Seidel' ring a bell?" I asked.

"Yeah, that's it," he said. "She used to help her."

"Line up the talent?" I asked, using the line that I had heard from Evigan.

He laughed. "Yeah, sure, man. Line up the talent. That's good."

"What about Angie?"

"Howe? What about her?"

"How long has she been hookin' and how does she fit into F&F?"

He looked at me with disbelief. "Hookin'? She don't hook, man."

I recalled how Angie had told me she was going to pay my retainer. That had been eating at me since I started the investigation. "You sure?"

"Sure, I'm sure." He half chuckled, half snorted. "She don't sell her body, man. It's her soul."

"What do you mean?"

"She models for Emma. Or...she *did* model for her. Then she went freelance for the company."

"F&F?" I asked.

"Yeah. She's still with the company as far as I know. She's deep in the business. That chick's got a drug problem like you can't believe. She needs the money. Her and Seidel had talked about going out on their own but Emma put the kabobs on that."

"So there were problems between Emma and Angie?"

"I don't know, man. I never got that involved. Taking pictures was extra income. That's all it was. Emma was the queen bee and she made sure that the other two knew it. I don't know if they were enemies or not."

I looked back at the apartment. "How do you live here?"

He moved his knee back and forth again. "I do odd jobs."

"Like what?"

"What do you think?"

I kicked his knee again. He let out a string of expletives.

"Drugs?" I asked. It seemed like the easy way to money these days.

He was near tears now. "Sure, man. Drugs, pictures, a little enforcing."

A strong blast of wind whistled as it climbed upward along the building. "I have no patience for you, Thornton," I said. "I don't like you and I don't like what you do. So trust me on this, it has taken a genuine effort to not kill you."

I holstered the Ruger and crouched down to eye level with him. "Tonight was just a talk. If you come near me or anyone that is close to me, I will kill you without compunction. Do you understand?"

He nodded his head.

"Okay," I said. "That's all I wanted." I stood and turned to walk away.

"Hey man," he yelled above the howl of the wind. "Don't leave me out here."

I left the apartment and closed the door.

THIRTY-FIVE

I was up by five the next morning and making my run around the park by five thirty. The air was cold but warmer than it had been the night before. I thought about my interrogation of Thornton and wondered how the girl had gotten him off the balcony when she returned. I was also wondering if I was going to have another meeting with him. Maybe the next one would be at a time and place of his choosing. If so, I would be ready. I had been threatened by better.

I finished my run and did an hour and a half in my basement gym. My energy level was still high. The confrontation had charged me, given me a sense of control over something—anything. But the events of the night before had also left me with more unanswered questions.

An hour after my workout, I was finishing breakfast and putting the dishes away when the phone rang.

"Mr. Parker, this is Elizabeth Diedrich. I'm Callie's principal," she said in a throaty voice.

The call had not taken me by surprise. After the conversation with Frank, I knew of the inevitability of a phone call from my child's principal.

"Is this about her grades?" I asked.

"Well, yes. So you are aware of that problem?"

"I'm aware of her grades dropping. Is that the problem we're talking about?"

"Well, no," she said, "it's a bit more complicated than that. Maybe we could talk in person?"

Carmel was about a half hour from where I lived. I would need time to shower and change. "Sure. An hour?"

"Let me see," she said. I could hear her leafing through a book. "Yes. I should be able to meet with you an hour from now. When you arrive, just tell the receptionist who you are and she will escort you right back."

"See you then," I said.

The drive to Carmel was a pleasant one. The precipitation from the day before had given way to a hint of autumn sunshine overhead. But the cold persisted, and rain-soaked leaves lined the roadways.

I was wearing a tan sportcoat, tie, and black, pleated pants. Not my usual fare since leaving the bureau, but when meeting the principal, a little glimmer and glow never hurts.

Anna had usually been the one to handle school issues—enrollment, parent-teacher meetings, or fundraisers—while I was glad to duck the responsibility. But Anna was dead, and I was going to have to meet my daughter's principal. Not for a fundraiser but because she was in trouble.

When I pulled into the parking space on the school grounds, I noticed the stark contrast to Tifton High. The courts were well maintained and there was no evidence of gang members or the graffiti they tend to generate. Instead, I saw groups of kids participating in a gym class on a field located to one side of the building. All of them seemed eager to be there.

As I entered the school, the contrast became starker. I immediately noticed that the floors of the hallways were shined to perfection, and the walls and lockers smelled of new paint. On one of the walls just inside the building, I saw a sign advertising a school dance.

Next to it, I saw a sign advertising the mother-daughter bake sale. The sign served as yet another reminder why I was here. The bake sale had been a joint venture between Anna and Callie, and they always seemed to command top dollar for their project. This year would be different though. Callie would go, but it would be with her grandmother this time.

As I scanned the wall, looking for directions, I found a sign that listed the way to the school's various offices. I followed the instructions and found Diedrich's office near the main entrance.

"Can I help you?" the receptionist asked.

She was about forty with shoulder-length blonde hair, a form-fitting, royal blue dress stretched over an excellent form, and large green eyes.

"My name is Colton Parker and I'm here to meet with Mrs. Diedrich."

"And which student is this regarding?"

"Callie Parker," I said.

She opened a large horizontal filing cabinet, fingered down to the middle of the second shelve and extracted a manila file folder.

"Right this way," she said.

I followed the receptionist into the principal's office, trying to hide the bulge of the Ruger under my left arm. The coat did not provide adequate cover for the gun.

"Mrs. Diedrich, this is Colton Parker. He's here regarding Callie."

The receptionist handed the folder to the principal and then quietly removed herself from the room. I watched as she pulled the door closed behind her, hoping she would glance back. She didn't. I never liked school anyway.

Elizabeth Diedrich was everything the receptionist wasn't. Short and thin with more gray in her hair than color, she wasn't as attractive as Presky and wore a pair of glasses suspended about her neck by a silver chain. But when she smiled and motioned to a chair in front of her desk, her pleasant demeanor immediately clashed with her stern, exterior façade.

"Have a seat, Mr. Parker," she said.

I sat across from the principal. A feeling of déjà vu swept over me.

"Mr. Parker," she began, placing the glasses on the bridge of her nose and opening the file. "You indicated that you were aware of Callie's grades."

"Yes ma'am," I said.

"But there are, I believe, more significant problems brewing." She clasped her hands and rested them on the open file. "Problems that may be tied to her seeming lack of interest in her work."

"What problems?"

"Callie has," she paused, searching for the right phrase, "found some new friends."

"New friends?"

"Yes. I'm afraid Callie has begun developing friendships with some of the other kids here who have had, shall we say, problems?"

"Have you talked with her about this?"

"I'm talking with you, Mr. Parker. I'm an educator with six hundred students. As much as I would like to, I can't be their parent too."

"Of course not," I said.

"I have talked with her grandparents. I believe she resides with them?" she asked, opening the file and scanning its contents.

"Yes," I said, shifting in my seat.

"Mr. Parker, I've always viewed the home life of my students to be off limits unless, of course, it was interfering with their studies. We're all aware of your wife's passing and the profound effect this has had on Callie. What we don't want to see is this time of grief permanently affecting her."

"Did you lose a parent at Callie's age?" I asked.

"No. I did not," she said.

"The effects of her mother's death will be permanent."

"Of course, Mr. Parker. I didn't mean to imply that it wouldn't." She leaned back in her chair and removed the glasses, allowing them to dangle from her neck. "What I mean to say is, we don't want Callie to find herself in an academic or legal situation that will affect her for the rest of her life. Not only has she lost her mother, but she has lost her at thirteen years of age. That is a challenging time for any young girl. This only compounds the...issues with which she must wrestle."

"Is she involved with anything that I need to be aware of?" I asked. "Is she in any trouble right now?"

She shook her head. "No, I can't say that we have uncovered any such activity. Our concern is that she not find herself implicated in such things."

"I understand and appreciate your concern, Mrs. Diedrich," I said.

She clasped her hands and rested them on the desk again. "Callie has always been a polite, studious, and pleasant young lady. And though we have seen changes in her personality and her demeanor, we can anticipate those as a result of her...what I am saying, Mr. Parker, is that I do not want to see her derailed by...the wrong crowd. She is hurting and vulnerable. As a result, she is open to undesirable influences."

"Neither do I. Thank you for your concern," I said. "I will talk with her about this."

"Thank you, Mr. Parker," she said, rising to extend her hand, "I'm hopeful that together, we can help Callie through a difficult time."

I stood and shook her hand. Her grip was surprisingly firm.

"Me too," I said.

THIRTY-SIX

I like a simple fix to problems. Got a headache? Take two aspirin. Need information from a pimp and a drug dealer? Handcuff him to a railing and kick the snot out of him. I was hoping for a quick fix during my meeting with the principal. Callie has a problem with her grades? Well, give her time to adjust to her mother's death, and she'll get back on track. I wasn't ready for the twist of new friends, though. Friends who were trouble. Friends who could influence a young girl who was still grieving over the sudden loss of her mother. I wasn't up to speed for this kind of problem. It was going to require skills I didn't have, based on a relationship that didn't exist. All in all, it seemed like the solution would be a lot simpler if I could take Principal Diedrich up to the balcony for a chat.

I drove back to Indianapolis, thinking along the way about Callie and how to best deal with an issue that, before now, Anna would have handled. That was assuming that this kind of problem would have even been an issue if Anna were still alive. Just one more reminder that Anna was gone and never coming back. One more reason to miss her.

I called the FBI office on my cell phone and asked for Mary. When she came to the phone, she sounded like someone who had run a marathon. Something she occasionally did, but with much less stress than I heard coming over the phone today.

"What's with you?" I asked.

"I'm burning up."

"Burning up?"

"Yeah. Mad. Angry. Burning up. You know?"

"Why? What's up?"

"You worked here. You know what it's like. I want to do one thing, the supervisor wants to do another, and the SAC, the *new* SAC, wants to do something else. Something else that is *entirely* wrong."

"You didn't go off, did you?" I asked.

"I would have if you hadn't called."

"Great. Then we could have opened Parker and Christopher Investigations," I said.

"Uh, no. I don't think so, Colton. No offense, but I've seen how you live. I'd just as soon stay here."

That stung more than it should have. "What are you doing for lunch?" I asked.

"Getting out of here. Why?"

"I need to talk," I said. "Can you meet me at Armatzio's?"

"Sure," she said. "When?"

I glanced at my watch as I moved onto the exit ramp. "About ten minutes," I said.

She told me that she would be there and hung up as I moved around the slower traffic, feeling a little lighter than I had just a few minutes before.

"So what did she have to say?" Mary asked when I told her of my meeting with Callie's principal.

I squeezed the lemon into my iced tea. "Just that Callie was connecting with the wrong element in school, and they're afraid that if some type of intervention isn't done soon, the damage could become permanent."

Mary nodded thoughtfully. "How old is she?"

"Thirteen."

Mary grimaced. "That's a crucial age for anyone. Especially for a girl and especially for one who has lost her mother."

"That's what her principal said too."

"She's right."

"I know."

"So what are you going to do?"

I shrugged. "I'm not sure. Anna always handled this kind of thing. I was never home enough to know what was going on or with whom."

"A lot of men are like that, Colton. My dad worked all the time too."

"Here we go," Tony said, bringing a salad for Mary and lasagna for me. He turned to Mary. "You should eat more. Like Colton here."

Mary smiled. "If I eat what he eats, I'll be broad shouldered like he is."

Tony thought for a moment. "Enjoy your salad," he said. "We don't need no broad-shouldered women in here. We like you just the way you are."

I waited for him to leave before continuing.

"I know it's been hard for her. Losing her mother. Losing her suddenly. Losing her after...she had seen her arguing with her father."

Mary took hold of my hand. "You can't blame yourself for her accident. We all clash with the ones we love. It doesn't make us responsible for what happens to them. It doesn't mean we don't love them."

"I know," I said. "But when you're on this side of the argument, that line of reasoning seems academic. The fact remains that Anna wouldn't have been in the car that night if we hadn't fought. And we wouldn't have fought if I hadn't lost my job. And I wouldn't have lost my job if I hadn't let my temper get the better of me."

"You saved a young girl's life," Mary said. "The truth is, everyone at the bureau admires you for what you did."

"I can't pay the bills with their admiration."

"If you hadn't forced her kidnapper to tell us where she was, that little girl would never have been found and that…" she paused, "that *suspect*," she nearly hissed the word, "would have *walked*—on some technicality."

"He *did* walk, remember?"

"Yes. But the girl is alive. Isn't that what's most important?"

I moved the lasagna around with my fork. "I'm glad the girl was found alive. But the fact remains that I lost my job. And my wife. So the fact also remains that if it wasn't for me, Anna would not have been in the car that night."

"No, but she would have been in the car again sometime. Right? And what then? Accidents happen every day. Are you responsible for everything that could have happened to her? I don't think so. I just think it was lousy timing. Nothing less, nothing more."

I shrugged. "Maybe," I said. "I'm just waiting for the day when I can believe that with my heart and not just understand it with my head."

For the next few minutes we were quiet as we ate and mulled over the situation. One of the things I had grown to admire most in Mary was her ability to recognize the moment. She felt no need to fill the air with mindless chatter. She was comfortable with silence. It was what made our partnership work.

"So," she said, "getting back to the subject at hand, what are you going to do about Callie?"

"I don't know."

"I might have a suggestion," she said.

I paused with my fork in mid-shovel.

"Let me talk to her."

"You?"

She sat back in her seat and folded her arms across her chest.

"Well, I didn't mean to—"

"I may not be someone's mother, but I have for sure been someone's thirteen-year-old daughter. It wasn't *that* long ago," she said.

"I hate to ask you to—"

"You didn't ask. I offered."

I finished the bite of lasagna.

"Listen, we can make this an innocent thing," she said. "Let's spend the day doing something light. Something fun. The zoo. A shopping trip, whatever. Just mention to her that I'm going along too and then, when the time is right, I will get her alone with me. Just the two of us. Girl talk."

"That's probably what she needs," I said.

"Excellent. So how about Saturday?"

"Sure," I said. "Saturday should work fine."

Mary smiled and began to dig into her salad.

"Mary?" I said.

"Yes?"

"Thanks."

THIRTY-SEVEN

Saturday dawned warmer and brighter than it had been in days. The city seemed to revel in the sun's splendor, and so did I. I finished my run and workout early, and I deferred breakfast again so I could pick Callie up at around nine thirty.

She was dressed in jeans, a T-shirt, and a jacket when I arrived.

"Ready?" I asked.

"Yeah." Her tone was flat, but that was to be expected after the events of the other night.

We began the drive from Carmel back to Indianapolis. It was quiet. We were twenty minutes into the trip and Callie hadn't said a word.

"I'm sorry about the other night," I said.

"I know."

"It's just that I'm concerned about your..." I paused. My conversation was drifting back onto the subject of her grades and, at this point, I wanted to build some bridges. Maybe even try to learn something from my error at the pizza shop. "I'm concerned about you."

"I know," she said.

"Mom's accident came out of nowhere. It's turned our life upside down."

She turned to look out the window.

"We're going to need each other to get through this," I said.

"Then how come I can't come home?" She kept her focus on the objects that passed by her window.

"I can't give you the things you need right now," I said. "Grandma and Grandpa can give you a nice home and a chance to go to a nice school." She put her elbow on the door's arm rest and set her chin on her hand. She kept looking out the window, saying nothing.

"It won't always be this way," I said. The truth was, I didn't know how long it would be. I had managed to accumulate enough money to start the business and run on a tight budget. It didn't leave a lot of room for financial luxuries. And there was the issue of the hours that I could expect to work. I didn't feel that I could leave a young girl home alone while I prowled the streets of the big city at night. She needed a better environment than that.

She remained silent, staring out the window.

I changed the subject. "Mary is coming along. Is that okay?"

"Yes. I like Mary."

Anna had been a true homemaker. She took considerable pride in decorating the house, cooking four-star meals, and entertaining. She would invite friends and coworkers to the house for dinner or a movie, and she had always made everyone feel welcome. Mary had been over several times and had always been a hit with Callie.

"Sure?"

"Sure."

"That's good," I said. "She likes you too."

The traffic along US 31 was light, making our progress toward the city easier than is typical during the week. The trees along the way had just begun to yield their leaves, painting the otherwise barren roadway in a kaleidoscope of color.

"It's just that Mary is still kind of new in town, and when I mentioned that we were going to spend the day shopping, she asked if she could come along." I didn't like lying to Callie, but I felt that the greater good would be served if she didn't know the whole truth.

"Okay," she said. Then, turning to me, "Dad, I'm sorry about getting so upset the other night. I'm sorry that I made you miss the game."

"There'll be other games," I said. "I just wanted to spend some time with you. Even if it is shopping." I feigned disgust at "shopping."

Callie smiled. It was the first one I had seen in quite a while.

By the time we arrived at the Circle Center Mall, it was already abuzz with shoppers, making if difficult to find parking. When we did, we met Mary at the food court.

"Hey guys," she said, smiling.

"Hi, Mary," I said.

"Hi, Callie," Mary said.

"Hi, Mary." Her tone, while pleasant, was still flat.

Mary glanced at me. I shrugged.

"Well...so, what are we going to do?" Mary asked. She was dressed in a gray vinyl jacket over a Donald Duck T-shirt and a pair of jeans that fit her athletic form like glaze on a donut. Her shoulder-length hair bounced with every turn of her head.

"I thought we would hit the shops...maybe get something to eat. See what happens," I said.

"Sounds like fun," Mary said. "That okay with you, Callie?"

Callie shrugged. "Sure. That's okay."

I looked around the food court. "What sounds good?" I asked.

"Johnny Rockets," Mary said. "I love their shakes."

"Okay?" I asked Callie.

"Yeah, I guess so."

We found a seat and placed our order. The smell of the cooking hamburgers, clinking dishes, and generally upbeat conversation should have made for a pleasant time. Instead, it was incredibly awkward. Mary tried in vain to stir the conversation as Callie barely talked, sometimes giving only a nod or shake of the head. Several times during the conversation, I would notice tears in Callie's eyes as she stared vacantly into the crowds around the restaurant. During those times, it would take a direct question to break her reverie and gain her attention. Mary shot me an inquisitive glance. I answered with my "I told you so" look.

After lunch, we strolled the mall and passed a sporting goods store along the way. Mary stopped to look in the window. One of the displays featured athletic wear for young women. A soccer ball was in the window.

"I love soccer," Mary said.

"You do?" Callie asked.

Mary looked at Callie. "Oh yeah. I played all through high school and college. I played all-star in my senior year."

"High school?" Callie asked.

"Yep."

"Where did you go to college?"

"Florida State."

Callie's eyes widened, and I knew instantly that Mary had flipped the right switch.

"That's where I want to go," she said.

"No way!" Mary said.

"Oh yeah. Mom said I might be able to get a scholarship playing soccer."

Mary smiled. "That's how I went."

They began talking a language that only the two of them understood. I didn't feel left out. I felt grateful.

"Hey, ladies."

"What?" they said, simultaneously, looking annoyed.

"I'm going to check out some CDs. Maybe we can meet here in say…" I looked at my watch, "…an hour?"

Mary looked at her watch. "How about an hour and a half?"

"Yeah. How about an hour and a half?" Callie said.

"That's fine," I said. "I'll meet you in an hour and a half, right here."

I walked toward the escalator glancing over my shoulder. Mary and Callie were locked in animated conversation. It had been a long time since I had seen my daughter so excited.

Exactly an hour and a half later I was waiting on a bench outside the athletic store where the three of us had agreed to meet. I had a bag containing a pair of jeans, a Tom Clancy paperback, and a CD of ABBA's greatest hits. Thirty minutes later the two of them showed up. Each of them had several bags, and they were wearing matching soccer jerseys.

"Where did you get—"

"Mary got it for me. It's cool, isn't it?" She was smiling.

I looked at Mary. She smiled. "Lighten up, Colton. This is supposed to be girl's day out, isn't it?"

"Well, yeah," I said, "but—"

"But, nothing," Mary said. "Callie and I had a good time, even if you didn't." She winked at me over Callie's head.

"Yeah. We had a great time. Mary's going to show me a video of some of her games."

I looked at Mary. "You videoed your games?"

She smiled. "I had a soccer mom. What can I say?"

Callie looked at the bag in my hand. "What did you get?"

I opened the bag and she reached in, pulling out the CD.

"Who are they?"

"Before your time," I said.

Mary looked at the CD. "They were before my time too."

I took the CD from her hand and dropped it back into the bag. "You're musically challenged," I said.

Callie looked at Mary, who rolled her eyes.

THIRTY-EIGHT

We strolled through the mall for another hour, leaving to have dinner at Armatzio's. Callie loved the place and hadn't been there since before her mother died. Mary was accommodating as always, but her body language made it clear that she would have preferred to go somewhere else. She kept mum about it for Callie's sake.

The drive from the Circle Center Mall to the restaurant took less than ten minutes. We were a little early for the dinner crowd, so finding a booth wasn't difficult. We had barely been handed menus when Tony came over. He pulled up a chair from one of the nearby tables and straddled it backward.

"Callie," he said. "It has been so long."

She smiled. "Hi, Tony."

"You are getting so tall," he said. "I remember when you were no bigger than this." He held his thumb and index finger an inch apart. Callie smiled again.

"A tad small wasn't she?" Mary asked. Tony ignored her.

"Francesca here tonight?" I asked.

Tony shook his head. "She is with Nick."

I lowered the menu. Francesca and Nick were quite close. Tony and Nick had had problems ever since Nick announced his desire to stay out of the restaurant business.

"Everything okay?" I asked.

Tony nodded. "Is okay," he said.

I wasn't sure that he was being straight with me, but it wasn't the right time to pursue it.

"So how are you doing in school? Good, no?" he asked Callie.

She looked at the menu, pretending not to hear him. He looked at me. I shook my head.

"You are…you are…" he said, "a…soccer player. Is that right?"

Callie looked up from the menu. "Yep," she said.

"Pretty good?"

"Very good," Mary said. "She'll probably get a scholarship to Florida State someday."

Callie looked at Mary and beamed.

"No doubt," Tony said. "No doubt."

"I think I'm ready," I said, handing my menu to Nick. "How about you two?"

Mary closed her menu. "I'm ready," she said.

"Me too," Callie said.

We placed our orders, and Tony went into the kitchen. For the next twenty minutes, I felt as useful as a screwdriver in a sewing shop. Callie and Mary talked soccer as Mary gave the younger version of herself tips and pointers on improving her game and obtaining the coveted scholarship to Florida State. When Tony finally brought our food, I felt like I had rejoined the living.

"Finally," I said.

"Oh hush, you big baby," Mary said.

"Yeah, Dad. You've been whining all day."

I looked at Tony. He smiled as he moved away.

After dinner, I asked if it was okay to drop by the office. It was close by, and I wanted to pick up my mail. I was expecting some information from F&F, and I didn't want my landlord seeing it accumulating outside my office door.

"Fine by me," Mary said. "If you don't mind taking me back when you're done. My car is in the parking garage at the mall."

I shook my head. "Sorry, but I thought that we'd just drop you off right here and you could use your Glock to hitch a ride back."

She smiled. "You are such a putz," she said, punching me playfully in the arm.

We drove to the office with Callie in the backseat and Mary in the front next to me. Six hours earlier this ride would have been awkward. Now it seemed almost natural.

When we arrived at the office, I parked out front, and the three of us went upstairs. The steps creaked.

"Dad, you ought to think about moving to a better place," Callie said.

"Really, Colton," Mary said. "This place…" she stopped midsentence. She was seeing what I was seeing. The door to my office was ajar. Not much, but definitely open. I looked at Mary, who already had her pistol in hand and was pushing Callie back toward the safety of the stairwell. I un-holstered the Ruger.

"What's wrong?" Callie asked.

"Stay here, honey," Mary said.

Callie stayed out of sight as Mary and I approached the office door. I took one side, Mary took the other. We paused to listen but heard nothing. I signaled to Mary and she nodded.

I kicked the door in the rest of the way and dropped to one knee. I swept the left side of the room with the Ruger and I knew that Mary, standing over me, was doing the same to the right side of the room.

"Good grief," she said. "Who did you tick off?"

The office had been tossed. Drawers from my desk and file cabinet were laying about the room, and the files they had contained were in various clusters on the floor. That is, if I'd had any true case files. As it was, the floor was covered in empty manila folders, coffee supplies, and a shattered coffeepot. Even the few books that I kept in the cabinet were torn to shreds.

"Well, if I had to guess right off, I would say Thornton."

"Dad? Is everything okay?"

"It's okay, honey," Mary said, re-holstering her gun. "You can come out now."

Callie eased from behind the wall and approached the office. She stuck her head inside the door.

"Wow! What happened here?"

"That," I said, sliding my gun back into its holster, "is a good question."

THIRTY-NINE

We spent the next hour and a half cleaning up and sorting out. Mary swept up the glass from the broken coffeepot while Callie and I tried to reassemble the contents of the drawers. Neither of us said much. Mary, trying to be upbeat as always, whistled "Whistle While You Work."

After twenty minutes I was growing tired of the song. "Mary?" I said.

She paused midsweep. "Yeah?"

"Is it possible that you might know another song?"

She glanced at Callie who was also growing tired of the song. "Sure," she said, and began whistling "Heigh-Ho" from *Snow White*.

I looked at Callie and shook my head.

"Here," I said, handing her a stack of folders, "put these files on the desk and then put this pile," I handed her another stack, "in the lower right desk drawer."

She looked at them. "But Dad, they're empty."

"I know," I said, "but that is where the empty files go."

"What makes you think Thornton was behind this?" Mary asked as Callie began to place the files into the drawer.

"He owes me," I said. "I roughed him up a little the…" I glanced at Callie who was busy enough filling my desk drawer with manila folders that she hadn't heard me. "We hooked up the other night," I said, lowering my voice.

Mary paused midsweep again. Her eyes widened. "You found Thornton?"

I nodded.

Mary glanced over my shoulder at Callie. "What happened?" she asked, in a near whisper.

I shrugged. "Nothing much, really. I kind of…forced my way into his apartment and told him that I wanted to talk."

"And?"

"And…he resisted."

"What did you do, Colton?"

"I overcame the resistance."

She studied me for a moment. "How did you leave him?"

"Alive."

She stood the broom against the wall and crossed her arms. "I would expect that you would. My question is more related to the overall state of his health."

"I left him handcuffed to the outside railing of his fourth-floor balcony."

"And?"

"And…maybe with a broken knee."

She shook her head. "Colton," she said, exasperated, "I didn't hear that. I'm an officer of the law."

"You're a federal agent, and defending myself is not a federal crime."

She shook her head again. "So now you think he may have tossed your office."

"Seems reasonable. I didn't rough up anyone else."

"Have you been annoying…" she paused to hold up her hand, palm out, like a cop stopping the flow of traffic. "Sorry, this is *you* we're talking about. *Who else* have you been annoying along the way?"

"Frankie DiCenza."

"Who's he?"

"He owns a strip joint called DeNights. He runs the numbers in this town. Any bookie who wants to stay in business deals with Frankie."

"Did you rough him up too?"

I shook my head. "No, but I had to slap his bouncer around a little."

She put her face in her hands and shook her head.

"I made it clear to Frankie that I would take it as a deeply personal insult if I thought he had anything to do with anything that might happen to me or mine."

"And you think that a threat from you is going to stop someone like him? Colton, these are bad men. They didn't get where they are by folding to every threat that comes along." She crossed her arms again and shifted most of her weight to one leg. It was apparent that she wasn't sure what to think. I had seen that look a thousand times. "Anyone else?"

"What do you take me for?" I asked.

"Dad?"

I turned to Callie.

"I don't know where these go," she said, holding a stack of maps.

"They go in the folder marked 'maps,'" I said.

"Maps?" she asked.

"I keep a map for all of the surrounding towns. Never hurts to be prepared."

She shrugged. "Okay."

I turned back toward Mary. "I will probably need to pay someone another visit," I said, realizing that I had indeed been knocking heads with some of the city's rougher elements. "Starting with Thornton."

Mary picked up her broom again. "Haven't you learned that violence begets more violence? Your need to be in control is going to get you killed."

FORTY

I had little doubt that it was Thornton who had tossed my office, which meant he probably also knew where I lived. After taking Mary back to her car and Callie back to Carmel, I drove home, arriving at nearly midnight. When I did, I found Mary parked out front. She got out of her car when I approached the house.

"Didn't I tell you I'd be careful?" I said.

She smiled. "A little insurance never hurts."

I sighed but didn't say anything. I knew it wouldn't do any good, and besides, I was glad to see her. As we approached the house, I bolted up the front steps, and Mary jogged around back.

The front door was still locked, and from peering in the window, I could see that the lights I had left on were still on.

I unlocked the door and went in, gun in hand. I walked straight through to the back of the house and let Mary in the back door.

"Okay?" she asked, re-holstering her Glock.

"Of course."

"Don't give me that," she said. "I know as well as you do that you were going to come in your house tonight with your gun in your hand, just in case."

I laughed. "I may be confident, but I'm not stupid."

She rubbed both eyes. "Why don't you make some coffee, and I'll tell you about my talk with Callie."

"You look tired," I said. "Are you sure you're up to it?"

She slid out of her jacket and draped it over one of the kitchen table chairs. "I'm up to it. Just make me some coffee."

She went into the living room and sat at one end of the sofa. When the coffee was fully brewed, I brought her a cup and sat next to her. I sipped my coffee and, like Mary, rubbed the strain from my eyes.

"How did it go?" I asked.

She blew on the coffee before drinking. "Colton, did I ever tell you about my dad?"

"Your dad? No, I can't say that you have."

She swirled the coffee around in her cup and took another drink before answering. "My mother died when I was seventeen. She died suddenly, just like Anna."

"I'm sorry," I said.

She shrugged. "Yeah, well…life happens. You know?"

I told her that I did.

"Anyway, after Mom died, I went through a very dark period. Dad did too. The problem was that we went through it separately. Dad had his job, and he turned to it to get his mind off of Mom's death. That left me alone with nowhere to turn."

"What did he do?"

"He owned a camera store. He sold Canon, Nikon, you name it. He serviced them too. But after Mom's death, he seemed to be busier than ever before." She paused to sip the coffee. "I was alone—a lot—and there were many nights that I would have dinner made, but it would get cold while I waited for him to come home."

"I'm sorry," I said again. "I wish that there was something that I could say, Mary, but—"

She shook her head. "Anyway, one night I got very, very angry and told him that she was my mom just as much as she was his wife. I told him that I got tired of him never being home and leaving me alone to deal with everything any way that I could. Do you know what he said?"

I shook my head.

"He said that he was trying to make a living for us." She turned to look at me. "He said that he was putting a roof over our heads."

I shifted uncomfortably on the sofa. "Mary, the situation is a little bit different between Callie and me."

"Dad concentrated on the camera shop and I concentrated on soccer. When I got my scholarship, I left home for Florida State and I haven't looked back since. Dad and I haven't spoken in over two years." She paused. "Is that what you want, Colton?"

"No, of course not. But I'm not your dad and Callie isn't you. Your dad had a stable source of income. He was using it to drown his sorrow and to provide an excuse for not doing the things he should have done. He left you to deal with your own grief any way that you could. The situation with Callie and me is different. I don't have a stable source of income. And I'm not leaving Callie to deal with Anna's death alone."

"Maybe not, but that's how she sees it."

"What did she say?"

Mary set the coffee cup down on the end table next to the sofa and turned to fully face me. "It isn't what she said, it's what she didn't say."

I shook my head. "Sorry. You lost me."

"She talked about soccer. *Only* soccer. Whenever I tried to steer the conversation to Anna, or you, or the issues at hand, she steered back to soccer."

"Yeah? So?"

"She's doing exactly what I did. She's focused on the future."

I made it clear that I didn't understand.

"She's focused on the future to the exclusion of the past. And the present." She paused to see if anything she said was taking shape. "Don't you get it? Her mother is dead, and her father, the only family she has left, has made his career his primary focus."

"That isn't fair, Mary. I'm not making it primary focus. I'm trying to make a living for us."

"That's what my dad said."

I sighed.

"Colton, Callie is a very sad little girl. She didn't just lose her mother. She lost her family too. And if you don't do something soon, she will find another. It may be soccer and it may be something else. But she will fill the void. Trust me, I know."

"You've done all right for yourself," I said.

She rubbed her eyes again. "No, I haven't."

"How can you say that?" I asked. "You're an educated, ambitious, highly trained FBI agent who has the respect and admiration of everyone that I know."

"Maybe I do now," she said, reaching for the coffee cup. "But there are things about me, about my past, that you don't know. There are things that I'm continuing to deal with that spring from things I've done in my life. Things I'm not proud of."

I could see tears in her eyes. I put my hand on her shoulder.

"Just before my senior year at Florida...I got pregnant."

"Pregnant?"

She nodded. "I was seeing a guy who made me feel like I mattered." Tears began to trickle down her cheek. "He was the right guy with the right line, and I was at the wrong place in my life and...the whole thing became one big stew and I fell into it."

"Did you have the baby?"

The tears began to flow. "No. I didn't. I had an abortion. And now..." she began to cry. I put my arm around her shoulder and pulled her close. She sobbed as she lay her head against my chest. "Now I look at you and Callie and I think how nice it would have been to have a daughter."

"Mary, I—"

"Did Pastor Millikin talk to you?"

"Millikin?"

She nodded, wiping tears from her eyes. "Did he tell you that I've been talking with him?"

I remembered Millikin's conversation about talking with Mary. It wasn't something I had forgotten to do. It was something I had been trying to avoid.

"He said you met at Anna's funeral."

"Yes."

"What did you talk about?" I was uncomfortable. I didn't know this side of Mary.

"Just what we've talked about tonight," she said. "I came to the realization that Anna was gone and that I could be gone just as quickly." She dabbed her nose with the tissue. "I needed to know if there was a better way to live."

"Is there?"

She shrugged. "I don't know, Colton. I just know that what he said makes sense. There has to be more to life than this. And if there is, doesn't it make sense to live for that?"

"You're starting to sound like Anna," I said. "After she got religion, she began talking to me about things like this. I'm not sure that I always handled it the right way. I probably caused a lot of tension, but…that was *her* thing, not mine."

"But that's the point, Colton," Mary said. "It is everybody's thing. If God made one of us, He made all of us." She sat up straight. "Millikin said that God wants a relationship with us. That Christianity is not a religion."

I was becoming increasingly agitated. "Sure seems like one to me."

"Did he talk with you about this?" she asked.

"He told me that I should talk to you," I said.

"Why didn't you?" She dabbed at her eyes. Mascara was beginning to run.

"I…don't know. I guess I felt uncomfortable."

She looked at me. "Why?"

I shrugged. "I don't know, really. Maybe it's the idea of you… going down a different road than the one I thought we…I…was going down."

She sniffled and smiled slightly, dabbing at her eyes with a tissue. "Misery loves company."

I hadn't thought of it that way, but she was right. I was miserable, and I didn't want to be miserable alone. "I never thought of you as miserable. I didn't know about the pregnancy."

"I've been miserable for a long time. Ever since Mom died and Dad went his own way." She lowered the tissue and turned to face me. "We are a lot alike."

"How's that?" I asked.

"We're very self-reliant people. You were shuttled from home to home yet made a life for yourself. Four years in the navy that helped put you through college. After that, five years with the Chicago PD, which helped you to eventually enter the FBI." She dabbed at her eyes. "And, despite the setback of Anna's death, you will try to come out of this situation by tapping into that unadulterated willpower of yours." I saw admiration in her eyes. It made me feel good. The first time that I had felt that way since before Anna died.

"And you bounced back from disaster to get your life back on track," I said.

She shook her head. "I'm not on track, Colton. That's my point. We are two very self-reliant people who are wrestling with problems that no one can wrestle with alone and expect to win."

"We'll come out of this okay," I said. "You'll work through this, and Callie and I will—"

She sighed. "Talk to Pastor Millikin."

"I already have."

She reached to take my hand. "I admire all you've done and all that you're capable of doing. I just haven't met anyone like you. But I'm learning that we can't even take our next breath, unless God allows it."

I was uncomfortable. I was seeing a side of Mary that I hadn't known existed.

"Talk to Pastor Millikin," she said again.

I shook my head. "No, I don't think so. The good Pastor and I have nothing to talk about."

"Then talk to God. I have. You just might be surprised by the result."

FORTY-ONE

I was back at Riley Towers by six the next morning. I was able to buzz an apartment on the fourth floor and convince a sleepy-sounding woman that I was Brad Thornton and had locked my keys in the car. I asked if she could buzz me in so that I could get an extra set from the apartment. She buzzed without question or argument.

When I reached Thornton's apartment I knocked. No one answered, so I kicked in the door. I scoured the place with the Ruger in hand, but Thornton wasn't there. As I was leaving the apartment, an elderly lady in a bathrobe and rollers was standing just inside her door. She saw me slip the gun in my holster and gasped.

"Pest control," I said.

I left Riley Towers and moved south on Pennsylvania, working my way around the county jail and then back onto Washington Street, heading east. Thornton hadn't been in, but finding him again wouldn't be difficult. For the moment, I had more important things to talk about. And that was going to involve Melissa.

I drove to her house, stopping first at the gas station that sat across the street. I bought two large black coffees and a box of donuts. When I got to the house, I eased over the fence and went to the front door with a cup in each hand and the box of donuts under my arm. Balancing the cups on top of each other with one hand, I knocked with the other. I hadn't seen Thornton's car parked out front. Since he wasn't home and wasn't with Melissa, it was probably safe to assume he was with the leggy blonde. Or someone else. It didn't really matter. At least not for the moment. It was Melissa I wanted to see now.

She opened the door. "Don't you ever give up?" No teddy this time. She was wearing a man's shirt and pajama bottoms. Her hair was pulled back and held in place by a rubber band. She had been asleep.

"Nope," I said. "But I do bring breakfast. Can I come in?"

She hesitated but finally opened the door and allowed me to pass.

"Where's Buster?" I asked as I moved past her.

She nodded toward the back of the house. "He's chained up out back." She pushed the door shut.

The shades were drawn, and the house had a musty smell. A piece of toast sat on the edge of the coffee table, and a fine coating of dust layered the room. Overall, not a real cheerful place.

"Kitchen's that way," she said, pointing to a doorway that was ahead and off to the right.

I went into the kitchen. A stack of dishes sat in a sink that had built up a layer of crust from years of hard water. A clock radio sat on top of the refrigerator with an extension cord that connected it to a socket over the stove. I sat on one of two chairs at the antiquated Formica and chrome dinette set and placed one cup of coffee on the table in front of the other chair. She stood with arms folded, leaning on the door frame. She was staring at me again.

"Better get it while it's hot," I said, removing the lid from my own cup and opening the box of donuts.

"Why are you here? If Brad finds you, he is going to kick your—"

"I don't think so," I said. I sipped the coffee and took a chocolate-frosted cake donut from the box.

"It don't matter what you think. It only matters what he knows."

I bit into the donut. "These are fresh. You really ought to sit and have one. At least have some coffee before it gets cold."

She hesitated for a moment and then opened the refrigerator and pulled out a carton of milk. She poured a little into the coffee and then stirred it with a spoon that she pulled from under the pile of dishes in the sink. She drank some and then sat in the other chair.

"I didn't come here to talk to Thornton," I said. "I came here to talk to you."

"What do you want with me?" she asked, hesitantly reaching for a glazed donut.

"I need to know more about Angie, F&F, Emma, and Billy. I think you're probably as good a source as any."

"Then why are you looking for Brad?"

I dipped my donut in the coffee and took a bite before answering. "I'm not looking for Brad. I've already found him."

Here eyes flickered momentarily. "When?"

"A couple of nights ago."

She studied me before resuming her stock expression of indifference. "And you're still here?" She bit into her donut.

"Looks that way, doesn't it?"

It was obvious that she had paused to think about what I had said. Her stoic demeanor momentarily thawed to reveal a real concern for the man.

"He's okay," I said.

"Of course he is," she said, reinstalling the screen of indifference.

"So?" I asked, pausing to drink the coffee.

"So what?"

"So, what can you tell me about Angie, F&F, Emma, and Billy?"

"I don't know what you're talking about," she said.

"Yes, you do," I said.

She glared at me.

"You and Angie are sex models for F&F's live programs, and Emma was a recruiter for the company. Probably recruited you as a matter of fact."

She set the donut down. "I think it's time for you to leave."

I shook my head. "Nope. Sorry. Not until I get what I came for."

Anger shot across her face as she jumped up from the table, causing the chair to tip over and crash to the floor.

"Melissa, please sit down," I said. "And don't try to get tough with me. It won't work."

She pointed toward the front door while keeping her eyes focused on me. "I said, get out."

"Emma had gambling debts. Was she blackmailing Angie?"

"That's it. I'm calling the cops." She moved toward the phone in the living room. I stood and followed her. As she picked up the receiver to dial, I pulled it from her hand and jerked the phone from the wall. I threw it into the kitchen where it clattered on the floor.

"I'm not playing games here," I said. She backed away. The façade of toughness had deteriorated. Before me was a woman who was fearful and vulnerable.

"Look," she said, "I don't want no trouble."

"Good," I said, advancing on her. "I don't either. So just tell me what you know about Emma and Angie and I'll be gone."

She had backed up to the sofa and was looking toward the hallway leading to the bedrooms.

"I'm not going to hurt you, and I certainly wouldn't hurt your child. I just want some answers to—"

She tried to flee down the hall but I caught her by the wrist and flung her onto the sofa.

"What is it with you and that boyfriend of yours?" I said. "I just want to talk."

She glared at me while holding her hand protectively in front of her face. "Maybe we don't want to talk to you," she said.

I could feel the anger welling up within me. I knew I had no right to force her to answer the questions I was asking. Yet I knew that I could. And that knowledge, coupled with the temptation it presented, was difficult to resist. It had been difficult to resist when I was interrogating Thornton. It had been difficult to resist when I beat the whereabouts of Amy Sandler from her kidnapper. But that beating had cost me my job. And my wife.

Now, here I was, out of control again. Standing over a cowering woman. A woman who was in her own home and who had a daughter asleep, not twenty feet away. A woman whom I had just promised that I wouldn't harm. Yet, I was poised to do just that.

The pause had given me time to reflect. My anger began to cool, and I became nauseated at the position that I had taken.

"Of course," I said, backing away. "If you don't want to talk with me—that's your right."

As I backed toward the door, she lowered her hand and looked at me with bewilderment. Her natural inclination to flee, to brace herself for the blows that she thought were coming, told me a lot about her relationship with Thornton, if not with men in general. And her belief that she had to protect herself and her child spoke volumes about me. I didn't like it. Not one bit.

CHAPTER
FORTY-TWO

Tifton High School was at the end of the day when I arrived in
Mrs. Presky's office. She gave me the room number for June
Seidel's family life science class, telling me that she had talked with
the teacher about my wanting to question her.

"She's agreed to talk with you. Emma was her friend and col-
league."

I thanked Presky for her cooperation and followed the directions
she gave me to Seidel's room. I obviously wasn't going to get anywhere with Melissa, so that left me with the Seidel option.

I peered through the window in the door and found a tall, thin
woman, fashionably dressed and about Emma's age, standing before
a group of teenagers who had gathered around an oven. Most of
them seemed thoroughly bored. A few were in deep rapture, learning
the nuances of baking bread.

The bell rang as classrooms burst open. I was knocked aside by
the opening of the door as the hall was instantly filled with chat-
tering kids and slamming lockers. From inside the classroom, I could
hear Seidel giving last-minute instructions.

"Remember people, there will be a quiz tomorrow. This is not an
open book, so study hard!"

I stepped inside the classroom and waited while two of the die-hards hung around to ask questions. The rest of the kids, girls in lowriders and boys in baggy jeans, filed out the door like zombies in a fifties horror flick.

The two students who had been hanging around got their answers and sauntered past me on their way out the door. Of the thirty or so kids in Seidel's class, none had shown any signs that they had noticed I was in the room.

"I don't think anyone even knew I was here," I said.

"You're over thirty," she said. "Far as they're concerned, you don't exist."

I walked over to where she was standing by the oven and extended my hand.

"My name is Colton Parker," I said.

She shook my hand. Her grip was firm.

"I know who you are," she said. "Bev told me that you might be coming around. Frankly, I expected to see you sooner."

"Bev?"

"I'm sorry—Mrs. Presky."

"Yes. I'm sorry too. I should have been here sooner. But I've been busy."

She gathered her books and walked to her desk. I followed.

"I'll bet that you have. I imagine that trying to extricate a murderer from his crime can be quite time consuming."

"You believe that Billy Caine is guilty," I said.

She raised an eyebrow. "Doesn't everyone?" She sat the books down on the desk.

"Seems that way."

She smiled. "So what can I do for you?"

"I'm trying to learn more about Emma."

"In hopes of finding some dark secret in her past that can point you to the real murderer?"

"If that happens, then we all benefit, don't we?"

"It won't. Emma had no enemies. If the police say that Billy killed her, he killed her."

"And what about you?" I asked.

She sat at the desk. "Me? What about me?"

"Who's list are you on?"

The change of her expression was stark. "Excuse me?"

"Emma was very heavy into Internet pornography. So are you."

Her face reddened. "I don't believe I heard you correctly."

I repeated what I had said.

She stood. "I think that you had better leave."

"I suspect that Emma and you were rolling young girls from this high school—and probably others—into the business. Kids who had no parental authority at home, or who needed money for college, or who were just too weak-willed to resist a favorite teacher."

The flush of her face deepened.

"I'm going to find out who killed Emma," I said. "I will do it with or without your cooperation. But if you decide to cooperate, I will do what I can to encourage leniency from the prosecutor."

She swallowed hard. Evil will deny its own existence until it's no longer possible. Then it wants to broker deals. I had just offered her the best one that she would get.

"Can you close the door, please?" she asked.

I moved to close the classroom door and took a seat at one of the student desks. Seidel sat behind her own.

"I will lose my job," she said.

"You should. But it's better than going to prison."

She nodded. Her bearing had changed. The confident teacher had become a withering confessor. "What do you want to know?"

"Tell me about Emma's gambling habits. How much did she owe?"

"Emma had few vices. All that she did with the business was for profit. Not enjoyment. You have to understand that about her."

"Sure," I said. "That makes all this so much better."

She hung her head. "Except for gambling. She did have a love for that. Not casinos—horses."

"She booked with Frankie DiCenza?"

She nodded. "We both did. Emma always had more money than I did, so her level of indulgence was considerably higher."

"She lose often?"

She nodded.

"How much was she in the hole?"

"I think it was somewhere in the neighborhood of twenty thousand."

"When was that?"

She paused to think. "Maybe seven…eight months ago."

"DiCenza pay her a visit?"

"Yes. A couple of times he had some of his men come around, nice like, and ask for the money. That went on for a couple of months. Then, when Emma didn't come up with it, DiCenza called her himself. He told her that she would be dead in a week if she didn't come up with the money."

"So she came up with twenty thousand? In a week?"

She nodded. "Yes. I think so. She might have been trying to accumulate it for a longer period of time, but, at any rate, the threats stopped. She never said another word about it."

"Did you have the same trouble? With DiCenza, I mean?"

"Yes."

"How much were you into him for?"

"Five."

"Thousand?"

She nodded.

"Are you clear with him now?"

She nodded.

"Did you and Angie try to put the squeeze on Emma?"

She pulled a tissue from a box on her desk and dabbed at her eyes. "I had my own debts with DiCenza. Angie had a drug problem." She chuckled slightly to herself. "That's a good one isn't it? Teacher and former student having addictions they can't pay for?"

"Yeah, that's great," I said. "Tell me about Angie."

She dabbed at her eyes again. "A loner. She was a student of mine and always seemed to be alone. No friends. No self-esteem." She sighed. "No father at home. No mother to speak of. Just alone."

"In other words," I said, "easy pickings for someone like you."

She dabbed again at her eyes but said nothing.

"Does the name Melissa King ring a bell with you?"

She nodded. "Of course. But you knew that before you asked, didn't you?"

"Tell me about her," I said.

She sighed, long and heavy. "The opposite of Angie. Feisty, aggressive. Always in trouble. And not very smart. Always seemed to have a hard time with the basics. But she had a body. There wasn't a boy in this school she couldn't have had."

I shook my head in disgust. The Melissa I saw had apparently been taken down a notch or two by the lifestyle she had chosen. "How did you two cook up the squeeze on Emma?"

"Emma was pulling down some serious money. Angie and I just thought that the two of us combined could do a lot better. We started to branch out. See if we could...enlist some of the girls on our own."

"Why didn't you?"

"We tried. But you have to understand how F&F works."

"Tell me," I said.

She dabbed at her eyes again. "It's like a pyramid scheme. Emma was at the top, I was the next layer down."

"And Angie?"

She shook her head. "She wasn't really a player at all. Just the talent. Her hold on Emma came from the fact that she was seeing Billy. Emma doted on that boy and couldn't stand the thought that someone like Angie might end up being related to her someday, even if it was by marriage. It used to drive Emma crazy."

"How did Billy feel about Emma?" I asked.

"I don't know. I only know that Emma cared deeply for him."

"So Angie was using Billy as leverage?"

She shook her head. "No. I don't think that she set out to use Billy at all. She actually cares for him. But when she saw the power over Emma that the relationship gave her, she wasn't above using it."

"Who approached who about taking Emma's position?"

She sniffled. "Me. I approached Angie. I said that we both needed the money and Emma was probably set for life. If we didn't bring any girls in, she would have nowhere to go but down."

"But Emma resisted that?"

She nodded. "Yes. She threatened Angie with telling Billy. He would have been deeply hurt by what Angie was doing, but it would have saved Emma's job and maybe her life. She still had the gambling debt over her head."

"Did Billy know what Emma was doing?"

"No. And that's what stopped her. Emma didn't want Billy knowing of her own involvement with F&F."

"So they reached a stalemate. But each was willing to pull the trigger if necessary."

She nodded. "Yes."

"Why didn't you go it alone?"

"I didn't have the ability that Emma had. If I worked with someone, I could make a go of it. But alone, I had no chance."

"So since you and Angie were effectively out of the picture, Emma won. She kept her position."

"Yes."

"Then Angie struck out on her own. If she could outwork Emma, she might be able to convince F&F to move her into position over Emma, or, at least, she could build her own pyramid."

"Yes."

"Except that she doesn't have the access to readily available young girls the way you and Emma did."

She lowered her head. "Yes," she said, barely audible.

"So Emma never saw Angie as a threat as long as she was on her own."

She nodded, keeping her eyes diverted away from me.

I stood from the too-small student desk and walked to the classroom window. I paused there for a minute, watching as students continued to drift out of the building on their way toward home, oblivious to the macabre nightmare that lay within the walls. Many of the young girls reminded me of my own.

"How many young lives have you ruined?" I asked, continuing to look out the window. I didn't hear an answer, so I turned to face her. "After Emma squelched this uprising, how did she get the money to pay off DiCenza?"

"I don't know. I do know that all of us got a heavy push from Emma."

"All of us?"

She nodded.

"How many of you are in Emma's pyramid?"

"I don't know," she said, dabbing at her eyes again.

"Any more from here?'

She shrugged. "I don't know. I've heard there are a couple more, but I don't know for sure."

"Presky?"

She shook her head. "No."

"When did this push start?" I asked.

"About six months ago. A couple of months later, it was clear that Emma was having problems with DiCenza."

"So," I said, moving from the window to where Seidel was sitting, "Emma put on this big recruiting push."

"Yes."

"And you believe that's how she paid her debts."

"Yes."

"Yet she was killed. Brutally."

Her eyes reddened. "Yes."

"Did it occur to you that you might know too much?"

She looked at me, slowly. "F&F does not employ killers, Mr. Parker."

"DiCenza does," I said. "And you know too much."

I could tell that she hadn't thought of it in that light. I moved toward the door. "I'm going to leave. I strongly suggest that you do the right thing and turn yourself in to the police."

"Turning myself in won't get your client off the hook," she said.

"Maybe not. But it will get these young girls off of your hook." I opened the door, "And it just might get you off of DiCenza's."

FORTY-THREE

A ngie fit the profile for the type of girl who would have been easy prey for someone like Emma. Alone and in desperate need of cash. Lots of it. If that was the profile for all of Emma's victims, then she would have plenty of young girls from which to choose. That would also explain the large number of girls that the Tooleys had seen coming in and out of Emma's home.

I climbed the same creaking stairs to my third-floor office that Mary, Callie, and I had climbed the night before and found mail in my box. Among the bills and increasing number of overdue notices was the package from F&F that I had been looking for the other night. It was wrapped in a plain brown wrapper.

"Of course," I said to myself, examining the package on the way into my office.

I removed my jacket and slid out of my shoulder rig, tossing both onto my desk. I opened the mailer and found a generic cover letter thanking me for my interest, along with a small catalog outlining the various products and services of the company. It seemed that "Fun and Frank" offered everything in the way of sexual content from photos of young girls "barely legal" to dating services for the "connoisseur of pleasure." A website and toll-free number were listed.

I hadn't examined the website. I didn't feel that it would offer as much of a preview of the coming attractions as a catalog would. And I had no desire to see young girls being degraded for the enjoyment of men who would have never allowed their own daughters to be photographed in the same way. The industry was built on hypocrisy. The kind of hypocrisy that would allow a guidance counselor to use her position as an access to young girls who wanted nothing more than a chance at life. The kind of hypocrisy that would bring profit to merchants who cared nothing for these kids beyond the dollars that they could earn. The hypocrisy of politicians who promised during each campaign to "make education and our children top priorities" and then proceeded to pass and enforce laws making it possible to do the very opposite.

How could I effect any change in the system when so many people simply didn't care? When so many were willing to write off one young girl, as long as she wasn't theirs, and continue to turn away in their ongoing attempts to ignore the problem?

I looked at the catalog again. On the cover was a photo of a young girl who was not much older than Callie. Described as "barely legal," she was posed to be enticing. Fresh-faced and smiling, her partially clothed body promised physical satisfaction but little else. There was no indication that she was anything other than two-dimensional. Born only to provide pleasure. A tool to be used and then, when the shine was gone, to be exchanged for another girl, a younger girl, who was equally willing and able. A fantasy come to life.

The girl in the picture, though, was not a fantasy. She was real. Three-dimensional. Someone's daughter. And she was there for a reason. Maybe it was the allure of fame. Or money. And maybe she no longer had the desire to be there but was held fast by the anchor of addiction. The type of habit that is costly to maintain and could be managed by just "one more movie," "one more photo."

Or maybe she had had true and legitimate desires. Desires that went outside the bounds of existing for someone else's sexual satisfaction. Desires for the legitimate things in life. An education, a career. Or a husband and children.

I spun my chair around and rested my feet on the windowsill. The sky was overcast with dark, rolling clouds.

I looked at the picture again.

Maybe she had wanted to be a nurse or an architect but didn't have the means to realize the dream. Or maybe her family structure wasn't much of a structure at all, and she had no support. No direction in life other than that provided by a wayward and self-serving guidance counselor. Maybe this girl, unlike Angie, could be saved before the despair took its toll and she grew into a hard, embittered woman. One who would see no redemption in any avenue of life and who would seek to live off the misfortunes of the others who would come behind her. Maybe.

I flung the catalog into the trash just as the phone rang. I turned partway around in my chair to answer it.

"Colton?" It was Mary. "I feel bad about the other night. I didn't mean to come off so strong."

"Mary, it's okay. Really. I appreciate your concern and all you did to help Callie. It's the first time in a long time that I've seen her excited about anything."

"I enjoyed being with her. I always do. And I didn't want you to think…that I think you're a bad father. I don't."

"Mary, it's okay," I said.

"And I just…opened up more than I should have. I told you more than you probably wanted to hear, and I'm sorry for spoiling an otherwise perfectly good day."

"You didn't spoil the day. You made it what it was. A very nice one. For Callie…and me. Okay?"

She hesitated and then thanked me for listening to her and hung up.

I kept my feet propped on the window ledge, contemplating the next step, when the phone rang again. Again, I turned partway in my chair and yanked the receiver off the hook.

"Mary, I said it's—"

"Colton, it's Corrin."

I lowered my voice. "Sorry about that, Corrin. I—"

"The school called."

"The school?"

"One of the teachers found Callie unconscious in the girl's restroom."

I spun my chair around and planted my feet on the floor. "Unconscious?"

Her voice began to crack. "She's on her way to Methodist Hospital. Frank and I are almost there now."

"I'm on my way," I said, hanging up.

Methodist Hospital is in the near downtown area, only a few minutes' drive from my office. I would arrive there before Frank and Corrin.

I grabbed my jacket and dashed down the stairs a lot faster than I had climbed them a few minutes earlier. The despair I had been feeling over the plight of Angie, Melissa, and other girls like them deepened.

By the time I reached my car, I had my cell phone in hand and was calling the FBI.

As I pulled away from the curb, the bureau's operator answered. I asked for Mary. She answered the phone on the second ring.

"Special Agent Christopher."

"Mary, it's Colton," I said, trying to sound controlled.

"Tell me I'm not slipping that much. Didn't we just—"

"Mary, Callie was found unconscious at school today."

There was a pause.

"I don't know any more than that," I said. "I'm on my way to Methodist now."

"I'll meet you there," she said.

The Minton-Capehart Federal Building in downtown Indianapolis is less than five minutes from the hospital. I expected that

Mary and I would arrive at about the same time. I was right. She was climbing out of her bureau-issued car as I pulled into the lot. She waited until I was out of my car so we could enter the hospital together.

"That didn't take long," I said. I was glad to see her.

"I told you I'd be right here," she said, gripping my arm.

The sliding doors hissed open as we entered the spacious waiting area of the emergency department. We walked to one of several open windows.

"Can I help you?" a round, middle-aged woman asked.

"My name is Colton Parker. My daughter, Callie, was brought in here a little while ago."

She swung the computer monitor to a position where she could better see it.

"How do you spell it?"

"C-a-l-l-i-e."

Her fingers flew over the keyboard like trained pigeons over familiar terrain. Then we waited while the computer searched to find the information we desperately needed.

"She's here and the doctor is with her now. Have a seat over there," she said, nodding to the sitting area of the waiting room, "and fill out these forms." She slid a sheaf of papers toward me.

I was beginning to protest when Mary took me by the arm and reached for the forms.

"Thank you," she said to the clerk as she guided me to a vacant seat.

"Why do they do that?" I asked. "Why do they always tell you to wait out here when your family is in there?"

"So you won't be in the way," Mary said.

"She's my daughter." I could begin to feel the despair slip away and the anger rise. Mary knew what was happening.

"When was Callie born?" she asked, directing me into a seat.

"What?"

"On the form. They want to know when Callie was born." She sat next to me and was beginning to complete the forms—trying to divert my attention.

I told her. She wrote it on the appropriate line.

"What do you think they're doing" I asked.

"Their jobs. This is one of the best trauma centers in the world. They know what they're doing. Okay?" She placed a hand on mine. "Okay?" she said again.

"Yeah. I guess it'll have to be."

"How tall is she and how much does she weigh?"

I shook my head. "I don't know," I said.

"Okay. We can skip that part for now. Address?"

I gave her Frank and Corrin's.

"She up to date on her immunizations?"

"I don't know," I said. "Don't the schools have to make sure of that sort of thing?"

"Insurance?"

I shook my head. "I don't have any, Mary," I said.

She was about to ask another question when a couple burst into the waiting room. The woman was crying. They talked with the woman at the window in hushed tones. She talked to them for a minute and then gave them the same stack of forms she had given me and pointed them toward the waiting area where Mary and I were sitting. They slowly moved to a row of empty seats like sinful passengers waiting for their train ride to hell.

Mary and I were trying to refocus our attention on the forms when Frank and Corrin came into the reception area. Corrin was crying, and Frank had tears in his eyes.

"Colton," Corrin said, hugging me.

"Is she okay?" Frank asked, standing with his hands in his jacket pockets. He looked as though he felt out of place.

"I don't know," I said. "We just got here and I…"

I noticed that their eyes diverted to Mary. Despite the desperation of the moment, their expressions revealed their dismay. They hadn't expected to see someone else with their daughter's husband. Particularly now, at such a crucial time, so soon after they had stood in this very room waiting to hear of their own daughter's fate.

"This is Mary Christopher," I said, introducing her to the Shapiros. "She was a coworker at the FBI."

Mary rose and extended a hand to each of them. She was clearly uncomfortable. "We met at the…at Anna's funeral," she said.

They returned the greetings without warmth.

"Colton, I'm going to get some coffee. Do you want any?" Mary asked.

"Sure," I said, knowing she felt uncomfortable. "Black."

She looked at the Shapiros.

"No thanks," Frank said.

Mary left as Frank and Corrin sat down.

"Has the doctor been out?" Frank asked.

"No. I haven't heard a thing. They told me to have a seat and to fill out these forms."

I glanced at the couple in the seats a few feet away. They were in obvious distress but were making attempts to complete their forms.

"Has she had any problems at home?" I asked. "Any fainting spells?"

Corrin shook her head. "No. That's what has got us so concerned."

"As far as I can tell," Frank said, "everything has been fine."

"We don't know what happened," Corrin said. "The principal called and said that some other girls found her in the restroom, lying on the floor. They couldn't rouse her."

I was about to tell them what I had seen in her during our visit to the mall, about the reluctance to talk and the tears that seemed to come out of nowhere, when Mary came back with the coffee.

"I saw a vending machine down the hall. It was closer than the cafeteria."

"Coffee is coffee," I said.

"Are you sure I can't get you anything?" she asked the Shapiros. They both shook their heads again. "We're fine," Frank said.

"But thank you for asking," Corrin added.

The doors leading to the emergency department's exam area swung open. A man that I guessed to be about thirty-five came through them. He was tall, gaunt, and dressed in green surgical scrubs.

"McPherson?" he asked.

The couple who had come in earlier stood.

"I'm Dr. Lindsey," he said. "Could I ask you to come with me?"

They followed the doctor to what I assumed was a private area. They moved as though they were walking the last mile.

"I wonder what that was about?" I asked. No one answered. Each of us was alone with our thoughts.

Within a few minutes, though, we heard wailing, and we had our answer.

The doctor returned. "Parker?" he said.

I stood and cleared my throat. "Here," I said.

"Folks, I'm Dr. Lindsey. Could I ask you to come with me, please?"

FORTY-FOUR

D r. Lindsey led the four of us into a small room several feet off the main corridor. He asked us to have a seat as he ushered in another man.

"Folks, I'm going to tell you about Callie, but then I have some questions."

"Is she alive?" Frank asked.

The question might have seemed oddly blunt coming from anyone else. But with the recent loss of his daughter, Frank's question was actually quite natural.

"She's fine," Lindsey said.

"Thank God," Corrin said.

"Do any of you regularly take narcotic pain medicine?"

"I do," Corrin said.

Lindsey nodded his head. "Okay, that explains some of this," he said. "Has Callie been under any stress recently?"

The question seemed surreal. We had all lost Anna only six months ago. Didn't the whole world know what it had lost? But then, of course, it didn't. Anna belonged to us. Our pain was not Lindsey's. It was ours.

"Yes," I said. "Her mother passed away about six months ago."

I could see a light go on in the doctor's head. "Ahh, okay," he said. "That answers the other question."

"Do you think you could answer some of ours?" Frank asked, voice indicating his agitation. "How is she?"

"She's fine, medically speaking. But it appears," he said, nodding toward Corrin, "that she has taken some of your medication, and she has experienced what we call an anaphylactic reaction."

"What's that?" Mary asked.

"That's a condition that develops when the body is severely allergic to something. It can happen with anything. Bee stings, milk, hair spray—anything. In this case, it happened when she took some of your medicine. The result is a closing of the airway, which can make breathing difficult, if not impossible. If she hadn't been found when she was, and if some very astute paramedics hadn't treated her as they did, that little girl may not have made it here in time."

I exhaled, allowing some of the stress to dissipate. "She's fine?"

He nodded. "As I said, medically speaking, she's going to be okay. But we have another problem."

"There's another problem?" Corrin said.

"Yes," Lindsey said. "The problem hinges on *why* she was taking your medicine."

We all glanced around the room, looking for an answer and hoping to see it in one of the others.

"I didn't give it to her," Corrin said.

Lindsey shook his head. "No, I didn't think you did." He turned to the other man. "This is Dr. Sebastian. He's a child psychologist, and I've asked him to consult on Callie's situation."

Sebastian smiled. He was a large man with a full beard and a pleasant smile. His appearance and bearing reminded me of the actor Sebastian Cabot. "Callie is taking the loss of her mother very hard."

"Of course she is," I said. "They were very close."

Sebastian nodded. "Yes, I know. I've already spoken with Callie." He sat in the seat next to Lindsey. "You see," he said, "what happened today is a cry for help. Callie—"

"Are you saying that she wanted to kill herself?" I said.

Sebastian nodded. "In a way, yes."

"In a way?" I said.

He put a hand on my knee. "If Callie had wanted to kill herself, she would have gotten it done. She didn't. She wanted all of you to know she's hurting and that she wants the pain to stop." He positioned himself so that he could speak to all of us. "Callie wants the pain to stop, even if it takes her death to do it. But she also knows that suicide isn't the answer. So she had made an attempt that was not designed to succeed."

"Except," Lindsey said, "it almost did. She didn't count on being severely allergic to the medicine."

"And," Sebastian added, "this isn't the first time. Have any of you noticed the scars on her forearms?"

I turned to Frank and Corrin, who were indicating that they hadn't noticed any scars.

"She has made many cuts on her arms. Superficial, but cuts nonetheless. These are common in adolescents who are seeking attention."

"She always wears long sleeves," Frank said. "We—"

"Don't beat yourself up," Sebastian said. "We have caught this in time and can intervene."

"What happens next?" Mary asked. I noticed her red-rimmed eyes for the first time.

"We will discharge her from the hospital in the morning," Lindsey said. "After that, we want to get her in to see Dr. Sebastian until we can get this worked out."

Sebastian stood. "Callie's not a bad girl," he said. "She's a young girl who's hurting." He turned to me. "She has some resentment toward you, Mr. Parker. She believes you to be responsible for the death of her mother."

His words hurt, but they explained a lot. The coolness of her demeanor when she was with me. Her flat, monotone voice.

Mary reached to take my hand. It didn't go unnoticed by the Shapiros.

"Is that why she did this?" I asked in a raspy voice.

Sebastian shook his head. "No. Apparently there is a mother-daughter bake sale coming up at school. She said she always went with her mother but this year…"

"I told her I would go with her," Corrin said.

"It isn't the same. Not right now, at least. The upcoming event, something that she and her mother looked forward to, triggered the events of today."

I stood. "Can we see her?"

"For a few minutes only," Lindsey said. "Her body has been through an amazing struggle and she needs time to recuperate."

"And," Dr. Sebastian added, "she's in a very fragile emotional state. Give her time to rest and don't bring up the events of the day. There will be plenty of time for discussion after she's discharged. Then the real work will begin."

FORTY-FIVE

We all had an opportunity to see Callie. Although she seemed fine, we handled her like a very expensive, very fragile piece of fine china.

Afterward, we were told that she would be kept in an observation bed and would be discharged late the next morning. Dr. Sebastian encouraged us to allow her time to sleep and recoup, and he advised us to not push her too hard.

"Give us time to help her," he said. "She can make an excellent recovery if she's given the proper time and support."

We all watched as Callie was taken to the observation room. After she was wheeled out of our sight, we moved toward the emergency waiting area on our way out of the hospital. The doors hissed open, and Millikin entered and began heading to the registration desk. He stopped short when he saw us.

"I just got the word," he said. "How is she?"

Frank told him everything. Her cry for help, how it probably was not the first attempt, and that she had been very lucky.

"God was certainly with us today," Millikin said, more to himself than to us.

The Shapiros and Mary seemed to agree. I was outraged.

"With us?" I asked. "God was with us today?"

The others gave me confused looks.

"Yes, of course," Millikin said. "He—"

"Don't, Dale," I said. "Don't go there."

"All I'm saying, Colton, is that God may have allowed this allergic reaction so that He could expose what she was doing. He enabled us to get her some help."

"He caused all of this," I said.

"He intervened in all of this," Millikin said.

"He took her mother."

"But He left her a father," Millikin said.

"He's destroyed her childhood."

"He gave her hope."

"He's ruined her life."

"He died to give her life."

The cannon was loaded, and Millikin was holding the match. I moved closer to him, crowding him. He didn't move.

"Do you want to hit me, Colton?"

Frank put a firm hand on my arm.

"You can, you know," he said. "If that'll make you feel better. But it won't stop me from praying for you and your family."

I was seething. I was angrier than I had been the night I confronted Thornton. Angrier, in fact, than the day I had assaulted Amy Sandler's kidnapper. But I had been angry all my life. Angry over the unfairness of my life. Angry with man and with God. But it was different this time.

Then, my anger had been fueled by a need to see justice. To see men like Brad Thornton and Amy's kidnapper receive the recompense they deserved for the sins they had committed. I was angry with God and wanted Him to own up to all He promised but then failed to deliver in the life of a small boy. A boy who was denied a loving family. Or a man who was denied a wife to grow old with. I wanted justice because of the indifference of God.

But this time was different. The anger I was experiencing with Millikin wasn't borne out of a sense of justice denied. Instead, it came from an overwhelming sense of helplessness. And an anger toward God for sitting passively by, again, as the events of a life that was out of control continued to escalate.

"Step aside, Dale," I said.

He stood motionless for a moment before stepping aside. As he did, his eyes locked on mine, and I saw something I hadn't seen before. It made me uncomfortable.

"I'll see you later," I said to the others.

I moved past the minister, through the retracting electronic doors, and into the cold night air. I needed to get away. To walk off the heat. Sure enough, as soon as I exited the hospital, the October chill began to soothe the emotional froth.

I turned left and headed toward Sixteenth Street and then turned left again. I walked aimlessly in the direction of Illinois Street, east of the hospital. I was headed nowhere and getting there quickly.

Night had fallen, and the normally busy street was unusually quiet. There were a few pedestrians scurrying for home, and only a smattering of cars, whose drivers were doing the same.

I watched as they commuted. They seemed blissfully unaware of the tragedy of life and how quickly it can go from bad to worse.

I crossed Capitol Street and continued moving toward Illinois. My destination wasn't geographical, it was emotional. I needed to escape the scene at the hospital and Millikin's incessant prying into my life.

As I moved along the street, I noticed an alley off to my left. It ran parallel to Capitol and Illinois and was bordered by tall buildings on either side. I paused and watched as an old man shuffled along the alleyway, his hands thrust into the pockets of his shabby coat, his collar turned upward against the chill. His shoulders were slumped, and he seemed bowed by the events of his earlier life. A life that had now left him alone and isolated. Nowhere to go and no one who cared if he arrived.

I glanced back at the towering hospital. Inside were people who loved me. The Shapiros, Mary, and a daughter who was slowly but surely sliding away.

I watched again as the old man moved toward nowhere, just as I had been doing a few minutes before. And suddenly, I felt very alone.

I turned and began my slow walk back to the hospital.

FORTY-SIX

I went home and slept, waking five hours later. After showering and shaving, I had a breakfast of eggs, bacon, and toast, and was on my second cup of coffee when I flicked on the television.

"Authorities are concerned about the possibility of foul play and are asking for anyone with information on the whereabouts of Ms. Seidel to contact the Indianapolis Police Department at..."

I flicked to another station. A gardener was giving tips on how to protect outdoor plants from frost.

I changed the channel again.

"Police say the woman, a teacher at Tifton High School, did not report for work the past two days, and efforts to locate her have not been successful. They're asking for anyone who may know something about the missing teacher to call IPD detectives at..."

I turned off the set.

Seidel was missing. Did this come as a result of my conversation? Had she decided to run rather than face the music? Or, like Emma, had she become the victim of foul play? And what, if anything, did this have to do with Billy?

I cleaned up, placing the dishes in the drainer. I wasn't up to combat readiness to be sure, but I had work to do, and it wasn't going to get done if I didn't do it.

I met the Shapiros at the hospital to arrange for Callie's discharge. Despite the events that had transpired the previous evening, she seemed her usual self—which, of course, wasn't her usual self at all. Her mind seemed preoccupied, and the general tone of her conversation, when there was a conversation, was flat.

We got her back to Frank and Corrin's house and decided to keep her out of school for the next several days. We knew that she was out of immediate danger now that the Shapiros could be with her, but we also knew that, ultimately, we would have to deal with the long-term issues. Our appointment with Sebastian wasn't until the next week.

After getting Callie settled, I drove back to IPD headquarters, and by eleven thirty I was talking with Billy again. We were in a room very similar to the one in which we had had our first conversation.

"I have a problem, Billy," I said.

He sat with his arms resting on the steel table. His hands were folded. "Don't we all?"

"You don't seem all that shook up about Emma. I mean, she was all the family you had. Right?"

He ran a hand over his skull. "Yeah."

"And?"

He nodded. "Yeah. She was all I had. Except for Angie."

"I don't think you're getting me here, Billy. I want to know why you don't seem more concerned over Emma's death."

He chuckled and shook his head. "Naw, man. You want to know if I killed her."

"Did you?" It was a question that I probably should have asked him at the outset.

"What do you think?"

"I think you're good for it."

He snorted. "A lot of people think I'm good for it. Why should you be any different?"

"Angie tells me that you and Emma were close. Very close. Yet she's murdered and you don't seem all that broken up over it. Then Angie tells me that you do a lot of odd jobs. And we both know the type of jobs you're capable of doing."

He was shaking his head. Not so much out of denial but more like disgust. "You think because I have a record, someone would pay me to kill Emma? Why? Think about it, man. She didn't have an enemy in the world."

I didn't want to tell him about DiCenza. If I was wrong and charges against Billy were dropped, I didn't want him killing Frankie over something that I said.

"Why would I kill Emma?" he asked.

"That's what I want to know," I said.

He stood and jabbed his forefinger at me. "If you think I'm guilty, then go for it. Prove it."

"So you're saying you didn't do it?"

"I didn't do it, man. I didn't kill her. She watched out for me like a mother hen." He moved from behind the table and began pacing the room with his hands on his hips. He was restless and clearly agitated; his breathing was labored.

"How did you feel about her?" I asked.

"I liked her. A lot. But I didn't like the way she was always buttin' in."

"How, Billy? How was she always butting in?" He had his back to me, facing the corner of the room.

"She was a teacher, man. I can't read. You figure it out."

"She was riding you about the fact that you can't read?" I asked.

He turned to me and rubbed a hand over his bald head again. "No, man. Well…yeah…kind of. She was always tellin' me that I needed to go back to school. Always tryin' to get me to do somethin' that just ain't natural for me. You know?"

"How did she feel about Angie?"

He shrugged. "Didn't like her. But I told her that Angie was my decision, not hers."

"Did you fight about it?"

"Yeah. A couple of times."

The Tooleys said they had seen Emma and Billy arguing on at least one occasion.

"How did Angie feel about Emma?"

"She never talked about her much. I don't think she felt one way or the other. You know?"

"What do you know about June Seidel?"

"Who?"

"June Seidel. A teacher at Tifton."

He shook his head. "Don't know her. Why?"

"It's not important," I said, standing and signaling the guard that I was done.

Billy was either an excellent liar or he had nothing to hide. Right now, I was inclined to go with the latter, but I couldn't entirely discount the former. If Billy killed Emma, it was a cinch that DiCenza had asked for the computer too. He would not have been able to ignore the possibility of a connection on it between him and Emma.

If Billy had worked for DiCenza as an enforcer, I was going to have to ask the other half of the arrangement. Something that I intended to do with vim and vigor.

CHAPTER
FORTY-SEVEN

D eNights didn't open until three in the afternoon. That gave the staff and dancers their downtime while allowing for deliveries and the necessary activities that come with running any business. I was betting that DiCenza would want to arrive near opening time, so I parked across the street in the parking lot of a bar that didn't offer the same "Nightly Attractions" that DeNights did. I positioned myself where I could see both the front and side doors of DiCenza's establishment, and since the only way in or out of the lot was by way of the opening onto Broad Ripple Avenue, I would be sure to see him when he arrived.

I didn't have to wait long. A black Lincoln Town Car arrived at precisely ten minutes till three. I watched as it pulled along the side door of the pink stucco building and a tall, broad-shouldered man emerged from the driver's side of the car. He was wearing a dark suit and tie and even had a chauffeur's hat perched on his head.

"Now ain't that just too cute," I said to myself as I emerged from my car. I pulled the Ruger from its holster and kept it in my right hand, down at my side, as I jogged across the street and into the parking lot of DeNights. The driver had the left rear door open and DiCenza was just stepping out of the car. He was wearing a blue pinstripe suit with an open-necked pink shirt and a pink silk handkerchief stuffed in the breast pocket of the jacket. The same wad of gold was showing in the same wad of black chest hair. He was surprised to see me.

"What're you doin' here?" he managed to say before I shoved him back into the car.

"Get in," I said to the driver, pointing the barrel of the gun at him. "Get in and drive until I tell you to stop." He paused for a moment as though he was weighing the feasibility of trying to jump me and wrestle the gun away. "Don't," I said. "You'll never live to regret it." He curled his lip in an expression of muted rage and climbed back into the car. I slid into the backseat next to DiCenza. "Drive," I said.

"Where to?" the driver asked.

"Anywhere. Just drive."

He backed the car out of the lot and onto Broad Ripple Avenue and began to follow the flow of traffic. I reached around the front seat, while keeping the Ruger trained on DiCenza, and searched the driver for a weapon. Chances were, he was more bodyguard than chauffeur. I was right. I found a shoulder holster under his left arm with a Smith & Wesson .357 Magnum in the holster.

"Nice piece," I said, popping open the cylinder and ejecting the cartridges onto the floorboard of the rear seat. "Adjustable sights, stainless steel with custom, shock-absorbing grips. You really know your stuff."

He focused on me in the rearview mirror. "Know this, tough guy. This ain't over till it's over."

I tossed the gun onto the backseat.

"It's over," I said. "Just drive and nothing will happen. To you, that is." I turned my attention to DiCenza. He managed to slide as far away from me as he could get. He was keeping an eye on the Ruger.

"What do you want?" he asked.

"Information."

" 'Bout what?"

"Emma Caine and June Seidel."

He continued to focus on the Ruger. "I told you. That old lady and I are cleared."

"You also told me that you didn't remember her. But you sent your goons—" I gestured toward the driver—"to give her an ultimatum."

"I don't know what you're talking about," he said. "I never—"

I rapped him across the face with the pistol. "Don't play games with me, Frankie. I know you threatened Emma. You gave her a week to pay up. And now the woman who told me that is missing."

"I swear, I had nothin' to do with that broad gettin' whacked."

I struck him again. "You're lying, Frankie," I said. "You're the big man in this town. You own the numbers here. There isn't anyone who wants in this business that doesn't pay homage to you." I saw the driver turn around to look at us. I nudged him between the shoulder blades. "Drive." He turned to face ahead.

"I didn't whack no old lady," DiCenza said again.

"You couldn't have her dissing you that way. Your reputation would be destroyed."

"No. That's—"

"So you got your money and then you killed her. And you took her computer because you knew that she could have information on it that would incriminate you."

"I didn't take nothin' man, and I didn't kill no broad."

"And now June Seidel is missing. She owed you money too. And she saw no way out."

He shook his head. "No."

"If her body turns up in an alley somewhere, that makes you good for it."

"No, you've got it all wrong. I didn't whack nobody. I got my money from the old lady."

"Her name was Emma," I said.

"Yeah, sure, Emma. She was good for a grand a week. Now why would I whack that?"

"Because she dissed you," I said. "And if you didn't make her pay for that, it would end up costing you a whole lot more than a grand a week."

He shook his head. "You give me too much credit. I ain't that smart. If I had thought of it that way, I probably would have killed the old...Emma. 'Cept I didn't. I ain't never killed nobody."

"You might be the first," the driver said, looking at me again through the rearview mirror.

"I told you to drive," I said. I turned my attention back to DiCenza. "You're not helping your case. You're going to have to give me a reason to not suspect you of killing Emma."

He sighed. "Go ahead and suspect me. There ain't nothin' I can give you to prove that I didn't have the old...Emma killed. Just logic. It's bad for business." He held up his hands. "I ain't sayin' that I'm above breakin' some bones. God knows I've done that and had it done a few times. But I don't go killin' people."

"You know Brad Thornton?"

He snorted. "Yeah, sure, I know Thornton. He used to do some work for me."

"Enforcing?"

"Yeah. 'Cept he liked it too much. Like I said, I don't kill my customers. It's bad for business."

I recalled how Lenny said that Thornton had given him his broken leg. "Remember a guy named Lenny?"

"Lenny what?"

"Just Lenny. Frail, skinny kid?"

DiCenza thought for a minute and shook his head. "No. I don't remember no Lenny."

"Southern accent. Hangs out at the Busy Bee?"

DiCenza thought again and his eyes widened. "Oh yeah. Now I remember. Mid-twenties. Came from Mississippi."

I nodded.

"Yeah. He's one that Thornton got too aggressive with. I told him to break the kid's leg. He was into me for five Gs."

"You maimed a kid for five thousand dollars?" I said, wondering to myself why I was so surprised.

"Like I said, it's business. Sure, I'll slap a customer around a little if that's what it takes to collect. But I do collect. And I try to keep 'em comin' back. Can't do that if I kill 'em."

"You said that Thornton was getting too aggressive?"

He nodded. "Yeah. Like with Lenny. I told Thornton to break the kid's leg. Use a bat. No big deal. What's he do? He drags the kid behind a car. Almost tears his leg off. That's when I told him, 'You've gotta go, man. You're bad for business.'"

"And he went? Just like that?"

"Sure. It's like I said, I don't kill customers. But I ain't above killing the help."

"What about Billy Caine?"

"Who?"

"Billy Caine. He ever work for you?"

"If he did, would I have to ask who?"

"Know about F&F?"

"Sure. Porn. Internet stuff, mostly."

"Ever dabble in it?"

He shook his head. "No, man. Too many players in it. It has gotten way too competitive. Too high profile. I stick to what I know."

"What about June Seidel?"

"Yeah, you mentioned her a minute ago. Don't know her."

I was ready to draw down on him again, when he thrust up his hands.

"Hold on, man. I mean, I don't remember her. Personally. If you say I did business with her, then maybe I did. It's just that I don't recall. Okay?"

"Not okay," I said. "She's missing and I want to know where she is."

"How should I know?" he said, his voice hitting the end of its upper reaches.

"Find out," I said.

"How?"

"Pretend she owes you money. I don't care how you do it, just do it."

He looked at the barrel end of the Ruger again. "Okay, man. Okay. I'll see what I can do."

I nudged the driver again. "Pull over here." He pulled along the curb and put the transmission in park.

"My talk here is done. I'm going to leave now. The advice that I gave you before still applies, Frankie. And tell your goon here, that it goes double for him." Neither said a word, but as I exited the car, I saw the driver watching me in the reflection of his mirror.

FORTY-EIGHT

I drove back to the office. I had been away for a while and needed to go through my mail. Mostly, though, I just needed to be alone. To think this thing through. I was sitting with my feet on my desk with another cup of coffee when the phone rang.

"I warned you." It was Bitterman's voice.

"Does Captain Wilkins know that you're playing on the phone again?" I asked.

"I told you to stay out of my investigation," he said, ignoring my jab. "And this time, you crossed over the line."

I figured he was probably referring to my questioning of Billy again. "Look," I said, "I—"

"Save it. I've already started the proceedings to get your license."

"Wow," I said. "You were really serious about that, weren't you?"

He hung up.

I was less sure than before of Billy's innocence, but given my interview with him and my conversation with DiCenza, I was also less certain of his guilt. This case was like a ball of yarn with one end exposed. But unlike a ball of yarn, the more I pulled on the loose end, the bigger the whole thing got.

I had just raised the cup to my lips when Harley Wilkins came through the door. A couple of IPD uniformed officers were with him. Unlike the two at the canal, though, these uniforms had the look of seasoned law-enforcement officers. None of them sat.

"That was quick," I said.

"What're you talking about?" Wilkins said.

"Bitterman just called, and you're already here. I must've really stepped on his toes."

"I don't know what you're talking about."

"Bitterman. He's all worked up over my interview with Billy." I glanced at the two cops with Wilkins. Neither of them took their eyes off of me.

"I don't care about Bitterman or Billy," he said. "It's you I want to see."

For the first time since Wilkins entered my office, I noticed the seriousness of his expression. "You don't look so good," I said.

"I ain't," he said. "I understand that you made contact with Thornton."

I looked again at the two uniforms standing on either side of the door. "That's right," I said.

"Want to tell me about it?"

"Not yet."

He leaned forward, resting his palms on the edge of my desk. "Here or downtown," he said.

"Well, since you put it so sweetly," I said. "I found Thornton. I asked him about his connection to Emma Caine." I didn't mention Angie.

"And?" Wilkins said.

"And what?"

"And what did he tell you?"

"Nothing useful," I lied.

Wilkins' eyes narrowed. He pointed his index finger at me. "Play funny guy with me and you're going away."

"Why don't you stop with the threats already," I said. "You know they don't work."

"Did you torture Thornton?"

"Torture?"

He didn't say anything. Just kept that cop stare focused on me. I swung my feet off the desk. "Are you for real?"

"Do I look like I'm fooling with you?"

"What did he say? That I pulled his toenails off until he squealed?"

"He didn't say anything. He's dead."

"Dead?"

Wilkins sighed and turned to the two uniforms. "Is there an echo in here?" He turned back to me. "Yeah. Dead. Like, no heartbeat, respiration has ceased...*dead*. Sometime between five and midnight."

"And you think I killed him?"

"The thought crossed my mind."

"Well, uncross it," I said. "I didn't do it. I was at the hospital with Callie then."

"Yeah, I know. I already checked. Except the nurses said you disappeared and didn't come back."

"I went for a walk," I said, appreciating the lameness of my alibi.

"Someone blew his brains out. Coroner says that he sustained a beating before he was killed." He leaned forward again. "Want to know the interesting part?"

I kept quiet. Until I knew more, I didn't want to say anything that could be misinterpreted or used against me.

"His girlfriend says that she came back from the store the other night and found him handcuffed to the balcony railing, half frozen to death."

I remained silent.

"And you know what else? His neighbor across the hall saw you coming out of his apartment with a gun in your hand."

"I can explain that," I said.

"I'll bet you can. Guess what else?"

"Why don't you quit playing games and just tell me, Wilkins."

"We dusted the place and found prints on the doorknob *inside* the apartment."

I hadn't killed Thornton. I had never planned on killing him, so I had not worn gloves during our meeting.

"And guess what else," Wilkins said, his voice getting shrill now.

"They're mine," I said.

"Bingo," he said, jabbing the same index finger at me. "Give that man a see-gar."

I sighed. "I was there, but I didn't kill him."

"You're good for it," he said.

"Come on, Wilkins," I said, raising my voice. "You know me. If I wanted him dead I would have done it the other night."

"Maybe you did."

"If I had wanted him dead, you wouldn't have a body."

"What were you doing there?"

"I found out where he was living. I went to talk to him about the case I'm working on—"

"Emma Caine."

"Right. And he was less than cooperative."

"In other words, you weren't going to let him get the drop on you again."

"Right."

"Even if you had to shoot first and ask questions later."

"I didn't shoot him. I forced him back into the apartment and... roughed him up a little."

"Then you chained him to the outside balcony."

"Something like that," I said.

"And left him there to freeze to death."

"I knew that his girlfriend would be coming back."

"How did you know that?"

"Because I heard her leaving, and she said that she would be right back."

"What if she hadn't come back?"

I shrugged.

He studied me, giving me that look that only veteran cops can give. The look that is supposed to make you melt and cry out your confession of guilt. It didn't work.

"I want your piece," he said.

I pulled the Ruger from my holster and ejected the magazine. I slid the gun across the desk toward Wilkins. He picked it up and pocketed it.

"We'll run it."

"Go ahead," I said. "The lady that saw me coming out of his apartment saw me before the time you say he was killed."

"I could still bust you for the assault."

"Sure. But you got bigger fish to fry."

He told me to stay in town and left. The two uniforms followed him, closing the door behind them.

I unwrapped myself from the empty shoulder rig and took two aspirin for a developing headache.

Guys like Thornton get killed every day. They ask for it. But I was willing to bet that whoever killed Thornton had probably killed Emma too. The strongest connection that I could make with everyone involved was F&F. DiCenza wasn't off the hook with me, but he had been truthful about Lenny. At least from the perspective that I could verify. But Emma had needed money right away, and she surely wasn't going to come up with twenty thousand dollars in gambling debt from her salary as a high school guidance counselor. That meant that she was probably pushing the F&F pyramid pretty hard. Just like Seidel said. My bet was that she pushed somebody too far. Somebody who saw the value in eliminating her.

June Seidel had said that others were involved in Emma's pyramid, but she and Angie were the ones who had tried to oust Emma. Now that June was missing I was left with one place to go.

FORTY-NINE

Angie was home, and when she answered the door, I barged into the apartment.

"I know it's not as nice as your place, but I deserve some respect," she said.

I had my backup piece, a Taurus .38 snub nose, in hand. "You played me for a fool," I said.

"What are you talking about?"

"Thornton is dead."

Her eyes widened. "He's dead?"

"Cut the act, Angie. You killed Thornton and you killed Emma."

"I haven't killed anybody," she said.

"Emma was squeezing you to let go of Billy. Threatening to tell him about the work you were doing. Billy thought you had a job. A normal job. And you couldn't have him finding out the truth. He may be a lot of things, but he isn't a voyeur. He wouldn't have been able to deal with it and he would have left. You wouldn't stand for that. So killing Emma got her off your back."

"No."

"You told me you're a hooker. But you're not a hooker. You perform on camera."

Her eyes diverted to the floor.

"And you wanted Emma's job. Enough to kill for it."

"No."

"So killing Emma was a win-win for you. Except that you didn't count on Billy getting fingered for it."

She shook her head. "No."

"Her computer was missing. You took it. You couldn't have the police finding your face on her computer. Even if it didn't point a finger at you, it would at least raise some uncomfortable questions. When I told you I wanted to talk with Thornton, you eliminated him. You couldn't take the chance that he would talk with anyone else."

"No," she said again, placing her face in her hands.

"You love Billy. That much is sure. And when you told me that he didn't kill Emma, you were right. And you knew that you were right because you are the killer. That's why you lied about being home on the night she was killed."

She shook her head.

"Where were you last night between five and midnight?" I asked.

She fell onto the sofa with her face in her hands as she thought.

She raised her head as if she had just experienced a "eureka" moment. "I was with Melissa. We were live online."

"For seven hours?"

"We do our bit and then break for fifteen minutes out of every hour. There are enough girls around the country performing so that when one or two of us disappears for a few minutes, no one notices."

"You're going to have to prove that."

"No problem. I can do that," she said.

W e drove to the same house where I had first seen Melissa meet with Angie. I parked the car in nearly the same spot as I had that day and killed the engine.

"What is this?" I asked, looking at Angie.

"This is the studio where we perform."

I glanced again at the dilapidated house. "You've got to be kidding."

We went into the house. The living room was furnished with a vinyl sofa, large-screen television, and Coke machine. A small kitchen was separated from the living room by a half-wall and contained a refrigerator and microwave. A telephone was suspended on the wall.

"This way," she said, leading the way to the bedrooms down the hall.

I followed her, keeping a few steps back with the revolver in my hand.

She led me into one of the two bedrooms in the house. A king-size bed filled nearly all of the floor space, leaving just enough room for a tripod-mounted camera and video lighting equipment. A file cabinet stood in one corner of the room, out of view of the camera.

"It's in here," she said, opening the top file drawer.

I pushed her out of the way as she opened the drawer. I found several file folders and a gun. I pulled the gun from the drawer.

"Looking for this?" I said.

I ejected the magazine from the gun and slid the slide back. There was a bullet lodged in the chamber. I removed it and tossed the gun on the floor.

"Honest to God, Mr. Parker, I forgot that that was even in there."

"Is this the gun you used on Seidel?" I was fishing. Baiting her to see if she would bite.

"Seidel? June? Is she dead?"

"Cut the act, Angie. I talked with Seidel. She told me about the scheme you two were running on Emma. Except Emma put the lid on it."

"I didn't know about—"

"So Emma ends up dead and now Seidel is missing."

"I didn't know about June, Mr. Parker. I honestly didn't."

I waved my revolver toward the bedroom door. "Come on," I said, "into the living room. I'm going to call Wilkins. You're going to jail."

"Please," she said. "Please let me get the file out. I can prove that I was here."

"Let's go," I said, motioning again for the door.

"Please," she pleaded. "Just take a look."

I hesitated and then glanced into the open file drawer. "Which one?" I asked.

"The blue one," she said.

I pulled the blue one and tossed it to her.

She flipped through it and pulled out a sheet of paper. She handed it to me.

"What's this?"

"It's a log. It's how we get paid. Melissa and I sign in and out."

On the paper, Melissa's and Angie's names were spread over the last several weeks. The times varied, but last night's entry recorded them as online at four fifty and off-line at ten minutes after twelve.

"I'm going to need more than this," I said.

"I can get you a copy of our performance," she said.

"A copy?"

"On disc. Melissa has it."

"Why does she have it?"

"She keeps a copy off-site for backup."

"What will that prove? You could have made it in advance like you could have done with this log."

"The show is encoded with the time and date. The disc will have that on it. You can check with the company if you need to."

I slipped the log into my pocket. "Let's go," I said, motioning with the gun. "And get your coat. We're going to see your friend."

FIFTY-ONE

We arrived at Melissa's in ten minutes. She was her usual cheerful self.

"What does *he* want?" she asked Angie.

"Melissa, we need to talk to you," Angie said.

She looked at Angie and then at me and back to Angie before opening the door.

The child was watching television again, eating a Pop Tart and sipping something from a capped drinking cup. She looked up at us for a second or two and then returned to her cartoons.

"What's going on?" Melissa asked.

"I think you'd better have a seat," Angie said.

Melissa gave us the back and forth look again. "What's going on?" she asked again.

"Thornton's dead," I said.

The expression on her face remained constant for a second or two but then took on a different texture as the realization of what I had said began to take shape.

"Dead?" she asked, looking to Angie.

Angie nodded.

"Brad's dead?" She turned to look at me. "You? You!" She lunged for me. I deflected her blows, shoving her to the sofa.

"Missy," Angie said, following her to the sofa in an attempt to restrain her, "he didn't do it."

"Yes, he did," she yelled with spittle flying from her mouth. "Yes, he did, and I'm going to kill him."

"He didn't," Angie said, struggling with the woman. "But he thinks I did."

I heard crying from the other side of the room. I saw the child, standing now, with one hand in her mouth. The Pop Tart and sipping cup were on the floor.

"It's okay, honey," I said, moving toward her.

"You leave her alone. You hear me? Leave her alone," Melissa screamed. The child began to cry harder.

"Leave Mommy alone," she said.

I looked at Angie. "Let her up."

Angie loosened her grip on Melissa but didn't entirely let go.

"Missy, listen to me. Brad is dead. He thinks that I did it," she said, nodding toward me. "I need to show him the disc from last night."

The look in Melissa's eyes was not human. Something else was manifesting itself. Something that had gripped her a long time ago.

"Who cares what he thinks?" she said. "He killed Brad and I'm going to kill him." She began to struggle again.

"I care what he thinks, Missy," Angie said, struggling again with the woman. "I didn't kill Brad. And if we don't show him the disc, the real killer will get away with it."

"No…he won't," Melissa said through gritted teeth. She was glaring at me.

I turned to look at the child, on her knees now, sobbing. Melissa seemed unaware.

"Do you want her to end up like you?" I said to Melissa.

She ceased struggling but continued staring at me, her face darkened with the bile of hatred.

"Melissa, listen to him."

"She can't hear you," I said. "She's too consumed with what *she* wants. Aren't you, Melissa?"

Her face remained contorted, her breathing labored. The child continued to sob.

"You don't care about this child, do you? Not you, no sir. The only thing you care about is yourself."

"I do care about Allyson," she said, her eyes narrowed with anger.

"Then help yourself so that you can help her."

She continued to glare at me.

"Look at her," I said, pointing to the girl. "Look at your child. Look at what this is doing to her."

Angie continued to maintain a grip on Melissa's wrists. "Missy, where is the disc?"

She kept her focus on me as she said to Angie, "It's in the file cabinet in the bedroom. Middle drawer."

Angie kept a rein on Melissa but looked at me.

"Go ahead," I said. I didn't like giving a second chance to someone who had tried to reach for a gun earlier. But for the moment, I felt like Melissa was the bigger threat.

"Missy, don't move. Okay? I'm going to get the disc. I'll be back in a second."

The child continued to sob, and for the first time, Melissa seemed to hear her.

Angie released Melissa. When she did, the little girl ran to her mother.

"I'll be right back," Angie said, leaving to go down the hall to the bedroom.

She returned in a few seconds with a CD in hand. She sat down at the computer in the living room and inserted the disc.

"Come take a look," she said.

I eased over to the computer, keeping an eye on Melissa and Angie. What I saw seemed to confirm that the two had been engaged in live acts on the computer during the time Thornton had been murdered.

"This is another reason that Billy would never tolerate what you do," I said, watching the two women at work. Angie lowered her eyes. "I want that disc," I said.

She ejected it and gave it to me. "Please, don't let Billy see this," she said. "It would kill him."

I slid the disc into my pocket and walked back to the sofa. Melissa was sitting upright now and embracing her daughter. The anger in her face had softened a bit.

"I know you think I killed Thornton," I said. "But I didn't. And now I'm less inclined to think that Angie did either. But it's a cinch that whoever killed him had a reason. Maybe it was connected to Emma's murder. Maybe not. But if you have anything that you think can help me, you better give it to me now."

She refused to look at me.

"Whoever killed Thornton may come after you too."

The child continued to sob.

I looked at Angie and sighed. "I'll keep this to myself," I said. "And you can be sure that I'll have the encryption of the time and date deciphered."

"It's okay with me. I'm telling the truth."

I looked one last time at Melissa and Allyson. Over the sobs, I could hear Buster barking from the backyard. "Think about what I said, Melissa. If Thornton meant anything to you at all, you've got to help me."

She said nothing as the child continued to cling to her mother.

FIFTY-TWO

It's clean. We checked you out. So I'm back to the beginning," Wilkins said, handing me the Ruger he had taken.

"I believe I told you that," I said, leaning back in my chair and propping my feet up on my desk. It was the next day, and I was doing what I had tried to do the day before. Think through the case.

"Don't push it," he said. He sat in the same chair Bitterman had sat in earlier.

I kept my mouth shut. I didn't see any reason to invite trouble.

"How's Callie?" he asked.

I told him.

"Good," he said, "Marla and I were concerned." He looked around my office. "How much does this place run?"

"Two fifty a month."

He nodded. "You're overcharged."

"Great view of the fountain," I said.

"I have a great view of the City Market," he said.

"Trade you," I said.

He snorted. "You can't afford it."

"Neither could you without the badge," I said.

"The badge is how I can afford it. Was a time when your badge bought you a nice view too."

"That was a long time ago," I said.

"Six months."

"A lifetime to me."

He nodded. "Got any coffee?"

"Sure," I said. I got up and filled the pot from the bathroom sink and poured the water into the coffeemaker's reservoir. I inserted a filter into the basket and added three scoops of coffee. I flipped on the switch.

"Be ready in a few minutes," I said, sitting again.

"Who do you think killed Thornton?" Wilkins asked.

I shrugged. "Could be anyone. The man was an expert in annoying people."

"So are you and nobody's killed you."

"Yet," I said.

"Yet," he agreed.

"Got any leads?"

"Not since you."

"You need to get out more," I said.

He nodded. "That I do."

I knew that he had come to offer an apology, though not in so many words. Wilkins didn't like being wrong and found it a hard thing to admit. But he would acknowledge his mistakes, and he was here to patch things up.

"Black?" I said.

"Cream, two sugars."

I got the coffee and handed him his cup. "I thought you were a diabetic."

"I am."

"What about the sugar?"

"What about it?"

I shrugged. "Nothing, I guess."

He drank some of the coffee. "You know, I kind of envy you."

"You?"

He nodded.

"The man with the badge and the power?" I said.

"You're confusing me with Bitterman. I've heard him use that line more than once."

"What's his problem?" I asked.

"What do you mean?"

"You've been a cop for a long time," I said. "You know the play. How is it that Bitterman can stay so gung ho?" I blew on my coffee before sipping. I waited as Wilkins paused before responding.

"Daniel is his own breed. He's a good cop. But he has his demons like we all do."

"Like what?"

"His insecurities, for one."

I laughed. "Insecurities? Are we talking about the same man?"

Wilkins sipped the coffee. "His family fell apart several years ago."

"I'm sorry," I said. "I didn't know."

"Well, Daniel is kind of private. Jasmine got tired of him working all the time and threatened him with a divorce if he didn't slow down. Threatening Daniel is the wrong thing to do."

"So he got a divorce?"

Wilkins nodded. "Yeah. And it was…how do they say it…hotly contested?" He drank some of his coffee. "Anyway, he lost nearly everything, including custody of his daughter."

"Wow," I said. "I'm learning more about this guy all the time. I'm almost starting to feel sorry for him."

"You might want to cut him some slack," Wilkins said. "The man lost his family, his daughter…the only thing left was the job."

"So he flung himself into it."

"You got it. Except his daughter got to be a little too much for Jasmine to handle. The kid got arrested for DUI and that angered Daniel to no end."

"I'll bet. Where is she now?"

He paused, fixing his gaze past me and out the window behind. "She's dead."

"Dead?"

He nodded. "Yeah. Shaneka died of drug overdose. She was sixteen."

"Whoa, Harley. I'm sorry. I didn't know. How did he handle it?"

"Like he did the divorce. He dug deeper into his work."

"How long ago has that been?"

Wilkins sighed. "Let's see," he said, "eighteen months…two years ago."

"So his gung ho work ethic is—"

"An escape, mostly. I think the psychologically correct term is *coping mechanism*. But Daniel was always one to make his work the focus of his life. As I said, it was part of the reason for his divorce."

We were both quiet for the next few minutes. I knew about coping mechanisms. Apparently, I wasn't alone.

"But take me on the other hand," Wilkins said, breaking the silence. "Being gung ho no longer makes any sense to me. Don't get me wrong. I do my job. It's just that I get tired of the rat race. Taking orders. Giving orders. Dealing with scum like Thornton." He drank some more coffee. "Why should I care who killed him? The man should have been wasted a long time ago."

"Can't argue that," I said.

"Except it's like you said. I've got the badge. That means I have to deal with it."

"In case you haven't noticed," I said, "I'm dealing with it too."

"Yeah. I guess you are. But you don't answer to anyone. You've got freedom."

"True."

He set the cup down on the desk and stood to button his coat. "For example, do you know how much paperwork I've got to do? Just on you alone?"

"On me?"

"You were a suspect until this morning," he said. "My boss wants to know why."

"Good question," I said.

He opened the door. "'Cause you were good for it."

"Or so you thought."

"Or so I thought," he said.

FIFTY-THREE

Two hours, two cups of coffee, and two chocolate long johns later, Angie knocked on the open door of my office.

"Come in," I said.

She came in and had a seat. A worried look was on her face.

"What's wrong?" I asked.

"Someone ransacked Melissa's house last night."

I eased back in my chair. "Where was she?"

"She was with me. After you left, we had to go online for a few hours. It was late, so she and Allyson spent the night at the studio. When she got home this morning, she called to tell me that someone had broken into her house."

It was the first part of her statement that bothered me most. "Where is Allyson when you two are doing your thing?"

Angie's eyes diverted to the floor. "She watches TV in the other room. Or naps. Or colors."

I shook my head. "Is anything missing?"

"She didn't think so, but she's scared."

"Understandable," I said.

"She's worried that someone might be after her."

Given what I knew of the lifestyle of Melissa and the late Brad Thornton, that seemed a distinct possibility.

"It could also be a random burglary," I said, verbalizing my thoughts. "Happens every day in every city in America. Trust me. I know," I said, looking around my office and not believing my own words.

Angie pulled her worn coat tightly across her chest. Her thin frame seemed to retreat within the fabric.

"Would you like some coffee?" I asked.

She nodded, and I poured her a cup.

"Black, right?" I said, handing her the cup.

She took it in both hands. "Black."

I sat in my chair without any coffee. Two cups is usually just a starter. But given the events of the past several days and the cups I already had, I was taut enough. I didn't need to pull the ends of the knot any tighter.

"Donut?" I asked, spinning the open bag in her direction. She shook her head.

"Angie, I feel for anyone who has been violated. I've been there myself. But what do you expect me to do about it?"

She sipped the coffee as she had done that first day we met, with both hands wrapped around the mug.

"Could you talk to her?" she asked.

I chuckled. "I think that Melissa and I have had all the conversations we're going to have. I'm not at the top of her list."

"She's scared, Mr. Parker. She thinks someone is after her. She doesn't know where to turn."

"Turn to the same place that everyone else turns," I said. "Call the police. They're very good at what they do."

"She's had too many bad experiences with the police."

Somehow, I could believe that. "Did she ask you to come here?"

Angie shook her head. "No. I just thought that maybe this was all connected to Brad's death. And since you think that he may have been connected to Emma and Billy..."

"You thought that maybe I would have an interest in talking with Melissa."

Angie nodded.

"Assuming, of course, that she will talk with me."

"She will. She has nowhere else to go."

"Sure," I said. "I know exactly how she feels."

CHAPTER
FIFTY-FOUR

A ngie called Melissa from my office before we left to tell her that we would be coming. The heads-up must have worked. When we arrived, she opened the door without hesitation and allowed both of us to pass into the living room.

"Where's Allyson?" Angie asked, looking around the room.

"She's asleep," Melissa said.

Melissa's eyes were red. A worn tissue was in her hands. She kept working it as she paced the living room.

"Missy, talk to him," Angie said. "If you won't go to the police, at least talk to him."

She paced the floor and said nothing. Angie glanced at me.

"Melissa," I said, "if you think that someone is after you because of the burglary, because of the circles that Thornton ran in...you just might be right. If you know anything that might be relevant, now is the time to tell me."

She sat on the worn sofa. Angie sat next to her and wrapped her arms around the troubled woman's shoulders. I stood.

"Brad knew a lot of bad people," Melissa said. "He always warned me about being careful."

"Did he ever mention anyone specific?" I asked. I was wanting to know what role DiCenza might have played. He still wasn't completely off my list for the murders.

She shook her head. "Just general talk."

"Did he mention any threats?"

"No one threatened Brad. At least not to his face."

"Did he owe anyone money?" I asked. I was fishing for DiCenza, but I didn't want to put his name in Melissa's mouth.

She thought for a minute and then shrugged. "I don't know. Maybe."

"Do you know of anyone he may have stiffed? In some way other than the money he might have owed?"

"Not offhand," she said.

I looked at Angie.

"Missy," she said, "is there anything here that might have belonged to Brad? Anything that might give us some ideas?"

She dabbed at her nose and thought. "No, I can't think of anything."

"Anything that could help us figure out who might be after you? Money, drugs?" Angie said.

"Address book, for example?" I asked hopefully.

"Wait," she said. "He kept a lockbox here. In case he ran out of money. He didn't trust banks."

"Can I see it?" I asked.

She got up and went into one of the bedrooms. Angie looked at me with a dejected look. In a couple of minutes, Melissa returned.

"Here," she said, handing me a metal locker the size of a shoe box.

I tried to open the box, but it was locked.

"Do you have a key?"

She shook her head. "No. Brad kept the key. I guess he didn't want me in the box. He said that it was for emergencies. Like if he had to get out of town right away."

Despite my skill at burglarizing Emma's house, I didn't think that I was going to be able to open the box with any finesse. My lock picks were at home.

"Do you have a screwdriver?" I asked.

"No. Would a kitchen knife help?"

"Sure," I said.

Melissa went into the kitchen and rummaged around a drawer. She returned with a partially bent knife. "Here," she said, handing me the utensil.

I took the knife and worked it under the lip of the box's lid. I pried and worked until the sheet metal of the box gave way. I shook the contents out onto the floor and knelt to examine them.

There was a white envelope containing a thousand dollars in twenties, a passport, a Missouri driver's license, and a computer disc. I looked up at Melissa. "Missouri?"

She shrugged. I looked at Angie.

"It's the headquarters for F&F, Mr. Parker."

"That's right," I said. "I forgot that."

The license and passport were in Thornton's name.

"Was he planning any trips?"

Melissa shook her head.

I examined the unlabeled disc. "Can I use your computer?"

She nodded.

I sat at the computer and inserted the disc. The machine hummed and clicked as it downloaded the bits of information encoded on the disc. Two file names eventually appeared. One read F&F One, the other, F&F Two. I clicked on One.

Immediately, the logo for F&F appeared, emblazoned over a purple background that was designed to resemble a theatrical curtain. Along the margins were various icons for "rooms" that catered to every fetish. Such things as Barely Legal, For the Discriminating Man, and Live Internet Action encircled the screen. I turned to look at Angie. She lowered her head. It was a reaction that I was getting used to seeing.

I turned back to the screen and clicked on icon Two. A spread-sheet appeared. In the left column were approximately a hundred fifty names with dates next to them that ran from as far back as the late nineteen nineties. The next three columns had initials at the top. I saw EC, JS, and BT. Emma Cain, June Seidel, and Brad Thornton. Under each of the initials, in rows that ran next to the names, were checkmarks indicating, I assumed, that the names on the left were recruited by the individuals who headed the corre-sponding column.

I scanned down the left-hand side of the spreadsheet and read the names to myself. It was then, about two thirds of the way down, that I noticed a sharp increase in activity under Emma's name. Her output of rolling young girls into the business increased dramati-cally and coincided with the time frame that Seidel had indicated as the period when DiCenza was putting the squeeze on Emma. That supported my theory that Emma was paying off DiCenza with a strong recruiting drive. But what I wasn't prepared for was one of the names that appeared on the list during the time of Emma's big push. I ejected the disc.

"I want to take this with me," I said.

Melissa looked at Angie then back to me. She nodded.

"Did you see something, Mr. Parker?" Angie asked.

"Maybe," I said. I picked up the passport, driver's license, and cash. I pocketed the license and passport along with the disc. I handed the envelope containing the money to Melissa. "You might as well have this," I said. "God knows you've earned it."

"I loved him," she said.

I studied her for a moment. As I did, my perspective of her changed. The inherent rage that had shown through her the last time we talked was gone.

I had known many women like Melissa. Like Angie too. At heart they were good. But they had been steered to a place in life from which there was no apparent escape. Often by the men they loved. Men who used them for gain, unaware or uncaring of the love and commitment they were receiving. I didn't want her to know about the woman that I had seen Thornton with that night in his apartment. There was nothing to gain but hurt.

"Of course," I said. "I'm sure he felt the same way about you."

FIFTY-FIVE

The disc was the first hard evidence I had that pointed to the killer. But even though it was good, tangible evidence, it was not invulnerable. I was going to need corroboration. So, like any investigator worth his shoe leather, I knew when to ask for help. I called the FBI.

I met Mary in the lobby of the sixth-floor FBI office.

"What wrong?" she asked. "Is it Callie?"

I assured her that Callie was fine. "But I do have a question."

"What?"

"Do you have a computer?"

She seemed taken aback. "Of course I do. What kind of a question is that?"

I pulled the disc from my pocket. "You need to see this."

She glanced the disc. "Okay, follow me."

The receptionist smiled and buzzed us through. I didn't know her, which meant she had started the job sometime within the last six months.

Mary led me down the long hallway to the rear of the suite and into a large room that housed most of the agents. Her desk, one of many in the room, was typical government issue, gunmetal gray, with a plastic nameplate that read SA Christopher. Her desk sat at the rear of the room, near the squad supervisor's office, and next to where mine had sat just six months before. It was lunch hour, so the room was largely empty. A couple of the guys that I knew were there. They smiled and said their hellos before returning to their work.

"We should be okay in here," Mary said, leading me into the supervisor's office. She closed the door, attracting the brief attention of one of the agents in the squad room.

"I don't think bringing me in here and closing the door is going to endear you to a lot of people around here," I said.

"I'll live with it," she said. "Let's see the disc."

I handed her the disc as she sat in the supervisor's chair. She slid it into the computer's feeder slot, and the file names appeared again as they had on Melissa's computer.

"What now?" she asked.

"Don't worry about F&F One," I said. "It's the cover sheet for the website." I tapped the screen over the second file name. "Click on this one."

She did, and the spreadsheet unfolded on the screen. "What's this?" she asked.

"It's a spreadsheet showing all of the girls that Emma and Thornton were able to recruit for F&F. See here?" I said, pointing to the initials. "This is Emma Caine, and this is Brad Thornton."

"Who's the other one?" she asked, nodding toward the initials JS.

"I'm pretty sure it's June Seidel. She's a teacher at Tifton and was involved with F&F."

"Was?"

I nodded. "Yeah. I interviewed her the other day, and now she's missing."

A light seemed to go on in Mary's head. "Oh, yeah," she said. "I saw something about that on the news. I guess I picked up on her having worked at the same school as Emma, but I didn't make the connection."

"Connection is right," I said. I then told her what June had told me about the conspiracy that she and Angie had cooked up against Emma, and about how Emma had squelched the thing before it got off the ground.

"And now," Mary said, "both Emma and June are dead."

"Technically," I said, "one is dead, the other is missing."

"Right. Missing," she said, correcting herself. "Who will probably turn up dead."

"Correct," I said, admitting the fallacy of my own statement.

"So why are you here?"

I reached over her shoulder and tapped the down arrow key, stopping when I reached the name that I had seen earlier. "Ring a bell?" I asked.

Mary looked at the name, and for a moment, nothing seemed to register. Then her eyes suddenly widened. "Is that—?"

"One and the same," I said.

"Colton," she said, turning in her chair to face me, "you've caught the tiger by the tail here."

"Gee, you think?"

She glanced through the window in the door, to the squad room on the other side. "We need to go somewhere else," she said, ejecting the disc.

"Where?"

"The second-floor cafeteria."

We sat opposite each other at a blue Formica-topped table. I was drinking a Coke, Mary was having iced tea.

"Now that I know all of this," she said, "what do you want from me?"

"The disc is evidence. But not enough to get a conviction. I'm going to need a wire."

She laughed. "Colton, I can't do that and you know it. And even if I did, it wouldn't stand up."

She was right. The evidence that I had, if taken to court, could easily be shot down based on the source from which I had obtained it.

"I know that my sources are impeachable. But the disc is relevant just the same."

She started to say something but then paused as she weighed what I had just said. "Okay. You've got a point. If this got to court, the disc would still have to be dealt with. But what I am saying is that you've got to go about this in a different way. And you're right in saying that you need corroborating evidence. A confession would be nice, of course. And the best way to obtain that would be with an incriminating statement made on tape, by way of a wire. No question. But it isn't going to happen. At least not on a federal level. So my advice is to go to IPD and tell them what you've got. Let them sort it out. It's what they do."

"This guy is good at what he does too," I said. "He's also a player. He's connected. That means that I can't waltz in there and say, 'Hey, guys, I've got the real killer, and by the way, could you prove it for me?'"

She sighed and leaned against the back of her chair as she brushed her thick mane from her face. "I'm not suggesting that you approach them in exactly that fashion. But I do believe you can take this to them. They'd follow through. They're good at this, you know."

It wasn't a question of how good IPD was. It was a question of how credible I was and how firmly the disc stood as evidence.

"The bureau has its limits," Mary said.

"So do I," I said. "And they're getting narrower and narrower by the minute."

FIFTY-SIX

My limits were indeed narrowing by the minute, so I decided to take Mary's advice and call IPD. I asked Wilkins to meet me at my office. By the time I arrived, he was sitting at the top of the steps.

"Nice of you to show," he said.

"Sorry for being late," I said. "I don't have a siren to speed through traffic with anymore."

He grinned, and I opened the door. The radiator was hissing, and the room was like a sauna.

"I know it's cold out and all, but don't you think that you've got the heat up just a bit too high?" Wilkins said.

I stooped and reached for the knob to turn the heat down. It dislodged, coming off in my hand. "Sorry," I said. "Looks like it's going to be a little warm in here."

He shrugged. "It's okay. There are a lot of people out there in health clubs paying a pretty penny for this kind of steamer. I'll just leave the door open."

"It might be best if you closed it," I said, sitting in my chair. "What I have to say is for your ears only."

His expression changed to the same serious one that I had seen the morning when he had taken my gun. He closed the door and sat in the chair across the desk from me.

"You know who killed Thornton, don't you?" he asked.

"Maybe," I said. "I might also know who killed Emma Caine."

"We've got the guy who killed Emma Caine."

I shook my head. "No, you don't. Billy is a lot of things, and there was no love lost between him and Emma. But he's not a murderer."

He leaned forward, allowing his forearms to rest on the edge of my desk. "Why don't we quit the sparring and you just be straight up with me. What've you got?"

I told him about my burglary of Emma's house. I told him about the missing computer, the fact that it wasn't on the evidence list from the property room, and I told him that Billy couldn't read. I told him about the disc—and about the sinking feeling I had when I saw that name on the spreadsheet: Shaneka Bitterman. And I told him about DiCenza, his threat against Emma, Emma's push to pay off her debt, and my theory that Shaneka had gotten swept up in Emma's drive to get DiCenza off her back. I asked him for a wire and to allow me to see this through to completion. When I was done, he looked like a man who has just been told that his wife is having an affair.

"That's a lot of stuff," he said. "And you think that just because his daughter's name is on the disc that Bitterman may be connected to the murders?"

"What would you do if your daughter's name was on that list?"

"I would probably kill whoever was responsible."

I waited for that to sink in and then said, "Emma's head was crushed by her murderer."

"Nature of our times. Kids are killing kids today for a pair of tennis shoes."

"Emma was killed in rage, Harley. And her computer was missing. I think it was to keep it from falling into police hands."

He shrugged. "Okay. I'll admit that there appears to be some circumstantial evidence here."

"Some?" I asked. "You marched in here the other day with a lot less on me. You checked me out and ran ballistics. All I'm asking is that we do the same with Bitterman." I paused again. "So how about it?"

"We have an internal mechanism for dealing with bad cops. *If* he's bad."

"Sure you do," I said. "Except that Bitterman won't talk to me about it. And he won't talk to you about it. And he won't talk to your internal mechanism either. And the only person I know who might be able to squeeze it out of him, won't talk to either one of you."

Wilkins sighed. It was the sigh of a weary man. "I'm assuming that you have thought this out," Wilkins said.

"As a matter of fact, I have. On the way over here."

"So you have a plan."

"Yes."

"Let's hear it," he said.

FIFTY-SEVEN

I called Angie and asked her to meet me at Melissa's. She agreed and was already at the house when I arrived.

I stood in the living room as Angie and Melissa once again sat on the sofa. Allyson was into a coloring book, blissfully unaware of our discussion.

"The disc that I uncovered from Thornton's box details a list of the names of every girl that he and Emma recruited for F&F. Both of you are listed as well as the names of some other girls who, I would be willing to bet, were underage. One of them was the daughter of the police detective who arrested Billy for the murder of Emma."

"Bitterman?" Angie asked.

I nodded.

"Why are you telling us this?" Melissa asked.

"Because I think Bitterman killed Emma and later Thornton in order to avenge his daughter's death." I told them that given the viciousness of the crime, combined with the evidence that existed on the disc, it seemed highly probable that Bitterman was the killer. An enraged father, seeking justice. An enraged father who just happened to be in a position to investigate his own crime and finger someone else for the murder. "It's bad enough that the daughter of a cop dies of a drug overdose," I said. "That may be pain enough. But to let the two who were responsible for leading her into that lifestyle continue to live…that would be unforgivable. His heart ruled his head, and he acted as a father. Not a cop."

"Was he the one who broke into my house?" Melissa asked.

I nodded. "Yeah, I think so. Broke into my office too. He was looking for anything that might point to his daughter's connection to F&F."

"So what do you want me to do?" Angie asked.

I shook my head. "Not you." I directed my attention toward Melissa. "You," I said.

"Me?"

"You're the only one who can logically pull this off."

She glanced at Angie then back to me. "Pull what off?"

I sat on the sofa next to her. "I'll have a wire. I need for you to wear it and to call Bitterman. Tell him that you have the disc and what's on it. Tell him that you want to leave town for the sake of yourself and your little girl," I said, nodding to Allyson. "Tell him you want five thousand for the disc. Tell him that's enough for you and Allyson to get out of Indy and make a new start. If he doesn't buy it, you will sell it to anyone in town who will meet your price, or you'll give it to the press. Or the police."

She shook her head. "Do you know what you're asking? Black-mail a cop? I won't be able to run far enough. No sir," she said, standing. "No sir."

Angie was looking at Melissa as she moved about the room.

"If you won't do it for yourself," I said, "or for your daughter, or for Thornton, then think of your friend. If you do this, we can put the right man away for a long time. Billy will come home to Angie, and you can move ahead with your life."

She turned to me, avoiding looking in Angie's direction. "And what if I refuse? Are you going to give him the disc anyway?"

I shook my head. "No. If you refuse, the disc goes to Bitterman's supervisor. It's still evidence, but you will not be in danger."

Her stance seemed to soften some.

"But there may be little that his supervisor can do without corroboration, and Bitterman will have gotten away with it. That means that Billy will do a stretch for something that he didn't do," I said.

Angie started to speak but hesitated. Melissa was pacing the floor.

"What if he didn't do it?" she asked as she stopped pacing. "Will I be in trouble for trying to blackmail a cop?"

"No. His supervisor is working with me. If Bitterman is innocent, the disc will be handed over to the detectives. They will probably want to interview the girls on the list and investigate to see if anyone else is involved with F&F's activities in Indianapolis." Seidel had said that at least two others at Tifton were involved.

Angie stood up. "Billy is all I have," she said to Melissa. "This might be the key to freeing him."

"And maybe to putting away the man who killed Brad," I said.

Melissa moved to pace the floor again with her face in her hands. Angie and I waited.

"If I do this, I need to know that I'll be safe. I have a daughter to raise," she said.

"I will be there with you," I said. "I'll personally guarantee your safety."

She looked at Angie then back to me. "Okay," she said, with some trepidation. "How do we do this?"

I looked at Angie. She was smiling.

"Let me fill you in," I said.

FIFTY-EIGHT

After leaving Melissa's, I was heading toward the office when Mary called.

"Irony of ironies," she said. "Your Ms. Seidel has been found."

"Where?"

"In a parked car at the airport's Day Parking terminal."

"Dead?"

"Of course. That doesn't surprise you, does it?"

"No. Not really."

"The airport police found her when they received complaints about a woman sleeping in her car. She had been there several days."

"How did you find out about this?" I asked.

"When you told me that she was missing, I called the morgue. I told them that I had an interest in her and would appreciate a call if she turned up."

"Which she did."

"This morning. Preliminary exam strongly suggests suicide."

"Note?"

"No. Nothing."

While I had no respect for Seidel or the life she had led, I did not want her to kill herself. I knew that my pressure had probably pushed her to act as she did.

"Thanks, Mary," I said.

"Take it easy, Colton. The body count is beginning to climb."

She was right. And if things didn't go according to plan, there would be more bodies on the way.

FIFTY-NINE

Melissa and I met with Wilkins in my office. He arrived a few minutes after we did, carrying an aluminum attaché case and a Styrofoam cup of coffee. After an awkward introduction—Melissa clearly not wanting to be here—Wilkins set the attaché case down on my desk and took a long drag on his coffee.

"What've we got here?" I asked.

"Hardware," he said, setting the cup down on the desk.

Melissa didn't say anything, but she was frowning as she looked at the attaché case.

Wilkins opened the case and extracted a digital recorder and a long coil with a suction cup at one end. Several other insulated wires and recorders remained in the case.

"First, we will have to contact Daniel. Make the pitch," he said to me. "And we will record the call."

"Sure," I said.

"If he bites, we set up a meeting. Probably in a public place."

"I thought they only did that in movies," Melissa said, shifting in her seat as she fidgeted with the buttons on her coat.

"It's done to minimize the chance of danger," Wilkins answered.

"We'll be nearby," I said to her. "You'll be safe."

Wilkins lowered the wiring that he had been trying to untangle and looked at me. "We?"

"I'm going to be there," I said.

He shook his head. "I don't think so. This is a police matter."

I shook my head. "I promised her that I would personally guarantee her safety. I can't do that unless I'm there."

"And you don't think that we're capable of doing that?"

"Sure," I said. "But you didn't make the promise."

Wilkins shook his head. "You're not going, Parker."

Melissa stood up. "If he doesn't go, I won't go."

Wilkins looked at her without saying anything.

"If she doesn't go, the disc doesn't go," I said. "And you'll never know if Bitterman is dirty or not."

"That disc is evidence. And tampering with evidence is a crime," Wilkins said, taking on the threatening tone that I was learning to recognize.

"Evidence gets lost," I said.

We held the standoff position for what seemed an eternity but was probably only a minute. Finally Wilkins folded and calmly went back to untangling the wiring. I nodded at Melissa and she sat down in her chair.

"Slide your phone over here," Wilkins said.

I moved my phone closer to him. He inserted the male tip of the wire into the recording jack of the digital recorder and attached the suction end of the wire to an area just above the ear portion of the phone's receiver. Then he sat in his chair.

"It's important," he said, addressing Melissa directly for the first time since their introduction, "that you follow the script to the letter."

Melissa looked at Wilkins, then to me, and then back to Wilkins. She nodded her head.

"The prosecutor is in on this, and it's important that we not appear to have entrapped Daniel."

She nodded again, and Wilkins looked at me.

"Ready when you are," I said.

He reached into the attaché case and pulled out a tabbed file folder that contained a small stack of papers. He pulled a single page from inside the folder and handed it to Melissa.

She took the paper. "What's this?"

"Read it to yourself and then out loud. Make it sound convincing; make it sound like you're not reading it," Wilkins said. He looked at me. "When she can do that, we're ready to go."

Melissa read the script for about fifteen minutes before she sounded convincing enough to pull off the sting.

"I think we're ready," Wilkins said.

I looked at Melissa. She nodded that she was ready.

Wilkins started the recorder and dialed IPD. When the receptionist answered he handed the receiver to Melissa.

"Detective Bitterman, please," she said. There was a pause. "No, I would rather not give my name." Another pause as she placed her hand over the mouthpiece of the receiver. "They're ringing his desk."

"Detective Bitterman? This is Melissa King." A pause. "Melissa King. Girlfriend of Brad Thornton. I have some information that might interest you." Another pause. "That's right. It seems that Emma Caine and Brad had an interest in some pornography. Ever heard of F&F?" Another pause. "Your daughter did." Another pause. "Don't play dumb with me, Detective. Shaneka was very heavy into some very nasty stuff. Lots of pictures. I have a computer disc that lists everyone from Indianapolis who is involved with F&F, and your daughter's name is on it." Another pause. "Don't threaten me, Detective; it isn't necessary. You can have the disc." Another pause. "Of course." Pause. "Five thousand. Five thousand and I leave town for good. You never hear from me again." Pause. "Look, someone trashed my place the other night, probably looking for this thing."

Wilkins' expression changed and he began to scan the script.

"If you don't take this thing, I know plenty of people who will," Melissa said, departing from her written lines. "I'm not into games. Do you want this or not?" Pause. "Monument Circle. The south steps at nine AM." Pause. "And Detective? Bring cash." She hung up.

"What was all that about?" Wilkins asked. "We gave you a script."

"Your script didn't work," she said, standing. "I need a cigarette." She fumbled in her purse and extracted a half-filled, partially crushed packet of cigarettes and a disposable lighter.

She lit the cigarette and inhaled deeply before blowing the smoke into the air.

"He will meet me at Monument Circle, south side, at nine tomorrow. He was not pleased."

I looked at Wilkins. "The trap is set," I said. "Now we see if he takes the bait."

"He'll take the bait," Wilkins said. "He believes that his daughter's reputation is on the line. The question is whether that means he's guilty of anything other than being a dad."

"It's more than that," I said. "He dispensed justice for her death, and he knows that disc is incriminating."

The room was quiet for a while. Neither Wilkins nor I said anything as we thought about the situation. Melissa continued to smoke the cigarette, flipping the ashes on my floor. After a few minutes, Wilkins pulled out another tangle of wires from the attaché case.

"Let's see how this fits," he said. "I want to hit the ground running tomorrow."

I was up early the next morning. After my run around the park, I showered, shaved, and dressed in a pair of jeans, a sweatshirt, and tennis shoes. I checked the magazine of the Ruger, counting fifteen rounds plus one in the chamber, before slipping into my jacket.

I wasn't really expecting trouble. I knew that a contingent of IPD detectives and uniforms would be nearby, but I wanted to be ready just in case. I had promised Melissa she would be safe. It was a promise I intended to keep.

Before I left, I called the Shapiros. Callie was hurting, and according to Dr. Sebastian, she blamed me for Anna's death. I wasn't sure that I could argue with her. I was still wrestling with that one myself. But her recent action showed a far more serious issue than any of us had suspected. We were not dealing with a young girl who was grieving over her mother's death. We were dealing with a young girl whose grief was close to becoming another tragedy. Sebastian had called it a cry for help. And that is exactly as I saw it. A cry that could be muted if I didn't intervene.

The work I had chosen was dangerous. The possibility of being killed was ever present. Today would be no exception. If that happened, Callie could go into a tailspin from which she may not be able to recover. At the very least, the Shapiros would be handed a serious problem. One that they were clearly unprepared to handle. Still, despite my anger with Millikin, I believed he would stand by them if something happened to me. His comment that "God has been good to *us* today" showed the level of identification he held with Callie, the Shapiros, and me. And though I had a deep-seated anger toward God and knew that He did not listen to people like me, I also knew that He did listen to people like Millikin. If divine intervention would help my daughter, I was solidly behind whatever Millikin could do to secure it.

Our conversation was short. Callie said she was fine and seemed improved from our conversation at the hospital the other night. I promised her that things would change and that I had a surprise for her. One that I hoped would help both of us to heal.

I told her that I loved her and ended the conversation. I hoped all would go well today and that I would be around for more.

As I stepped outside, I looked at the sky. It was gray, and the cold wind was brisk. The stillness made the atmosphere seem artificial, like a stage that was set for the next act, scripted and beyond my control. I was getting used to the feeling.

I stopped for breakfast at La Peep's on Illinois Street and then walked to Monument Circle, several blocks away. The monument, a one-hundred-eight-foot obelisk, was built between 1888 and 1901 as a war memorial and is surrounded by fountains and reflecting pools. It sits in the center of a brick-lined, circular thoroughfare that serves as a site for ceremony and celebration. Today it would be a site for neither. Although the rush hour crowd had begun to thin, the circle was still heavily populated with pedestrian traffic.

I positioned myself on the south side of the monument, several yards off the southwest corner where Meridian Street intersects with the circle. The buildings that surrounded the area did little to break the wind, which hurled downward through the concrete alleyways, swirling around the man-made circle before ascending again. I raised the collar on my jacket and blew into my cupped hands for warmth. I did not take my eyes off the steps of the monument.

At nine o'clock I saw Melissa ascend the steps of the war memorial. She surveyed the circle from her perch before sitting near the top step. Like me, she blew into her cupped hands.

I positioned myself behind a streetlight to better shield my position and studied the portion of the circle that was within my view. I saw no evidence that IPD had staked out this area. But then I had not expected to see them. Wilkins, like the men under his command, was a professional. If Bitterman had the slightest hint that he was being tailed or was otherwise under surveillance, he would bolt, and our chance of nabbing him would disappear.

At half past nine I was getting concerned that he had changed his mind or had made us, but he suddenly appeared, coming from the east side of the monument's bottom step. I turned away, facing a shop window that allowed me to observe him in the glass' reflection.

He walked up the steps of the monument, passed the area where Melissa sat, reached the top of the staircase, and continued around the base of the obelisk. He made a full pass around, reemerging on the west side. This time, he glanced around and began his steady descent of the steps toward Melissa's position. She stood, hands in her pockets, as calm as though this were a day in the park.

I turned and ran across the street toward the monument, weaving in and out of the circling traffic. I stopped at the bottom of the steps. If Bitterman were to turn, he would see me.

There was no prearranged signal from Melissa. She was to engage Bitterman in conversation about the disc. If he tipped his hand, IPD would rush him, allowing Melissa to walk away unscathed. I watched as clouds of condensation escaped from them. Melissa remained calm, blowing into her hands for warmth.

Bitterman, on the other hand, became quite animated, waving his hands around and jabbing his finger at her chest. She remained calm.

Then she moved. She handed him the disc.

Suddenly, I saw two IPD uniforms emerge from the west and east sides of the obelisk at the top of the staircase. Melissa turned to walk away, and for a brief moment, Bitterman appeared confused.

Then, like a cornered animal, he reacted. He grabbed Melissa's wrist and jerked her toward him, spinning her around as a shield. In his right hand was a semiautomatic. He had the barrel resting against her right temple. I drew the Ruger and raced up the steps. IPD officers, uniformed and plain clothes, appeared from everywhere like a thin blue line of ninjas. Wilkins was to my left, emerging from the top step on the west side of the obelisk.

"Everybody just take it easy," Wilkins said. "Just take it easy."

I was about fifteen steps down from Bitterman. I kept the Ruger trained on him.

"Let the girl go, Daniel," Wilkins said. "Let her go and put the gun down."

I could hear Bitterman's voice and see the cold blast of his breath, but because he was facing away from me and toward Wilkins, I couldn't make out what he was saying.

"No. It doesn't have to be that way. There is always another way, Daniel."

Bitterman shook his head. Melissa turned her head so that she could see me. For a moment our eyes locked, and in that moment I did not see fear but instead a willingness to surrender. A willingness to capitulate and allow fate to have its way. I understood that feeling. I had felt it many times as I stood at Anna's grave. And as Bitterman turned to see what Melissa was looking at, I saw it again. But in his eyes, there was also anguish. The anguish that comes from a pain that will not go away. Chronic pain. The pain of failure and self-doubt. The pain that a father feels when he has failed. I understood that feeling too.

"Let her go," I said, setting the Ruger down on the steps. "Let it end here, Daniel."

"Daniel," Wilkins yelled from atop the staircase, "let her go."

Bitterman didn't look back at Wilkins and the others. He cocked the hammer of the semiautomatic. Melissa clenched her eyes shut. She was preparing to die.

"Don't," I said. "There's a better way."

Suddenly, without warning, he shoved Melissa aside and pointed the pistol at me. He held it in both hands, his feet spread shoulder width apart, aiming it directly at me. I made no move to pick up my own gun.

For a moment, time seemed to stand still. In the distance I could hear Wilkins yelling for him to drop the gun.

A flock of pigeons scattered overhead, reacting to the echo of a sudden gunshot.

For all of her toughness, for all of her willingness to surrender to death's siren call, Melissa sobbed, rocking against me where we sat, midstep on the stairs of the Circle's monument.

"She okay?" Wilkins asked.

I nodded, keeping my arms around the traumatized woman.

"Captain?" a voice said. It belonged to one of the uniforms. "Take a look at this." He handed Bitterman's gun to Wilkins. It was a Walther PPK.

Wilkins ejected the magazine and locked the slide in place. "Well, I'll be…" He turned to me. "It's empty."

"Suicide by cop," I said, recalling the anguish in the detective's eyes. "If it didn't work out, he had no intention of going on. Life had gotten too painful."

Wilkins pocketed the weapon. "This officer will drive you both to headquarters. Plan on being there awhile."

SIXTY-ONE

I sat in an interrogation room drinking a Coke. Wilkins sat across from me with a digital recorder.

"How's the girl?" I had asked when he came into the room.

"She'll be okay," he said. "She's in the next room, giving her statement."

I nodded and drank from the can.

"She did well," Wilkins said. "Talked to Bitterman like a pro. He made a confession of murdering Caine and Thornton. Threatened to kill her too if she didn't give him the disc."

"Emma and Thornton had initiated his daughter into their world. Thornton supplied the drugs and Emma supplied a way to pay for them. When he found out, he couldn't take the pain," I said.

"So he snuffed the old lady. Made sure that he was the one assigned the case. When he found out that the neighbors had seen Emma and her nephew arguing, he had a suspect."

I nodded. "She had lent Billy the credit card when he visited. The purse had been spilled during her struggle with Bitterman. He took the computer because he couldn't leave anything behind that might point to his daughter's involvement with F&F. That would lead back to him. So he searched my office and Melissa's house to see if there was anything he missed.

"He could handle the pain of her death. But he wouldn't live with the fact that those who were responsible, and who had profited from it, were still walking around." I took a long drink from the Coke. "And he knew that there was always a chance that they could walk, assuming that he could gather enough evidence to get to trial in the first place. But I suspect that when he was alone, in the quiet of the night, he couldn't live with the murders."

"Daniel was a good man," Wilkins said. "An honorable man. And," he added, "he loved Shaneka. It was his love for her that drove him to do what he did. And it was his honor that made what he did impossible to live with." He paused for a moment as he stared blankly into space. Then, more to himself than me, he said, "He probably knew we were on to him. He knew that she was wired, so he made a confession."

"Good for the soul," I said.

Wilkins shook his head. "I should've seen this coming. The evidence against Billy was too light. I kept thinking that Daniel had something more. He was such a good cop that when he spoke, I listened."

"He was willing to frame Billy," I said. "He had lost his family for the job. Lost his daughter to the very thing he had fought against all of his life. He probably saw Billy as a negligible cog in the wheel. One small price to pay to find some level of justice."

Wilkins was dejected. "It didn't work. He was doing things he knew he could never live with. When it all came to a head, he took the quick way out." He shook his head. "I should've seen this coming," he repeated. "Daniel was hurting."

"A lot of guys are hurting," I said. "A lot of men who are not involved in their kids' lives." I rolled the can between my hands as we both sat silent for a moment. "It's always a lot easier to see the other guy's situation than it is to see your own."

Wilkins nodded again. "Listen," he said, "get out of here. Go see your daughter. Just be back tomorrow. I'll need your statement."

I finished the Coke and stood.

"By the way," he said, "June Seidel's body turned up."

"I know," I said.

"Then you know that the coroner's report is listing suicide as the cause of death."

"No, I didn't. I only had the preliminary."

"Mary's out in the lobby," Wilkins said. "I called her for you. Figured you might need a ride home."

"Thanks," I said.

He shook his head. "No, thank you."

"For what?"

"For helping me to find my way again." He looked at me from his sitting position. "I have a daughter too."

SIXTY-TWO

Mary drove me to the parking garage next to La Peep's, where I had left my car. She parked in an empty stall next to mine and killed the engine. I filled her in on the events of the morning.

"So what about Billy?" she asked.

"He's off the hook," I said.

"That'll make Angie happy."

"Uh-huh," I said, staring out the side window at nothing in particular.

She leaned forward to get a better look at my face. "Something wrong?"

I shook my head. "Not anymore."

"Not anymore?"

"Not anymore," I repeated, turning to look at her. "Do you know what Emma and Angie have in common with me?"

She shook her head. "No. Not really."

"None of us had a father in our lives. Not one of us could point to any man and say, 'That's my dad.' And look what it has brought us."

"What?"

"Lives that have been void of any correcting and guiding influence. Lives made miserable by choosing the wrong paths."

"Colton," Mary said, smiling. "I wouldn't classify your life as miserable. Maybe some days seem that way. But—"

"I would," I said. "Think about it. Think about how the choices that I have made have spilled over into the lives of others."

"You're thinking about Callie, aren't you?"

I nodded my head. "A little, I guess," I said. "But I'm thinking mostly about what Millikin said. About Adam being the father of us all and how his sin, his poor decisions, his desire to follow his own will, has affected all of us." I turned to look vacantly out the window again. "Just the way mine have affected Callie," I added.

"You're doing it again," Mary said.

"Doing what?"

"First you blamed yourself for Anna's death. And now you're blaming yourself for Callie's actions."

"No, I'm really not. I'm thinking beyond that. I'm thinking about how Adam, and the rest of us for that matter, have dropped the ball because we insist on our own way. When the truth is, we don't know the way. We need help." I turned to face Mary again. "I've never been good at meaningful relationships because I was never allowed to develop any. So I forged my own road. I've tried to control anything that threatened me. I've never learned to rely on others. I've always chosen to do things my way."

"But—"

"Adam did that too, didn't he? Because of his sin, the original sin, he lost his relationship with God. And we all pay for it." I turned to gaze out the window again. "No wonder we are the way we are." I changed the subject. "Callie's doing better, by the way," I said.

"I know," she said. "I called the Shapiros and talked to her earlier this morning."

We sat quietly for a few minutes, watching as the condensation from our breath formed on the inside of the windshield.

"I couldn't do it," I said.

"Couldn't do what?"

"Kill Bitterman." I turned to face her. "What I saw in his eyes this morning was the same thing that I have seen in my mirror for six months. The man was hurting. And when he turned to face me, I just…couldn't do it."

"Yet you had promised to protect Melissa."

I nodded. "Yeah. Does that mean I failed again?"

She shook her head. "Remember when we were talking about those little hairs that pop up on your neck? The ones that tell you to listen to that inner voice?"

"Yes."

"That's what you did. You sensed something that you can't describe or explain. But you went with it and you were right. That's what makes you good at what you do." She took my hand. "Some people go through their entire lives and never develop that intuition. Be glad that you have it. It made you a good cop and it will make you a good father."

CHAPTER
SIXTY-THREE

The teachers from Tifton High School that were arrested, were
they part of that case you worked?" Bucky asked, lighting a
cigar.

"Yeah," I said. IPD had arrested two other teachers at Tifton for
their involvement with F&F. Emma had been busy. The extent of
her reach would not be fully known for several months.

Two weeks had passed since the shooting. Bucky Kravitz had
come to the house to pick up his cigars and play a few hands. He
brought most of the old gang with him—Dave Chastain, a Marion
County Sheriff's Department homicide detective; Pete LeRoy, a
local newspaper reporter; Ernie "Cod" Williams, cab driver and
part-time fisherman; and Tom Hoskins, retired IPD patrolman and
close friend of Bucky. Each of them were sitting around my kitchen
table, smoking cigars as Pete shuffled the cards. News of the arrest of
two of Tifton's teachers had made the news, as did information that
IPD and the Marion County prosecutor were looking into F&F's
dealings in Indianapolis. The postal inspector was looking at them
again too, which now made it a federal case.

Pete began to deal the cards.

"What happened to the Caine boy?" Hoskins asked.

I watched as the cards made the rounds. "All charges were dropped and he went back to Angie."

"Did she get out of the business?" Chastain asked.

I took my cards. "Yeah. She and Melissa are working with IPD and the Feds now, telling them everything they know."

"Good for them," Hoskins said. "I spent a big chunk of my career watching young girls like them get eaten up by that industry. It's about time they turn the tables."

"Amen to that," Cod said. "Been watching girls like them on street corners for thirty years. It's why I like fishing so much. No problems there. Just you and the fish." He scooped up his cards.

"No problems for the fish either, as long as you're the one looking for them," Pete said.

We all laughed at the good-natured ribbing, when we heard a clatter in the kitchen. Callie had come in to get a bowl of ice cream.

"Hey, doll," Bucky said. "How you doing?"

She shrugged. "I'm okay," she said, opening the refrigerator with one hand while reaching simultaneously for the ice-cream scooper with the other.

She was better, to be sure. But not where she needed to be. Since the revelation of the extent of her grief, there was a seriousness about her that she no longer attempted to hide. A change in her demeanor and conversation that was years ahead of her age. And there was the underlying bitterness too. Bitterness toward me. Not the kind that revealed itself in hostility. At least not yet. But the kind that springs to life in apathy. A strong signal that she no longer seemed to care if I was part of her life or not.

Still, she had wanted to come home. My surprise for her was a room made up just for her. I had bought the furniture after my talk with Melissa and Angie. It was not as nice as what Frank and Corrin had provided, but it was hers nonetheless. And she was with me.

I wasn't sure yet how we would make it. But I knew that if she didn't come home with me, neither of us would make it. Or even care if we did.

She was tired. Very tired. The events of the past several months had all taken their toll. Her life had gone from that of a middle-class, secure, American teenager to one of uncertainty. The very core of her identity had been shaken. But it had not been destroyed. It could be rebuilt, although it would not come easily.

Our first appointment with Sebastian had helped both of us to understand her need for help. And it was a start.

Millikin had offered to help too. And he did. His connection with Anna served as a springboard for one with Callie. And the two of them spent time in conversation. Conversation about Anna, Callie, and God.

I wasn't entirely sold on all the things that Millikin had said, and years of resentment toward God would not go away overnight. I was still a loner, fighting an uphill battle in life, and I would not surrender control of my life easily. But I came to understand that Millikin was right when he said that God had allowed the incident to give us a chance to save Callie. I was grateful for what He had done. It had given me hope. And it had given me pause to think. I knew that in the days to come, I would do plenty of that.

I looked at my hand. Aces and eights, the infamous last hand played by Wild Bill Hickock, known as the Dead Man's hand. I smiled at the irony. For six months, I had felt like a walking dead man. Now, with Callie's return, I had hope. And that helped me to feel more alive than I had felt in a long time.

I watched as Callie moved out of the kitchen. She looked over her shoulder at us and smiled. It was weak, but it was enough. And I knew that despite the challenges ahead, we would be fine. Just fine.

About Brandt Dodson

Brandt Dodson was born and raised in Indianapolis and comes from a long line of police officers spanning several generations. Dr. Dodson is a writer and a board-certified podiatrist, specializing in peripheral nerve surgery. He and his wife and their two sons live in Newburgh, Indiana, where he serves as an elder at the First Christian Church. *Original Sin* is his first novel.

ೞ

Coming Soon....

The second book in the **Colton Parker, P.I.** series, *Seventy Times Seven.* Available in bookstores everywhere August 2006.

Lester Cheek had everything a man could want. A beautiful home, a thriving business, and money to burn. But he was alone—very alone. Until he met Claudia. The attractive and effervescent Claudia is everything that Lester could hope for. But then she mysteriously disappears, and Colton Parker is hired to find her. The investigation soon leads Colton to discover the dark truth behind Claudia's disappearance as he races against time to locate an international hit man and stop a murder for hire.

Other Excellent Fiction
From Harvest House Publishers

❧

FORGIVING SOLOMON LONG
Chris Well

Crime boss Frank "Fat Cat" Catalano has dreams of building a legacy in Kansas City—but a coalition of local store owners and clergy have banded together to try to break his stranglehold. Detective Tom Griggs is determined to bring Fat Cat down, no matter what the cost. Even if that cost is neglecting—and losing—his own wife. Hit man Solomon "Solo" Long is a "cleaner" flown in from the coast to make sure the locals get the message from Fat Cat. It all adds up to a sizzling page-turner that crackles with wit and unexpected heart—and hits the reader in the gut with a powerful message of forgiveness.

THE CHAMBERS OF JUSTICE SERIES *by Craig Parshall*

THE RESURRECTION FILE
When Reverend Angus MacCameron asks attorney Will Chambers to defend him against accusations that could discredit the Gospels, Will's unbelieving heart says "run." But conspiracy and intrigue—and the presence of MacCameron's lovely and successful daughter, Fiona—draw him deep into the case...toward a destination he could never have imagined.

CUSTODY OF THE STATE
Attorney Will Chambers reluctantly agrees to defend a young mother from Georgia and her farmer husband, suspected of committing the unthinkable against their own child. Encountering small-town secrets, big-time corruption, and a government system that's destroying the little family, Chambers himself is thrown into the custody of the state.

THE ACCUSED
Enjoying a Cancún honeymoon with his wife, Fiona, attorney Will Chambers is ambushed by two unexpected events: a terrorist kidnapping of a U.S. official...and the news that a link has been found to the previously unidentified murderer of Will's first wife. The kidnapping pulls him into the case of Marine colonel Caleb Marlowe. When treachery drags both Will and his client toward vengeance, they must ask—*Is forgiveness real?*

MISSING WITNESS
A relaxing North Carolina vacation for attorney Will Chambers? Not likely. When Will investigates a local inheritance case, the long arm of the law reaches out of the distant past to cast a shadow over his client's life...and the life of his own family. As the attorney's legal battle uncovers corruption, piracy, the deadly grip of greed, and the haunting sins of a man's past, the true question must be faced—*Can a person ever really run away from God?*

THE LAST JUDGMENT
A mysterious religious cult plans to spark an "Armageddon" in the Middle East. Suddenly, a huge explosion blasts the top of the Jerusalem Temple Mount into rubble, with hundreds of Muslim casualities. And attorney Will Chambers' client, Gilead Amahn, a convert to Christianity from Islam, becomes the prime suspect. In his harrowing pursuit of the truth, Will must face the greatest threat yet to his marriage, his family, and his faith, while cataclysmic events plunge the world closer to the Last Judgment.